PRAISE

"An incredible first novel."

—El País

"Forces the reader to keep reading."

—El Mundo

"An outstanding debut."

—FNAC

THE
WARNING

OTHER TITLES BY PAUL PEN

THE
WARNING

PAUL PEN

TRANSLATED BY SIMON BRUNI

 AMAZON **CROSSING**

Text copyright © 2011 by Paul Pen
Translation copyright © 2020 by Simon Bruni
All rights reserved.

Previously published as *El aviso* by RBA Libros, S.A. in Spain in 2011. Translated from Spanish by Simon Bruni. First published in English by Amazon Crossing in 2020.

Published by Amazon Crossing, Seattle

www.apub.com

Amazon, the Amazon logo, and Amazon Crossing are trademarks of Amazon.com, Inc., or its affiliates.

ISBN-13: 9781542004572
ISBN-10: 1542004578

Cover design and interior illustrations by Damon Freeman

Printed in the United States of America

THE
WARNING

AUTHOR'S PREFACE

I set myself a goal of getting this novel translated into English when it was first published in Spain almost a decade ago, back in 2011. However, when Amazon Crossing proposed the project this year, all this time later, I had some doubts as to whether it would be advisable to go ahead with it. I even considered passing up the opportunity. Why? Well, because I wrote this book that you're about to read more than ten years ago. It was my first novel, but it will reach you, English-speaking readers, as if it were my fourth, after *The Light of the Fireflies*, *Desert Flowers*, and *Under the Water*. And naturally, it worries me to think you'll be reading a text written with much less expertise than you'd expect from an author with four novels published.

The Warning is a story that I adore, with characters I loved creating, especially the boy Leo and his problematic relationship with his mother, Victoria, but also the ill-fated couple Andrea and Aarón. It's also the book that began my career, so all my early memories as a writer are associated with *The Warning*, which makes it something more than just a book for me: it's a crucial turning point in my life. To top it off, the book still brings me joys such as this translation and its recent film adaptation (the movie is available on Netflix, by the way—you can see it, but only *after* reading the book).

In spite of all this, I reread *The Warning* today and suffer when I discover certain passages that I'd never write in the same way now. I wince at each confusing shift in point of view, I roll my eyes at certain similes and metaphors, and I cringe at characters' intrusive thoughts. It's like watching an old VHS of a school show: you know the child dressed as a raccoon and trying to sing, dance, or act is you, and you also know that, at that moment, you were giving it your best, really trying hard, but even so, you can't help covering your eyes now and again in a fit of embarrassment.

In a way, what the offer from Amazon Crossing forced me to do was decide whether to show this old VHS tape to the world. Whether to let you all see me dancing dressed as a raccoon. In the end, despite my doubts, the decision was yes. Most of all, because of my desire for the story of Leo Cruz, a boy who dreams only of seeing shooting stars, to reach as many readers as possible. Because neither he nor Aarón nor Andrea is to blame for the fact that I was unable to bring them to life and tell their story as well as they deserved. They have the same right as the characters in my other novels to be read in English (I will also take this opportunity to explain that my excellent translator into English, Simon Bruni, has been as faithful as ever in his translation, so any strange sentences or constructions in the text are my fault and from the original version in Spanish).

So I ask you to completely forget who wrote this and simply enjoy getting to know Leo Cruz, a very special nine-year-old boy. I hope you'll be there with him through the hard times and give him the support he doesn't receive from his mother. I also hope you appreciate the chamomile scent of Andrea's hair, feel the heat of the pavement on your bare feet, and try to understand how overwhelming Aarón's feelings of guilt must be for him. In short, I invite you to meet the inhabitants of a strange Spanish town that an apprentice writer imagined ten years ago. A town overshadowed by a strange pattern of death and intersecting destinies . . . or perhaps just an unlikely series of coincidences.

Paul Pen

PROLOGUE

Tuesday, September 12, 2006

After his first day of school, Leo came out of the classroom with his head down, staring at the ground. He let himself be carried along by the stream of children. Surrounded by screams, laughter, and running, he progressed toward the main road, more than a step behind the rest of his classmates. The September sun in Arenas seemed to melt the pavement, creating pools of nonexistent water on its surface. The white stripes of a crosswalk were an invitation to cross to the other side, where the American's store was. The place that, every afternoon, became a promised land of sugar and fun for the schoolchildren. The *Open*. The store was actually called something else, but the word *Open*, written in yellow and purple neon lights shining above the door, had become its true name. Some said that Sr. Palmer, the owner, had brought the sign from the United States.

Leo stopped at the crosswalk when the crowd of children halted. He looked up, barely lifting his head. The pedestrian signal was red.

"See this scar?" said one of the boys, pointing at his chin. "They gave me four stitches." He filled his chest as he held up a hand with the thumb gathered in. "That's why they call me Slash."

The introduction elicited sighs of amazement and cries of admiration. Slash received them with his arms in the air. Over his head, the signal changed to green.

"To the Open!" he yelled.

Having appointed himself their leader, Slash ushered his new classmates over the road. It was the first opportunity for the class to go on the school pilgrimage that took place every day. They all followed Slash. A boy ran up to him and grabbed him by the shoulder. "I'm Edgar," he said. At just six years old, he seemed to know who it would be good to make friends with. Behind them, two girls looked at each other, unsure what to do. Frightened, they took each other's hands. And they started walking.

Leo noticed that the group was vanishing around him.

He also felt the pressure of his feet against the pavement. He bent forward slightly, like anyone would to start walking, but his toes increased the responding pressure. His feet were left fixed to the ground. While his torso returned to its upright position, Leo wavered one last time between obeying his mother and crossing to the Open with the rest of his new classmates. That morning, she'd asked him to wait for her to pick him up from where he was now. Then she'd given him the first meaningful goodbye kiss of a child's life.

Forcing his good eye up again to look forward while barely lifting his head, he could see the other children advancing along the crosswalk.

Leo only wavered for a few seconds.

But those few seconds proved decisive.

The kid who'd grabbed Slash by the shoulder looked back, toward the entourage the boy with the scar had made his own with a simple gesture. He smiled when he saw that everyone was following them. Then he noticed Leo, motionless on the other side of the road, his head bowed. The boy shook his leader's shoulder. Slash turned around to see what was happening, then set off back toward Leo. The rest of the group changed direction as well and milled around near the two of them.

"What's the matter? Are you deaf or something?" Slash asked.

Leo didn't answer. He kept looking at the ground.

"Hey, I'm talking to you," Slash persisted. "Are you deaf?"

Leo shook his head, then replied, "And if I was . . . how would I answer your question?"

A murmur broke out and then rose in volume among the group of children. Slash held up his arm and shushed them.

"Ooh, it's the class smarty-pants," he said. "That's why you wear that patch on your eye, is it?"

"It's called a lazy eye," Leo said in an attempt to defend himself. "And they're taking it off in less than a month."

"*It's called a lazy eye, it's called a lazy eye,*" chanted Slash, pitching up his voice. "Is that why you won't come to the American's store? Because you can't see properly?"

Leo shook his head again.

"Then I know why." Slash fell silent for dramatic effect. He stretched it out for several seconds. When he spoke again, his voice was deeper. "You're scared of the Open. You're scared you'll get shot."

The announcement made the children fall silent. First a few murmurs, then nothing. Heads turned and mouths opened. Everyone looked at Slash first, and then at Leo, who shrugged. Finally, Leo looked up at the group. At Slash. He held a hand over his forehead to shade his one open eye.

Slash tried to keep his gaze fixed on Leo's, but his nerves betrayed him and twice his eyes flicked from one side to the other. He wanted to know how the group was reacting to his words. Because what he'd said wasn't just any old comment. He'd voiced the unmentionable secret of the Open in front of everybody. The secret that made the American's store the ideal setting for the stories made up by the children of Arenas. The scene of the shooting, years ago. And the boy who died. In reality, they had all heard their parents or older siblings talking about it at some time. Their mothers recalling it in the supermarket. But the look they gave the children right after, and the sudden change of subject they always then imposed, had made it clear that it was something the children shouldn't speak about. Just as nobody spoke about the dark shape that had been seen behind the curtains of the main room of the house at the end of the dirt road. The Open's secret was one that couldn't be shared. Much less shouted out in broad daylight at the school gates.

To break the silence, perhaps, but most of all to avoid showing even a hint of uncertainty or weakness, Slash filled his chest for a second time, fixed his eyes on Leo's, and said, "You're a scaredy-cat." Then he yelled it: "Scaredy-cat!"

Slash looked at the boy who'd grabbed him by the shoulder. He gestured at Leo with his head and insulted him again. Edgar understood the command.

"Scaredy-cat," he aped, adding his voice to Slash's. "Scaredy-cat! Scaredy-cat!"

Between the two of them, they began to repeat the phrase as if chanting a slogan. A third voice joined the chant. Then a fourth. The two frightened girls who'd held each other's hands started yelling the insult as well. Before long, the whole group was shouting at Leo. At some point, someone switched to the word *chicken*, and the new insult was copied until the whole choir was intoning the new attack.

A car began hooting its horn at the crazed pack. The pedestrian light had turned red again, but the children were still in the middle of the road. The driver was tapping the accelerator with her foot. She was also clicking her fingernails together mechanically, hooking the one on her forefinger onto her thumbnail before releasing it. She hit the center of the steering wheel again, harder this time, and kept the hooting constant so that the sound would be heard over the children's noise.

The yelling eventually subsided, and when Slash decided to cross to the American's store, the group followed him. Leo was left alone at the school gates while the kids, who might that very morning have become a gang of friends with whom he could let off firecrackers in the teachers' mailboxes, went away forever, trading stories—true or false, it didn't matter—about the legendary shooting at the Open.

The woman who'd been honking her horn tried to drive on. She had to brake several times to give way to more stragglers. Her top lip went up, showing her gums. When she'd managed to position herself on the crosswalk, she looked at Leo.

He got in the car.

"Mom, promise you'll always come get me," he said.

Victoria saw her son's sad expression. This was the same boy who'd woken her that morning, tugging on her sheets, anxious to start his new school life. She also observed how, on the other side of the road, a large group of children were rolling around on the grass outside the store. She felt a twinge in her stomach and hugged her son in the passenger seat.

"I promise," she said.

Over his mother's shoulder, through the driver's window, Leo saw Slash guiding the last of the children into the store with arm movements similar to a traffic cop's. When Slash found Leo looking at him from inside the car, his eyes narrowed, and he pointed at him. Using the same finger and unfolding his thumb, he formed an imaginary pistol. He held it to his temple. And fired.

1.

AARÓN

Friday, May 12, 2000

In the passenger seat, Andrea flicked the usual lock of hair from her face. She placed a finger on his lips.

"Don't say it."

Aarón just shrugged, sucked in the smell of chamomile that filled the parked car, and had to look away when the light changed in her eyes.

"Don't say it," she repeated. "It's not true."

Andrea looked straight ahead for a few seconds, through the windshield at a moonlit Arenas —it was little more than a village expanded with housing developments, a sea of residential tranquility. She clenched her teeth to contain her words, then opened a fist and revealed a stone.

"No . . . ," requested Aarón. "Please."

"It's up to you," said Andrea. "You can give it back to me whenever you want."

She left the stone on the dashboard. Then she stroked his hand on the gearshift and got out of the car.

Aarón heard the door close. He struck the steering wheel with his left fist while Andrea switched cars. The sand crunched under her tires when she left. He sighed, his forehead resting on the steering wheel. It was a few seconds before he sat up straight again. When he did, he looked at the clock on the instrument panel. It was after nine. Then he remembered. He'd promised Sr. Palmer he'd take his medication to him at the store after he left the pharmacy.

He thought about what to do, biting his bottom lip. He took his cell phone from the dashboard and pressed one of the buttons.

David answered. "Hey, man, how did it go?"

"Good," Aarón began to say, but he corrected himself. "No, actually, not good."

"Did you tell her?" David asked without needing a reply. He had detected in Aarón's voice that he had. David Mirabal was very good at knowing what was going on in his friend's head. Just like his mother, Ruth, was good at knowing what went on in the mind of Ana, Aarón's mother.

The two women had met at the university—standing in line to register for an administrative degree they never completed, just as they hadn't ended up marrying the boys' fathers—three years before bringing the two of them into the world on the same day. Coincidence decided both youngsters would be born on the same Wednesday. An extraordinary Wednesday in the early seventies that Madrid celebrated with the most spectacular blizzard seen in years.

"I think she took it badly." Aarón opened the car door and turned to hang his legs out, resting the arm he was holding his cell phone with on the steering wheel, just as he'd rested it so many times on David's shoulder to measure the depth of a puddle with a stick before leaping over it. "But she went off in such a rush. We barely spoke. You know what she's like. When Andrea doesn't want to listen . . ."

"I'll head over and you can tell me all about it." The last word sounded stifled, David exerting himself getting up from somewhere. "Are you where you told me, up at the viewpoint?"

"Hang on. That's why I was calling you. I just want to go home. Seriously, I want to lie on the sofa, eat a massive pizza, and watch any old crap on the TV." He paused before continuing. "Trouble is, I promised the American I'd take his medicine to the store."

Sr. Palmer, a Kansan who'd arrived in Spain on a ship, had spent more than half his life running the store. He bought Arenas's old gas station at a bargain price and hung the neon sign he'd stolen from a tyrannical boss—at the other store where he'd worked, in Galena, his birth city—over the door. When he arrived in the mid-seventies, Arenas was still no more than a single street and a couple of housing development plans. The watch factory set up years before, fifteen kilometers away, had brought the first workers to the village, but the road links with Madrid were still too poor to attract more people.

Then they improved the A-6 and Arenas began to grow. From the counter in his store, Sr. Palmer began serving an ever-increasing number of young couples. On match-day Saturdays he sold sunflower seeds and beer to the men, first-time fathers appearing in the store wearing their soccer team's scarf around their necks, radios stuck to their ears and their firstborns sitting on their shoulders. Whole families arrived the next day, on paella Sundays, when the fathers bought newspapers to read the reports on yesterday's match, the mothers asked Sr. Palmer to select the crustiest bread for them, the children yelled requests for packs of cards to complete their collections of soccer-league players, and a grumpy grandfather looked suspiciously from under his beret at the young foreigner who still hadn't learned to deal with pesetas. And it was from the same counter—where he finally managed to familiarize himself with bills that were too colorful and whose denominations were too high for someone accustomed to dollars: a hundred, a thousand,

and even five thousand pesetas—that Sr. Palmer watched the village grow. Arenas became a town with a private university, a water park, and as many houses as there were tears from the eyes of Sra. Palmer, who missed Kansas so much it was as if she and her husband had emigrated to the Land of Oz, not Europe.

"I don't know why you always take the American his medication," said David. "Let him go to the drugstore himself, like everyone else. We're not Telepizza."

Aarón looked at the stone on the dashboard.

He remembered how Sr. Palmer had sold him his first beers. It was that time he had wanted to impress Andrea, when they weren't even together yet. Aarón couldn't have been any older than seventeen. The American knew his age because he knew his parents and had seen him grow up, but he let himself be fooled. He gave Aarón the beers and asked him to come closer so he could whisper something in his ear. *Fight for that girl*, Sr. Palmer said to him, dragging out his *R*s more than he did now. And Aarón had listened to him. Two years later, he started dating Andrea. Ten years after that, today, he had decided to end it.

Sitting in the car, he remembered her laughter after the second beer.

". . . to be worrying about anyone else," David continued on the telephone.

"What?" asked Aarón, trying to pick up the thread again.

"I said you have too much on your plate to be worrying about anyone else. You shouldn't have gotten him used to you taking it to him."

"Buddy, it's no bother. The poor guy spends the whole day stuck in the store . . . and he lets me fill the car up without paying."

"Seriously? He lets you do that?"

"Sometimes."

"I knew there was something weird going on."

"And I told him this morning I'd take him his medication as soon as the pharmacy closed, but with . . . with all this stuff with

Andrea"—Aarón closed his eyes when he heard himself refer this way to what had just happened—"I forgot. I left the medicine there. I don't even have it with me."

"So take it to him tomorrow, no?"

"It's antihypertensives and vasodilators."

"Bad heart, or what?"

"High blood pressure," Aarón specified. "I should take them to him today. I just really don't feel like going back to the pharmacy, or going to the store . . ." He left the sentence up in the air.

"You want me to go, in other words."

"Could you?"

Aarón heard David sigh on the other end of the line.

"I could. Of course I could. On my day off. Provide a service we don't even have to provide. If he wants, I'll give him a foot massage as well," said David. "All right, for fuck's sake, I'll go. But I'm doing it for you, because I can guess how you're feeling. Hang on—will the boss be at the drugstore?"

"Nah, he left early today. He wasn't there when I locked up. The American's medication's on the counter, I left it there."

"I hope the boss doesn't show up. I have zero desire to see his face on my day off, and—"

"You weren't so worried about him showing up when you took Sandra there the other night," Aarón cut in.

"Bastard," replied David, before laughing. "Though I still don't see what's wrong with getting it on in a drugstore. It's the first time in twenty-nine years a girl's left me half-done. I'm sure my brother doesn't have that problem when he takes girls out in the patrol car."

"I don't think Héctor goes with girls in his patrol car. Cops don't do that . . . do they?"

"You don't think? I wouldn't be so sure. We Mirabal brothers will do whatever it takes to get some action."

Aarón heard David's sentences ending more and more slowly, as if he was thinking about something else.

"What're you doing?" Aarón asked.

"I can't find the drugstore keys, man. One day away from there, and I've lost them already."

Aarón heard drawers opening and doors closing.

"Got them," David finally announced. "I got the keys. And I just found the photos of the first time we got drunk, in a drawer. Can you explain to me what we were doing buck naked up a willow tree at the lake?"

"Your brother had to pick us up in the patrol car." Aarón was surprised to find himself laughing. "That was a long time ago." He made a calculation and the laughter died in his mouth. "And I was already with Drea by then."

"OK, you need to go home," decided David, who also stopped laughing. "Do I have to go now to do the American's thing?"

"If you can, yeah. I told him I'd go as soon as we closed, but if—"

"I'll go now, then," David interrupted. "I'll be there in no time. And I'll tell him to fill my car up for free."

"Hey," Aarón shot back, "that's a secret."

"I know, man, I know, I was joking. But hey, should I come by later with some beers and you can tell me about Andrea?"

"No, don't bother. I'll be asleep. Talk to you tomorrow."

"Up to you. I'm going to buy the beers anyway. We can start saving for the trip another day."

The mention of the trip made Aarón feel bad. Because he hadn't said anything about it to Andrea.

He shook his head and said, "Thanks for going, seriously. I don't think I . . ."

He stopped talking when he knew he wouldn't be able to finish the sentence with the way his throat was tightening.

"Go on, hang up, it's no big deal. And us guys don't cry, all right?" said David, when he understood what was happening.

Aarón smiled at the floor, blinking hard. He returned the cell phone to the dashboard and rested his elbows on his knees.

He looked out at the town, which, seen from up high, was like a model. He searched for Aquatopia, the water park that boasted the biggest slide in Europe, visible from anywhere in Arenas. The outline of the Giga Splash and the other slides were part of the town's skyline. Like the hundreds of houses that gave Arenas its characteristic appearance of the perfect suburb for family life. The Noroeste University, whose opening Sr. Palmer had witnessed in the early eighties, brought the students first. Their families came after them. Then more families. The construction industry saw gold, building residential developments an ever-increasing distance from the old village's historical center, which lost all its importance. As did its real name: Arenas de la Despernada, a name that all the inhabitants shortened for convenience and perhaps also to avoid referring to the noblewoman who, according to legend, lost both legs when the village was founded.

The population lived in houses with front and back yards, neat fences, and little swimming pools in original shapes. The Moreno brothers hit the jackpot with their family pool business, their slogan, "A different design every time," working to perfection. The municipal council also capitalized on the situation, offering free university enrollment to young people completing their secondary education at the local school. That measure ultimately determined the demographic of Arenas, just forty kilometers to the northwest of Madrid: it was made up of young families, couples with money coming from the big city to live someplace where their children could start at kindergarten and graduate from college without leaving the town. Youngsters who would also enjoy a happy childhood growing up on Lake Arenas, another local landmark, and throwing themselves down the slides at Aquatopia.

Not far from the silhouettes of those slides, Aarón, from his car parked up high, identified his apartment building. Then his eyes made out the green light of the sign on the front of the drugstore where he started his internship during his final year of college. And where he had continued to work to this day.

Aarón squeezed the steering wheel. The plastic squeaked under his skin in the silence of the night on which he'd mustered the courage he needed to cast from his life the woman who was all smiles and indecipherable hip movements. A woman who had even forgiven him his indiscretion with Rebeca Blanco, a student doing an internship who helped Aarón at the drugstore for a few months and in whom Aarón had sought the sense of adventure that was lacking in his life. An indiscretion he ended up admitting. And Andrea forgiving, because she preferred the pain of betrayal to the pain of loss. A demonstration of love that wasn't enough for Aarón. Because Aarón still wanted to find out what life without Andrea would be like. To go away from her to know whether he loved her as much as he thought. To know it before making a family and never having the chance to know the truth again. *Do it, then, man. Tell her,* David had urged him a few weeks ago. *Tell her everything you just said to me. That what happened with Rebeca might be a symptom, that you feel like you've missed out on a lot of things in the ten years you've been together. And that you're not ready to be a parent. If you're not ready, you're not ready. It's not something you can force,* he'd insisted. Then, just to try to motivate Aarón, he'd proposed a trip. *Let's ask for a week off and go somewhere. Anywhere. I don't know, Cuba,* David had said, as if the island was on the moon. *Just you and me. To celebrate your new life. Or cry together. Whatever you prefer.*

Still hypnotized by the green light shining in the distance, Aarón closed his eyes and tried to block out his memories. Then, though he wanted to avoid it, his gaze escaped to the dashboard. There it was, the stone they found at the lake the night it all began. The night when he first told Andrea he loved her. Aarón had planned the moment to coincide with the solstice that marked the beginning of the first summer of the nineties, the two of them sitting on the blanket he laid out on the Lake Arenas shore. What he hadn't planned was the uncontrollable urge to throw himself, fully clothed, into the water and yell to Andrea what in reality she already knew. With arms outstretched and water dripping from them into the sparkling lake, Aarón held out a hand and said, *Come in the water.* It was an invitation that replaced the usual declaration of love forevermore. Because from that night on, the shortest night of that year, they never said the conventional three words to each other. Instead they simply said *Come in the water.*

Aarón suddenly sat up in the seat. He started the car and headed back down the highway that led up to the viewpoint. He drove on through Arenas's tranquil streets, negotiating its many traffic circles. He turned the corner onto the main road. In the distance he recognized the neon sign of the American's store and the silhouettes of the gas pumps. He again remembered the first beers he'd bought for Andrea.

"Thanks, David, I really needed to go home," he whispered to the empty car.

He had barely managed two slices of pizza. He lay on the sofa without intending to sleep, resting his left forearm over his eyes, still perceiving Andrea's chamomile smell that somehow always lingered on his skin.

The first ring of the telephone sounded remote, like a daydream within the real dream he'd slipped into without intending.

The second ring arranged each reality on its proper plane.

Aarón remembered that he was on his sofa at home, with his forearm over his eyes, most of a pizza going cold on the table, and a telephone ringing for the second, no, the third time, near the front door. Without knowing exactly why, because normally he was quite happy to remain impassive while someone somewhere despaired at the tenth unanswered ring, he ran to the telephone and answered it.

"Drea?"

"Oh God, Aarón, listen."

Andrea's voice sounded alarmed. Aarón didn't have the strength to
go back over what they'd spoken about.

"Drea," he interrupted, "Drea, please."

"It's David."

Then he fell silent and let her continue.

"David's been shot." She choked when she tried to go on. "At the
American's store."

2.

LEO

A mosquito exploded on the murderous fluorescent lamp that hung next to the neon sign at the American's store. The blue light flickered for a few seconds before returning to its constant deathly glow. Leo looked up when the insect, its abdomen bulging with blood from some local resident, was fried with a brief crackle. His face was colored by the yellow reflection of the word *Open* in casual type, and the purple that framed the word. The door-opening system detected his presence and the two panels slid in opposite directions to allow him in. A gust of icy air hit his skinny body, making him tear his eyes from the hypnotic brilliance of the murderous lamp.

He looked inside the shop and took a step back so the doors would close. He stood out there not knowing what to do, grabbing the straps on his new space backpack at the shoulders. His father turned around.

"Son, what're you doing?" Amador offered Leo his hand. "Come on, what's up? You'll feel better in here. There's air-conditioning," he said.

Amador pulled on Leo's arm. The doors closed behind them.

It was the first time Leo had been in the American's store. Two whole years had passed since his new classmates had made fun of him in unison and left him at the school gates. The Open was open to everyone—that's what the sign indicated—but for Leo, each day after school, it was as if the store were empty, the lights were off, and it had been declared under quarantine with a couple of boards nailed across the entrance. His classmates gathered there at the end of each day. The same classmates who always forced him to sit in the front row and who threw balls of paper at him. Sometimes with a stone inside. The owners of the laughter that always broke out at his expense. Slash and the rest of them shot out in the direction of the American's store as soon as the school bell rang, to buy some Cokes—sometimes they added a pack of Mentos to make them explode in a fountain of foam—to decide who had the best bike, and to play-fight on the grass by the gas pumps, imitating the latest video game.

Sometimes they also looked at Leo. They pointed at him. From the other side of the street that was an entire world away, Leo saw them laugh and mimic him. He knew they were doing it when they put their heels together and took little steps with their feet pointing outward, like a penguin, though that wasn't how he walked. Every afternoon he waited alone for Mom to pick him up, to honor the promise she made him on the first day of school, though she often had to go back to the office and would leave him at home with the housekeeper, Linda.

"Ground control to Major Leo." Amador interrupted his son's thoughts.

Leo examined the store's interior, lit with fluorescent tubes, like a boy who'd snuck behind the curtain of the adult section at the video rental store. His hand slipped from his father's. To his left, the wall beside the door caught his attention when he saw the candy boxes piled on top of one another in a colorful wall of transparent bricks. He approached them. This was the spot they looked at him from. He turned his head and, like the others must have done so many times, he searched for the crosswalk in front of the school entrance. From there, following the white stripes that seemed to shine in the darkness, his eyes moved on to the place by the traffic lights where "lame Leo" always stood. His own form was projected onto the empty sidewalk, through the store's transparent doors. A ghostly reflection. The image that was seen from here every afternoon by Edgar, Slash, and all the other children who would never be anything but the mass of kids who rejected him from the first day of school. For a moment, he could feel them materializing in his vicinity. They crowded around him, grabbing piles of candy and laughing at the weird boy who watched them from outside. Unable to control himself, Leo took a sugar-coated gummy strawberry. He wanted to know what it was like to be one of them. When he put it in his mouth and chewed, he tasted the sourness of self-betrayal. He swallowed with his eyes closed. He shook his head. He was alone again in front of the stacks of candy. His condensed silhouette evaporated on the street. Only he and his father were in the store. Summer emptied the town of students.

"You've just had dinner. You can buy yourself some of them tomorrow, if you want," said Amador, speaking over the television voices flooding the store.

"It doesn't matter, Dad." Leo turned around and approached his father's legs. "They're not very nice."

"Did you eat one without paying?" Amador scolded him. He crouched down and cleaned Leo's mouth with his thumb.

From behind the counter, Sr. Palmer observed the gesture. The familiarity of the scene flicked a switch abandoned somewhere in his mind. Like the fluorescent light outside the store, a memory flickered in his head, fighting to come on. It failed and went out.

"We didn't come here for you to take candy," Amador declared before standing back up.

He walked toward the store's aisles. Leo followed him, keeping his distance. They passed the newspapers and magazines on their left—the last few copies of some papers, on the floor, barely preserved their front pages. Next to this section was a large display, refrigerated but open, of sodas and prepared food. At the back, several freezers contained pizzas, ice cream, and other frozen products. When it first opened, the store only stocked accessories for the cars that stopped to refuel. Then there were bread and newspapers. Later, US chains combining a store and a gas station open 24-7 landed in Spain—old acquaintances of Sr. Palmer's that he knew as 7-Elevens, which already existed in Kansas when he left. Adapting to the times, the American gradually expanded the store and its hours to meet the town's growing demand. It had been years now—since he'd begun hiring students part time—that he'd been selling pretty much everything and was open until midnight. Sr. Palmer proudly told people how he'd turned down offers of millions from Shell and Repsol.

Leo and his father bypassed the first aisle, stocked with car products. He observed the bottles of oil and antifreeze, the pine-tree-shaped air fresheners. Passing the second aisle, he barely had time to see what the cans contained. Amador turned down the third aisle.

"Which one are we supposed to be buying? Skim or whole?" Amador asked with a confused look, examining the shelf of dairy products.

"The pink one, I think," said Leo. "That one with the picture of the cow on it."

"We'll take some whole as well, just in case" was Amador's final decision. "Will the rocket take all this weight on the way home? Earth's so far away, we could easily end up orbiting without being able to reach it."

"The gravity force is lower on this planet," Leo responded, projecting his voice. "It shouldn't be a problem."

Father and son had used astronautical jargon since the day Amador gave his boy a pack of glow-in-the-dark stars, which were the trigger for Leo's burgeoning interest in astronomy. Some time ago, the two had stuck them on the boy's bedroom ceiling, with Victoria complaining about the marks the adhesives would leave on the paintwork. Leo had directed the operation with a star chart in his hands. He knew the various constellations and where each star had to be positioned. Amador would have distributed them in no particular order around the room, but Leo wanted his artificial sky to be exactly the same one the other kids his age—everyone except him—looked up at from the fires at their summer camps, discussing with their friends which was the best of the ten original aliens that Ben 10 could turn into with the Omnitrix. Too bad that, in the pack of stickers Amador bought from the American's store, there weren't enough stars to complete the chart Leo held excitedly in his fingers. *That must be a black hole,* Dad had improvised, seeing his son's face when they stuck the last star on an unfinished Cassiopeia.

With the two cartons of milk, they headed toward the counter. The store owner had his back turned. He was searching for something in some drawers that overflowed with paper and colored wires. With his shoulders bent, his shirt collar almost touched his white hair, perfectly combed from the bald patch on the top of his head to the back of his neck. The pictures on the television located somewhere under the counter were projected onto his body, and the sound was so loud that, now that they were close, it was unpleasant in the ears.

Amador noticed a little device on Sr. Palmer's left ear. He dropped the two cartons of milk noisily on the counter. The old man's shoulders jerked upward. He slammed shut one of the drawers in which he hadn't found what he was looking for and turned around, frowning. The elastic jowl that hung under his chin continued to jiggle after he turned.

"Sorry," Amador said.

The old man came to the counter, switched off the television. His round cheeks swelled even more when he smiled.

"Don't be sorry, it's no problem." Sr. Palmer spoke Spanish almost without an accent now, but the peculiar vibration of his *R*s and the occasional strange construction gave him away. "It's this damned gizmo," he explained, indicating the device over his ear. "It doesn't work like they said it would. I can't even hear the doors when someone comes in. The other day, I had the fright of my life when Gloria, the woman from the library, appeared at the counter. Quite big, that lady. You can't imagine what it's like to suddenly find her in front of you—"

"Don't worry," Amador cut in. "You carry on. I saw you were looking for something."

"That's a similar story. My damned heart, it's going to stop on me one of these days." Sr. Palmer hit the left side of his chest. "No smoking, no drinking—it's quite the sacrifice, worse than putting up with my good lady wife all these years," he added, rounding off the joke with a double cough. "And my pills aren't showing up, *dammit*." His curses, onomatopoeia, and counting still sometimes came out in English. "One day my good lady wife will have to come and close the store because I've dropped dead right here." He turned back to the drawers. "Like what happened to the man at the bar on the corner, one of the owner's brothers. Did you hear? They say he died while he was closing out the register. They found him next to the slot machine. They say he dragged himself there on his elbows."

Amador didn't know whether Sr. Palmer was talking to them or himself.

Leo, who was resting his backpack against the counter and hidden behind it, pulled on his father's shirt. He held his finger to his temple and drew circles with it. Then he turned back around. Behind eight of his fingers, Leo's eyes emerged over the counter. Amador cleared his throat to catch the old man's attention.

And Sr. Palmer turned around again.

His gaze, which had been fixed on Amador, now moved to the boy.

Leo had gone on tiptoes and was looking at him curiously, biting his bottom lip. His initial innocent curiosity turned to astonishment at the inexplicable recognition he noticed in Sr. Palmer's eyes.

The old man felt his heart change position when the light of memory, which earlier had only flickered, now came on.

The boy's expression when he frowned, the way he kept one eye more open than the other, was unmistakable. It was the boy. It was him.

For a moment, Sr. Palmer's vision blurred. He thought he was going to fall, but regained his senses. The image of Leo's face struck him in the deepest part of some forgotten place in his brain. A cold sweat broke out on his forehead. He heard his heart beat in his ears. His pulse accelerated in the way his doctor had told him it mustn't.

"Are you all right?" asked Amador. "You look like you could really use those pills."

"The pills, yeah," Palmer muttered. "The pills."

He opened one of the drawers for a third time. He rummaged through the papers, letting them fall onto the floor. Maybe his subconscious, which did remember where he had last seen the pills, now guided him, in this event of dire necessity, to the box of medication. He took out a pack of five capsules. He extracted two and put them in his mouth. He swallowed hard, almost without saliva. He felt them go down, sticking to his esophagus. Though there was no medical reason to experience an instant improvement, the placebo effect removed his anxiety for the time being, enabling Sr. Palmer to hide his tension before turning back around.

"*Wow*, that's better." His voice only trembled at the beginning. "That'll be"—he did the mental arithmetic in English—"three euros fifty."

"No, add one of those gummy candies as well," said Amador, gesturing at the entrance. "My son, he ate one."

Palmer barely reacted to the comment. He kept his eyes on Leo as he took a green plastic bag out from under the cash register and put the cartons of milk in it.

Amador searched in his wallet for a five-euro bill. He handed it to Sr. Palmer. After receiving the change, he wished the American a good evening and headed to the exit.

"Come on, Leo!" he yelled on the way, seeing his son still standing there looking at the old man. "Let's go, or Mom will get mad. And Pi will be waiting for you."

Leo swiveled on his heels. He started following his father.

"Hey, kid!" he heard the voice behind him say. "Your dad left his change."

Leo froze for a few seconds. He retraced his three steps and stretched his arm out over the counter to receive the coin that Sr. Palmer placed in his hand. After they gave each other a final look that the old man understood but Leo did not, the boy turned away.

His space backpack hit the counter on his way out.

He headed to the Aston Martin parked outside, from which his father was giving two long blasts on the horn.

"What did you go back for?" Amador asked when Leo climbed into the passenger seat, positioning his backpack between his legs.

"You left money." Leo held the coin up in front of his father's eyes.

Amador thought about it for a moment, shook his head, and said, "That's strange. The old man must have wanted to give you the candy. But it's the last time you steal. Understood, Commander? Over."

"Understood. Over and out."

Leo burst out laughing.

The silhouette of a high five between a father and son at rearview-mirror height was the last thing Sr. Palmer saw from the store's entrance.

When the neon changed over his head, a violet glow left his face in shadows.

3.

AARÓN

Friday, May 12, 2000

The water splashed the bathroom mirror and floor when Aarón tried to wet his face. The uncontrollable trembling in his hands made it almost impossible. He looked at his feet, at the puddles on the marble floor.

"David, no," he whispered to his own face, disfigured by the drops of water on the glass.

He turned and had to grip the door to avoid slipping. He left the apartment while the boy he'd climbed trees and lit fires with fought for his life on a gurney medics were pushing through the corridors of the University Hospital.

Aarón got in his car and drove down one of the town's long avenues. It was silent and almost deserted on a weeknight. As silent as a family car parked by the sidewalk. As deserted as the skeletal framework of a half-built housing development. On the streets surrounding the town center, the only signs of life were the illuminated windows of kitchens and bedrooms of houses protected by fortifications of Arizona cypresses. Or the occasional night jogger or the sound of bottles falling into the green containers for recycling glass.

Andrea was waiting on the street, at the door to her house. Aarón made out her slight figure from the car. Her face was hidden behind a tangle of hair.

"Go," she said as soon as she was in the car. She was holding a white handkerchief screwed up in a ball. Aarón waited for her to look at him. He heard her sniff, her eyes fixed straight ahead. "Go," she repeated. This time she shook her head to remove the hair from her face and spoke directly to him. The green of her eyes that was normally bright seemed to have dulled to a brown. The small, round nose of a little girl grown up without realizing it was red from using the handkerchief she held. She rubbed her lips together, lips that had smiled at him so many times. Andrea's smiles were so wide her eyes almost closed. The moisture on her face reflected the orangey light from the streetlamps. Aarón wanted to hold her. The engine revved when he used his right foot to lean over. He let it roar while Andrea's slender body shook in a sob that made his neck wet.

"Tell me you're crying because of what I said up there earlier," he said.

But she shook her head, her brow pressed against his shoulder. Eventually, the movement changed and the shaking became a nod. Aarón blew out. He opened his eyes wide in the hope the air would dry them. He returned to his seat. The engine stopped groaning.

"We're going to stay calm for now, OK?" he said.

He gripped her hand and she wiped her nose with her handkerchief. She nodded, rubbing her lips together again. This time she also used her teeth.

Aarón turned off the hazard lights. The car moved off.

"It's going to be fine," he said to the steering wheel.

They drove on through several traffic circles on a May night that was warmer than usual for Arenas. They said nothing. When Aarón instinctively turned down the street the Open was on—one of the two that led to the hospital—Andrea tried to stop him, but reacted too late.

"Take the water park road instead. This one's going to be"—the car slowed to a stop—"closed."

In the distance they could see the rotating lights of two police cars. Aarón recognized the one Héctor always used. He'd been driving it around the town for more than ten years, never imagining his own brother would one day—today—be the victim at a crime scene he'd have to attend. The blue light from the police vehicles was reflected on the Open's glass front. On the two gas pumps near the store's little parking area. On the school windows on the other side of the street. On Andrea's pupils when she looked at Aarón as if the scene had suddenly reminded her of something important.

"Please, no," was what came out of Aarón's mouth when the image at the other end of the street forced him to take on board the full implications of what had happened. A deafening thought hit him for the first time: *It's my fault.*

At that precise moment, in the hospital, the boy who'd taught him how to kiss a girl and to get a bat drunk, the man who'd offered to take the medication to the American's store for him a few hours ago, was spilling his blood onto a gurney and peering into the abyss of a coma through the hole opened up in his chest by a bullet that entered him on the left side of his back.

It was Héctor himself, a blurred amalgamation of brother and police-man, who rushed to them at the hospital with the first news on David's condition. He hugged Aarón first. Then he grabbed Andrea's face by the cheeks and kissed her on the forehead before stretching his arms around both of them. Aarón and Andrea's hands interlocked. Héctor shook his head.

No.

"He's gone into a coma," he told them. He was being the cop who gives bad news only to other people. "They said he's grade four, something about a Glasgow scale. They told us no. That they don't think"—he said the remaining words in the sentence in a brother's voice—"they don't think he'll come out of this."

One person at the hospital who would come out of it was Sr. Palmer. After the gunshot, he had collapsed in the store. He'd fallen onto his knees, keeping his balance for a few seconds by using his hands as a third and fourth means of support. It didn't prevent the pain in his chest from pulling him down and leaving him lying faceup. Now he was hooked up to a drip, his life translated into an intermittent beep. His wife was holding his hand, with her forehead resting on the mattress. When she heard her husband say, *I promised I'd never leave you alone, didn't I?* Sra. Palmer opened her eyes, thanked God out loud, and replied, *I just wanna go back to Kansas.*

"No one can go in to see him for now," Héctor added.

Throwing her head forward, Andrea made her hair hide her face.

Andrea moved Aarón out of the way with a gentle push with her right hip, the one he'd rested his face on so many times to play with her pubic hair after making love. With the usual twist of her wrist, she managed to open the door.

Aarón's home was on the second floor of one of the few apartment blocks in Arenas. It was Andrea, an architect, who had advised him to buy it. She had completed her architecture degree at the Noroeste University in Arenas. The university itself offered her, newly graduated, a position teaching descriptive geometry to cover a period of maternity leave for an associate professor. This turned into sick leave due to postpartum depression, and it continued for reasons unknown to Andrea. When they offered her a permanent contract, she stopped worrying about what might have happened to the other professor. The day they celebrated her new job, Aarón joked that the woman could be dead, for all they cared, making Andrea spit a jet of champagne out as she slapped him on the shoulder.

Now, years later, the memory made Andrea smile while she observed how Aarón had left the house when he set off for the hospital. On the TV, a home shopping channel was advertising a revolutionary neck pillow. The pizza, now completely cold, was hardening on the table. The kitchen lights were on, as were the living-room ones. There was water on the bathroom mirror and floor.

Andrea placed a hand on Aarón's face. She stroked the pronounced bone of his jaw. Then she closed the pizza box and took it to the kitchen. She left it on top of the trash can because the extra-large size Aarón always ordered wouldn't have fit even in the container outside. Had it been a normal night, less than half an hour would have passed before he complained about the lid on the trash can not opening when he stepped on the pedal, asking her to leave the box to one side next time. Had it been a normal night.

Aarón was lying on the sofa now, his forearm covering his eyes. She sat on the edge, at his waist. She rested her right hand on his stomach. Aarón took his arm away from his face. He wasn't looking anywhere in particular, but his eyes were fully open. He was chewing the inside of his bottom lip, like he did when he was reading the directions on some medication she'd bought without consulting him. It was a gesture that had always touched Andrea and that, at this moment, she didn't know whether she should miss.

She held a thumb to Aarón's lips. Had it been a normal night, he would have bitten it, barking like a dog. He let her rest it on his mouth, without reacting. A tear rolled down one of Aarón's temples before falling onto the sofa, making a dark spot on the blue upholstery.

"We were going on a trip," he said.

Her thumb was still on his lips, so the sentence sounded as if a child had said it. She didn't know anything about any trip. She thought of

David. A wave of something very dark came up from her stomach and broke in her throat, where a stifled sob set her off crying again. She lay on Aarón's chest. She wished that night didn't really belong to her life.

When Andrea got up, separating her cheek from his chest, she tried to smooth down his T-shirt and noticed it was wet. She saw that Aarón still had his eyes open. He was looking at some nonexistent place, beyond his apartment's ceiling. She gripped his chin, forcing him to look at her.

"Please." Her voice was gentle but firm.

"I asked him to go to the store," Aarón managed to say.

He only just finished the sentence when his lips curved downward, the complete opposite of a smile. He squeezed his eyes shut, trying to contain the liquid that spilled between his eyelids regardless. Andrea couldn't find any words. She just dried his eyes with her index finger. Then she went over his face, starting with the straight, thick eyebrows of someone always thinking about something important. She ran her finger along the contour of his broad forehead, framing it from his temples along the hairline, where the chestnut hair that sometimes seemed blond began. She massaged the point between his eyes in little circles. Then she went down the broad, straight bone of his nose, skipped his lips, and landed her finger in the dimple in the middle of his chin. From there she kept going down toward the mound of his Adam's apple.

Andrea stood up and pulled on Aarón's arm. Helped by the tug, he let himself be led. While she guided Aarón's body, slim and with his stomach still flat though he was almost thirty, Andrea remembered the day he moved. *This house is perfect for you to come live with me*, Aarón had said. Then he'd grabbed her from behind and rested his chin in the hollow between her shoulder and neck. *Aarón, you know already, as far as my mother's concerned, there has to be a wedding*, Andrea had said.

I don't understand your mom's insistence on getting married. How long did her marriage last? Six years? he'd said.

Seven. I was seven when Dad left. But that's not the point. So, shall we get married, then? He had evaded the question, and she had escaped from his arms.

Now, she was practically carrying Aarón in her arms when they reached the bed. He fell onto the mattress like a dead weight. She took off his sneakers but didn't suggest undressing. She knew from experience—on Thursday nights, she arrived home exhausted after teaching eight hours of classes without a break—that going to bed without the usual rituals or dental hygiene was a treat you had to award yourself from time to time. At any rate, he was only wearing jeans and a T-shirt. As always. She did ask if he wanted some acetaminophen, an idea he found comforting. Aarón, in defiance of his own pharmaceutical expertise, thought there was no better sleeping pill than a painkiller.

"You'll stay over, right? I'm scared of getting up tomorrow. I might not even sleep," he said, his mouth pressed against the pillow. "Make it a thousand milligrams."

He was already asleep, snoring gently, like on so many other nights, when Andrea returned with the glass of effervescent water. She lay a sheet over his legs, opened the window above the bed, and went over to the bedside table to put down the glass. She had to move some papers aside, and they fell to the floor. She picked them up in the darkness and tried to put them back on the table. It was impossible with the glass of bubbling liquid there.

On her way out of the bedroom, she recognized the enormous T-shirt she'd left hanging from the television when she'd gotten up that morning. She took it to use as pajamas again. She closed the bedroom door and turned on the light. She undressed in the living room, took off her bra, and put on the T-shirt. It almost reached her knees. She surprised herself when she decided to keep her panties on. She returned to the kitchen. Unlike Aarón, she wasn't going to be able to sleep without the help of one of the few pills he kept in his surprisingly empty medicine cabinet. She wandered around the apartment taking little sips from her glass, shaking two capsules in her fist.

Among the papers from the bedside table she'd just left on the sofa, she made out a long, rectangular silhouette with a logo on it she immediately recognized. A large red and yellow *B*. She frowned. She sat down, stretched the T-shirt's material over her bent knees, and picked up the folder.

Two airline tickets. One in David Mirabal's name. The other in the name of Aarón Salvador. One week. In Cuba. Leaving on June 10, 2000. Less than a month from now.

"Were you going to celebrate our breakup, or what?" Andrea murmured before throwing the capsules to the back of her throat. "Idiot," she added before swallowing, not knowing whether the insult was directed at Aarón or herself.

4.

LEO

When they returned from the Open, Amador automatically kissed the corner of his wife's mouth while she spoke on the cordless telephone.

Leo went up to his room to undress.

Pi was waiting for him there, rubbing himself against the doorframe. He sounded like an idling engine. Leo crouched down and offered him a PEZ that he took from his pocket. The animal sniffed it and decided to bite into it.

"The cherry ones are the best," Leo said as he dropped his backpack by the desk and took off his shoes. "Have you been chewing my gray slippers?"

He found the slippers under the bed. He put them on after his pajamas. When he knelt next to Pi to ask him if he wanted another PEZ, he caught sight of one of his backpack's side pockets. Leo had asked if he could take his space pack when his father told him they'd go to the American's store that night to buy some milk for breakfast. During the last days of the school year, he'd imagined that the backpack really did belong to an astronaut and that he could fire himself into space from his desk. To a place where there was no one who would put glue on his classroom chair. Where he wasn't always the last one to be chosen for team games.

Now Leo fixed his eyes on the backpack's zipperless pocket, where the capital *S* of the words *Space Commander* was printed. The *R* at the end was on the identical pocket on the other side, with the words running right across the front. The blue-and-red-striped corner of an unfamiliar envelope was sticking out from the first pocket. Leo could never be bothered to empty his backpack at the end of the school year. No doubt it was still full of his belongings, but this envelope wasn't one of them.

Curious, he stretched over and took it out.

A memory came to mind. The time his classmates left a dead frog in his sneakers. He felt some relief when he held the envelope in his hands and found there was no way it could contain an animal.

He opened it.

He took out a piece of paper that had been folded in half twice. Maybe it was another fake declaration of love from one of the girls in his class, really written by Slash. He was about to read it with the resignation of someone who knows the joke is always on him. He even felt fortunate that he hadn't found the envelope on the day they must have put it in his backpack pocket—at least he avoided the laughter of dozens of children, contained at first and then exploding at his expense. In his room, under the light of the glow stars his father had given him, only he and the books on his shelf would witness the humiliation that would never be his last.

Then Leo read the note.

A film of cold sweat covered his body, which separated itself from his rational thought in a surge of panic that took his breath away. The rest of the world, his mother yelling downstairs and a sports commentator letting rip in a high-pitched voice, suddenly seemed as if it were submerged in an ocean of liquid glass.

Absently, he walked to the stairs.

The big toe on one of his feet recognized the first step, and he began going down.

His right hand was as cold as a stone. With his left hand, he twisted the leg of his pajamas nervously at the hip. He continued, his old gray slippers rubbing against the carpet. He held the envelope in the marble fingers of a hand he could barely feel.

Leo took a lot longer than usual to go down the stairs. When he arrived at the bottom, he crossed the hall and peered into the living room, which was accessible through tall, open arches. The television was loud, broadcasting the overexcited observations of the sports commentator. And fighting against the television in a battle of sound, his mother was discussing politics on the phone with a friend.

Leo's face was pale. His eyes, black, all pupil, were unblinking. He just stood there, hoping to catch his parents' attention, trembling like he did when he read adult horror novels.

Seeing him, Victoria yelled her son's name.

She threw the cordless telephone onto the sofa to go to the boy. Amador was alerted by the unexpected movement behind him. His wife knelt beside an absent Leo, who was twisting his pajama leg and looking nowhere in particular, unresponsive to his mother's increasingly rough shaking. As if in slow motion, Amador approached them.

"What the fuck's going on?" he yelled at his wife.

He knelt and grabbed his son's face with both hands. He didn't know what to do and, without much thought, imitating his own father, dealt him a hard slap.

Leo burst instantly into tears. Victoria held the boy.

"Son, please, what is it?"

Leo looked his parents in the eyes.

In an attempt to calm him down, Victoria separated his sweaty hair from his forehead. She rearranged his pajama top, pulled his gray slippers back on.

"Put your heel in the slipper, too, or you'll step on them and they won't last three months," she said, wanting to blank out other thoughts with the sound of her voice.

Holding one of her son's ankles and stretching the back of the slipper, she saw the moist envelope Leo had in his hand.

"What've you got . . . ?" She didn't finish the question.

With a gentle tug, she separated the envelope from Leo's fingers. The boy was barely whimpering now. He was sniffing up the snot under his nose and on his top lip, wiping off the rest with the back of his hand. A large curl of wet fabric stood out on his pajama leg.

The envelope bore no stamp or postmark. Nor an address. Nor the name of any sender.

"It's airmail," Victoria thought out loud when she saw the blue and red stripes along the edge. "What's this letter, angel?" She spoke with her face near Leo's.

She intended her tone to be soothing, but her choked voice sounded quite the opposite. She turned to her husband.

"Do you know what . . . ?" She was unable to finish the sentence again, as the sight of words written in blue on the front of the envelope interrupted her.

Amador observed his wife's eyes opening in a look of incomprehension before her eyebrows arched in an expression of total confusion. She passed him the envelope so he could read it, too. They were capital letters, written in a clean and tidy hand. Six words:

FOR A NINE-YEAR-OLD BOY

For a second, Amador felt relieved. His heart slowed. It wasn't so bad. Victoria was exaggerating, as always. The envelope wasn't addressed to Leo, who had celebrated his eighth birthday just a month ago. Then it occurred to Amador that, if the envelope had put his son in a state this close to a panic attack, there must be something more. At that moment his fingers ran over the rectangular form of what seemed like a piece of paper folded in half twice.

"Where did you get this?"

He asked the question looking at his son's frightened expression. Leo was between his mother's crossed legs now. She had sat on the floor and was trying to smooth down the creases on the boy's pajama pants in a nervous gesture that she soon replaced with another much more personal one: clicking the nails of her forefinger and thumb together.

Victoria noticed how old Leo's slippers were. It soothed her to imagine herself choosing some new ones with him at the Centro Oeste, the town's shopping mall. The thought obscured a deeper one that certainly existed but that she refused to process: that something wasn't right with her child. She forced herself to fill the main stage of her mind with images of varicolored house shoes: gorilla feet, bees with antennae, a lion's paw.

Amador lifted the envelope flap and took out what indeed turned out to be a standard piece of paper folded in half twice.

Leo remained crouched between his mother's legs. The sweat that soaked his back was beginning to dry. He was cold, and reacted with a slight chatter of his teeth.

"Take it easy." His mother hugged him from behind.

Amador unfolded the piece of paper. Once he had unfolded it, he had to turn the letter around because he'd opened it the wrong way up.

Amador read with eyes wide, moving his lips in an expression that allowed Victoria, for a few seconds, to see a reflection of her son, who moved his lips in the same way when he read the books that were never for children.

The transformation of Amador's face was brutal. Worry gripped Victoria's stomach and quickly turned to fear.

"Honey, what does it say? You're scaring me," she said.

"I don't know. Leo," he said to his son, "where did you get this?"

"For God's sake, Amador, let me see it!"

Somewhere in the house, Linda recognized the yell of the woman she called *señora*, and she assumed the *señores* were arguing again.

Amador got up. His knees, which had been resting on the wooden floor, had begun to hurt. He passed the note to his wife, keeping his eyes fixed on her.

Victoria grabbed the piece of paper with a trembling in her hand she couldn't hide from her son. The first thing she noticed, before even reading it, was the single paragraph's excellent presentation. She hadn't noticed her eyes moistening. She had to blink several times before she could make out the letters. Her reading vision was still good, despite the hundreds of pages of reports she had to study for each of her cases, almost always in relation to intellectual property—singers, writers, and artists in general, none of them very successful, made up her portfolio of clients—and she only put on her glasses when she thought her workday could stretch beyond ten hours. The excellent presentation took on a macabre significance when Victoria read the contents of the letter:

> *I don't wish to frighten you, but it's impossible to explain any other way. Please, do not go to the gas station in Arenas. The American's store. Do not go there on August 14, 2009. I don't want to scare you, but it could be the day of your death. Don't go. I'm sorry, I had to warn you.*

Victoria laughed. A false laugh, a little unhinged, similar to the one she forced in court sometimes when she wanted to pour scorn on a witness's statement. Or the one she directed at her husband when, after she rejected for the nth time the sex that they'd been crazy for years ago, he accused her of having lost interest in him.

Amador looked at her, pressing his lips together, until Victoria gave up her theatrical performance.

"Up you get, Leo, come on," she said.

She ruffled her son's hair to prompt him to stand up so she could, too. She got up nimbly, rearranging her shirt and adjusting it under her skirt around her slim waist. Then she knelt in front of Leo so that their eyes were at the same height.

"Angel, what the hell is this?"

Leo looked at her without responding.

"It was the kids in your class, wasn't it? Why do you always wait for me by yourself at the school gate? Why aren't you playing with everyone else, huh?" She gripped one of his shoulders. "Look, sweetheart, if those children are doing something to you, I need you to tell me. Will you tell me?"

Victoria still had the letter in her hand. While she spoke, she decided that the words written in it were so savage they could only be the work of some irresponsible little brat, though deep down she knew the handwriting was clearly an adult's.

Leo also knew the writing was an adult's. It was why the letter had frightened him so much. Because none of his classmates, not even the most advanced in basic writing, could have imitated an adult's hand with such precision. And none of the older kids at the school, not even the most ignorant teenager, would have collaborated in such a mean joke perpetrated on a boy whose only crime was being unable to do the vaulting horse in gym class.

"You can tell me and Dad anything. You know that. You do know that, right?"

Leo said nothing.

At first, Victoria had been very happy with how attentive, quiet, and obedient the boy had been from a very young age. For a long while, she had allowed him to keep his light on after going to bed. More than once, she'd found him asleep with a book in his hands. Victoria would lean against the doorframe and smile at the image of the seven-year-old boy who still slept under a Buzz Lightyear comforter but who read adult crime novels or horror stories, devouring the pages without even asking what the words meant. She would kiss him on the forehead, tuck him in, and enjoy her feeling of superiority over her colleagues at the law firm who despaired at their children's slow progress with reading. Sometimes it worried her that such a young boy was reading stories about serial killers or the paranormal, but she knew he was going to do it anyway, that he'd find the books behind her back, so it was better to encourage him to read than to forbid it. She had never seen the attraction of reading for pleasure after all the reading she had to do for work, and at first she admired the way Leo was able to immerse himself in a story and spend hours on end turning pages and moving his lips, a childlike mannerism on a face whose expression was decidedly grown up.

But a few weeks ago, Victoria had started to turn off his light at ten on the dot. His license to read in bed at night was over. Because a few weeks ago, Victoria had also begun hating all the things that made Leo different. Now she was unhappy that her son didn't go out to play with his classmates more. She regretted not signing him up for a team sport, the ones that had training sessions after school. It might have made Leo less fixated on mathematical curiosities like palindromic numbers, or have meant he would spend less time on that ridiculous multicolored cube or watching the sky through his telescope while the heat from another sunny day escaped through the window, taking his entire childhood with it. Victoria no longer boasted to her colleagues at the office. And when one of them recounted her son's exploits in a soccer tournament, Victoria fell silent, picturing Leo bent over his desk, reading books his father gave him and, when she wasn't looking, turning back on the light she had turned off.

"Where did you get this letter?" Victoria insisted.

"It was in my backpack," he whispered.

"What do you mean, in your backpack?" Victoria replied. "What was it doing in your backpack? Who put it there?"

Victoria, a victim of her own powerlessness, was shaking her son. Amador had to grab the boy to separate him from his mother.

"I'm sorry, angel," she said. "It's just that I don't understand."

She stretched out her arm to rest her hand on Leo's chest. Then she grimaced with anger and abruptly stood up.

"Enough is enough. I'm going to speak to the principal tomorrow," she decided, forgetting that summer vacation had begun and the school was closed. "They'll have to do something with those monsters. And I'll speak to your teacher, Srta. Blanco. What was her name?" she asked Amador. "You know, the one who was a classmate of yours."

"Alma," said Amador. "But it's July. Who do you think you'll find at the school?"

"In that case . . ." Victoria bit the tip of her index finger for a few seconds, realizing her mistake. "In that case I'll have to speak to the kids' mothers. Leo, angel, do you have any of your classmates' numbers?"

The three of them knew the answer to the question. Leo lowered his head in silence. He took a step sideways to separate himself from his father's legs, as if he wanted to disassociate Amador from the shame that belonged only to him, the class weirdo who hadn't managed to make a single friend.

"Well done, Mom," said Amador.

He went down onto his knees and hugged the boy. Leo pressed his face against his father's chest. Over his son's shoulders, Amador looked at his wife in disbelief. She held three fingers to her lips in a gesture of regret that she maintained for the duration of the hug to which she didn't feel invited and that she refused to participate in.

Amador stroked Leo's face with both hands. He proposed taking him to bed and staying with him until he was asleep.

"And we'll talk about the letter tomorrow," he said. "What do you think?"

"No, Dad, it doesn't matter," an ever-more-grown-up Leo answered before heading back to his bedroom.

He didn't look back even once. Before he climbed the stairs, a heel came out of a slipper. He stopped for a moment in front of the first step.

"Good night, Mom," he said.

Although he knew his mother had heard him, she didn't answer. He climbed the stairs, leaving his parents behind.

The knot in Victoria's throat seemed to tighten even more. Amador gesticulated at her, urging her to respond to Leo, but she shook her head with her three fingers on her lips, trying to stop herself from crying.

Victoria sat on the sofa and allowed a single tear to roll down her face. She diverted her gaze, turning her husband into a blurred shape that went to the kitchen first and then disappeared upstairs. Then she remembered the day Leo was born. The night when she went into premature labor. When they dashed around the house, searching for the suitcase they had ready for the occasion, and she tripped on the very stairs her husband was now climbing. That night, Amador was left with his arm outstretched after the silk of his wife's nightdress slipped through his fingers as he desperately attempted to stop her fall. He was unable to prevent Victoria from ending up sprawled at the bottom of the stairs with an open wound on the left side of her forehead and a large amount of blood flowing from between her legs. Luckily, University Hospital was very close, and Victoria gave birth to a healthy boy just half an hour after the incident. A drop of blood from the wound still open on her brow had landed on her son's face in an unusual maternal scene.

Sitting on the sofa, her back upright and the envelope resting on her thighs, in her hands, she saw herself holding Leo in her arms for the first time in the early hours of that hot June night when she became a mother. When Victoria decided it was time, she got up. She put the cordless phone she'd thrown against the sofa back on its base, turned out the light, and climbed the stairs in the darkness.

5.

AARÓN

Saturday, May 13, 2000

The smell of coffee woke Aarón. The aroma had infiltrated his dream world to catch him and pull him back to the reality of a very specific morning: the morning after the night someone had tried to murder his best friend. It was a few seconds before he felt the stab of pain from the memory inside.

The familiar sound of Andrea—her short steps and her feet brushing against the parquet flooring, the way she gently closed the microwave door, the two clinks of the spoon against the cup when she served the coffee, and the mournful hum of the refrigerator that always remained open while she cooked—allowed him to think it could just be any normal day. But the acetaminophen dissolved in a glass that was still full on the bedside table, the smooth sheet that betrayed how far away they had slept from each other, and the horrifying echo of last night's thoughts forced him to accept that this was no normal day.

From the doorway to the kitchen—where there was a small break-fast bar facing the dining area, on which Andrea had laid out an over-sized buffet—Aarón watched her for a moment before she noticed him. When she did, she put the frying pan she had in her hand down on the ceramic cooktop. She approached him with a face swollen from tiredness and tears. There was no good-morning kiss. Just a tender stroke of his face, which was prickling with a beard of several days.

"You're up. How are you?" she asked, before brushing away the usual lock of hair. "Me, I'm not good at all. Look at the breakfast I've made." She let out a faltering sigh. "I thought it'd do you good to eat. I think I've overdone it, and I was about to make an omelet."

She looked at the table she'd laid out, like an artist seeing for the first time a piece painted in a trance. She shrugged in an attempt at an apology that Aarón found charming.

"I still can't believe what's happened to David." Andrea let out the forbidden word and fell silent, waiting for his reaction. "And it's eleven o'clock. I'd like to get to the hospital. Let's have breakfast and go. They'll let us see him, won't they?"

She gripped Aarón by the arm and pushed him toward the table.

"See him?" The words escaped his mouth.

"Of course." She pulled out a chair so Aarón could sit down and sat in the one opposite. "I want to see him, see how he is."

Aarón stared blankly into his cup, as if the coffee were as deep as the ocean. The echo of his own voice inside his head, repeating to him that everything that had happened was his fault, drowned out Andrea's words.

"Aarón, what is it?" She rested a hand on his.

"I need to eat, that's all."

He smiled with half his mouth. When Andrea took away her hand, he wanted to grab it. But he took the cup instead, the large white one they bought at Ikea. He took a sip of the bitter coffee.

"I went down to see if the building manager already had the newspaper. I wanted to see if it said anything."

A torrent of jealousy struck Aarón when it occurred to him that the old busybody downstairs with the hairy ears would have seen Andrea as she was now. Dressed in the T-shirt she always slept in when she was staying at his apartment, the one that was enormous on her and had a pi symbol printed on it.

"And?"

"He did. He gave it to me. And he said he was sorry." She took a deep breath, and her nipples showed clearly through the worn gray fabric. "I bet everyone knows by now. It'll be the story of the year in Arenas."

Andrea gave him the newspaper, open to the relevant page, folded in half. Aarón saw the black-and-white photo of the American's store and recognized Héctor's patrol car, one of the two parked at the establishment's entrance. He began reading quickly, skipping some words and jumbling others into an indecipherable mumble.

"Did you read this about something similar happening in the same place thirty years ago?" Aarón asked when he was halfway through the article. "It says here that when it was just a gas station there was another robbery and they killed a boy. It must've been before the American opened the store, right? It's an account from a man who was present when it happened."

"I didn't want to read it," said Andrea. "I don't want to see David's name in initials."

Sure enough, the article described R. Palmer as recovering well in the University Hospital but stated that the young man D.M. remained in "very serious" condition.

Andrea bit into a slice of toast. She had to make an extraordinary effort to swallow it. She felt each crumb of bread pass through her tight throat, as if two large hands were trying to strangle her. Aarón remained immersed in his reading, silently now, moving his lips slightly. As if it were a completely normal breakfast, Aarón asked for the sugar. After glancing at the table, he got up to fetch it.

"It's always me who has to open a new bag," he said from the kitchen with his back turned as he poured almost a kilo of sugar into a reused Nescafé jar. When he'd finished, he went to throw the bag in the trash. "Drea, you've got to leave pizza boxes to one side. You can't open the lid otherwise."

The sob that came from the table made him turn around right away.

He saw Andrea with her forehead resting on both hands, her elbows on the table. She was looking at her plate and the rectangular slice of toast, a little semicircle from the teeth she'd bitten into it with at one corner. The woman who never took things too seriously sniffed and said, "You worry about the sugar if you want. I'm going."

Aarón grabbed one of her shoulders. He hugged her and rested his head in the hollow of her neck.

"I can't go so soon," he said to the back of her head. "I need to know he's going to get better first. Imagine if we go and they tell us he's . . ."

A diminishing morning erection brushed against her, and the smell of chamomile enveloped him until he lost all understanding of why he'd decided to end his relationship with her. Then his eyes fell on the small pile of papers Drea had left on the breakfast bar the night before. The maroon wallet from the travel agency had been placed on top. Aarón understood that Andrea had wanted him to know she'd seen the tickets. It was typical of her, he thought, to say nothing but make it known to him in some other way. Maybe it wasn't so difficult to find reasons for them to break up. His immediate reaction was to let out a flurry of explanations, but he knew they were no longer necessary. The thought of the week's vacation that he and David would no longer be able to spend together made him hold Andrea harder.

She moved her head away and looked him in the eyes. She wet her lips, and Aarón smelled strawberry jam. She opened her mouth. She could only breathe. She said nothing. When she swallowed, the muscles in her neck tightened. On the second attempt she found her voice and said, "Aarón, David's dying."

And in Aarón's head, Andrea's lips continued to move, adding, *It was your fault.*

He separated himself from her body like she had separated herself from his on so many nights after finding out about Rebeca. Aarón rested a hand on the breakfast bar. He shook his head, his eyes still on Andrea, while his mind reverberated with the accusation.

"I'm going," she said. "I need to see him."

She turned away from Aarón and looked back at their breakfast. The sight of her crazy spread seemed to make her uncomfortable.

"I'm going," she said again. "I hope to see you there."

Aarón heard the door open and then close. He was still shaking his head.

After thinking about it for a few seconds, he went out into the corridor. Andrea was standing there, paralyzed, her legs naked under the enormous gray T-shirt. Barefoot.

"I'd better get dressed," she said.

When he was alone again a few minutes later, Aarón contemplated the apartment. Still wearing the clothes in which he'd decided to break up with Andrea an eternity ago, he felt as if he were peering into an unfamiliar abyss. He put the brakes on his dark thoughts by shaking the guilt from his head like a dog shakes off water.

He returned to the table and finished reading the report on the robbery. He reread the name of the local who'd recalled the events of thirty years ago for the newspaper. Samuel Partida. Aarón tried to remember if he knew the name from anywhere. Then, he thought of David, and took his cell phone from one of his pockets.

Héctor's exhausted voice answered.

"Aarón, buddy, thank God it's you. I didn't know David was so well known in Arenas." His joy at hearing a familiar voice sounded genuine. "A bunch of people we don't even know have been calling us."

Aarón paid special attention to the nuances and inflections in the voice that had broken up the night before, as if he could decipher

David's situation in them before asking the question he didn't want to ask.

"Is there any news?"

"There is."

Aarón held his breath and imagined the worst. He remained on edge as Héctor continued.

"Well, no, nothing about my brother yet. There's no change. They've barely let us in to see him." Aarón heard him breathe through his nose before going on. "I haven't been home yet, man. I'm still in my uniform. But Carlos came a while ago—do you know Carlos? My partner, I think he studied with you guys. He told me some stuff."

Still sitting down, Aarón was rubbing his stomach hard with the hand that had held the newspaper. He didn't know what to say and wasn't sure how long he could maintain the conversation. He didn't feel ready to listen to too many details about the incident. Not from the mouth of Héctor, who probably felt like yelling at him that it was all his fault. That his brother was in the condition he was in because Aarón had been too lazy to run an absurd errand.

"Turns out they've caught the son of a bitch who shot him. He's younger than David, can you believe it?" Rage made the last two words slip on his vocal cords and sound high pitched, like a teenager whose voice was breaking. "He's just a kid. But at least he's legally an adult—the bastard will pay. He'd better hope my brother . . . he'd better hope my brother doesn't die."

Without knowing why, perhaps just to fill the silence, Aarón asked him whether the kid had acted alone.

"The hell he did. There were two others waiting outside the store in a car," Héctor replied, as if it were the end of a bad joke. "What a bunch of assholes."

Aarón could hear footsteps as Héctor paced up and down a hospital corridor.

"They wanted to steal a crappy cash register in a worthless store, and the bastard ended up shooting my brother. He says it was a mistake—he got nervous and didn't know how to react. Apparently David made a strange movement to protect a young boy who was waiting in line . . . and fuck it!" Aarón heard a slam and assumed the blow was Héctor punching a wall. "The guy goes and fires. He didn't know how to react, he says."

He was speaking through clenched teeth, and Aarón could picture atomized saliva shooting out of his mouth like shotgun pellets. Aarón thought it wouldn't be long before a nurse showed up to give him a tranquilizer. As if he'd read Aarón's thoughts, Héctor lowered his voice and added, "But I know what I'm going to do to that motherfucker if I get him in front of me. He'll find out what happens when you mess with a cop's brother. He'll get a nice surprise when he finds out he's not the only one with a gun." His voice dropped to a whisper, as if he was aware he was saying too much, but continued. "And that when I shoot, it's legal. Do you know what I'm saying?"

Aarón confirmed that he did.

"Fuck. And how're you doing?" asked Héctor.

"Andrea and I are in bad shape. She's on her way to the hospital. I didn't want to go with her. I don't think I'm ready to—"

"Don't worry. I know what you're going to say. It's fine. I'll stay here with my parents. If anything happens, I'll call you."

Aarón hoped there would be no reason for him to call.

"Anyway, he's in fate's hands now. I'm going to leave you now, all right? I think they're letting us in."

Héctor hung up.

Aarón left the cell phone on the table, near the black crumbs from a burned piece of toast. He'd only been up half an hour and all he wanted to do was go back to bed.

He's in fate's hands now, Héctor had said. And Aarón thought that perhaps it was his own destiny he'd evaded.

Questions swirled around Aarón's head with no apparent logic. *Racing thoughts*, he called them. The swirl stopped with a still image of David at the Open, protecting a child and being shot in the back.

Then another image of yet another child, thirty years earlier, also at the Open and also witness to a shooting that, as an adult, he would recall for the purpose of filling out a report in a newspaper that had almost gone to print when news of the incident reached the editorial office.

Pinching the bridge of his nose, as if trying to remember the surname of an old classmate, Aarón had the feeling he was about to realize something important. And while he tried to persuade himself that what he was beginning to imagine was absurd, the result of a bad night's sleep, at the same time he sensed that his most recent and profound fear could be justified.

"It was my fault," he said to the empty room.

His cup of coffee spun on the edge of the table and fell onto the floor.

6.

LEO

Monday, July 21, 2008

As Victoria passed by Leo's bedroom, she crouched to check whether any light was emerging from under the door. In her right hand she gripped her heeled shoes, in the other, the airmail envelope. She pressed her ear against the door and held her breath. She deduced that Leo must be asleep.

She headed down the hall to the master bedroom. Her tights crackled with static electricity when her thighs rubbed together. She opened the door without caring how much noise it made—she knew Amador was awake. She didn't find him naked with the sheet up to his waist, as she had on so many nights in the early years of their marriage, but sitting at the foot of the bed, bent forward. He was resting his elbows on his thighs, his hands interlinked as he circled his thumbs. Just as he'd sat one night three months ago when he'd thought bringing up the absence of sex in their marriage for almost six months might be a first step toward fixing the situation.

Victoria approached her husband, threw her shoes onto the bed, and sat next to him with her arms stretched out behind her, her legs crossed. After they exchanged a look, he said, "What was that?"

"Oh, please," she said. "Do you think I wanted to make him feel bad? I asked about his friends without thinking. I know our son isn't the most popular kid at school." She unfolded her legs. "But I'm certain they wrote the letter." She paused and rested one of her hands on Amador's knee. "What else could it be?" she asked, with no real desire to speculate on any other possibilities. They were all too terrifying.

Amador fixed his eyes on Victoria and tried to remember why he loved the woman who'd given him a son. Only one image, of the night they met, came to mind: his father, Amador Cruz Sr., at a boring convention of weary old lawyers in Prague, gesturing at Victoria Cuevas with a hand that held a double whiskey and telling him that she was the type of woman it was in his interest to marry. The ice cubes in his father's glass jingled, as cold as the look she gave them with her green eyes before approaching to ask them if they were talking about her.

At that moment, with the two of them sitting on the bed, Amador couldn't remember whether he'd ever fallen in love with his wife in any way other than the attraction he felt for the woman his father had considered to be of interest. In reality, Amador had always lived the life his father had wanted to see him live.

"I know you didn't want to hurt him," he said.

He stroked her cheek clumsily. He picked up the envelope with the same hand and took out the letter, placing it between their legs in an exhausted invitation to read it again.

"How could anyone do this?" he asked.

He stressed the *anyone* with a strange inflection, unable to believe that any normal person would want to frighten a child in such a cruel way.

"It was his classmates." Victoria wanted to sound convinced. "Look how worried we are, and I bet it's a few little brats playing a stupid prank on him." She squeezed her husband's leg. "I'm sure that's all it is."

"Do you really think they'd go this far?"

"Honey, I've seen them making fun of him. When I pick him up in the afternoons, he's always by himself. There, outside the school"—she waved a hand in the air—"separate from all the others. They're all in the store over the road."

"In the Open?"

"Yeah, the American's store, the gas station, the one"—it took her a few seconds to grasp the meaning of the question—"the place in the letter." She constructed the sentence word by word, as if translating from another language. "See? It was them."

She jumped up and held her hand to her forehead to massage it.

It all seemed to make sense now.

It was less than ten years ago that the young man had died in the American's store. The Open, as everyone called it. A young man whose mother remained shut away in her home, without the strength to go out. She only got up when she knew it was night to kiss her son's photograph, always in the same place. Over the years, her dry, almost dead lips had erased part of the face, just as little details of her memory of her son were erased from her soul. But outside that mother's room, the event had become the favorite horror story of the town's children. The older ones told it to the younger ones while they ate their churros and hot chocolate at the lake every August 20, Arenas's public holiday. The story splintered into different versions on school playgrounds and soccer fields. And year after year it was retold as children came out of class, or at the entrance to the Open itself.

The shooting that night had become local folklore, a "tale from the crypt" that the children reinvented year after year at their summer camps, sharing chilling stories at campfires as they passed flashlights around to illuminate their faces from below. The little ones didn't dare go to the American's store. The kids who went in to buy candy and soda and then spent the afternoon outside the store's door, their bikes lying on the grass, were no longer children in the other kids' minds. That's why Leo was still just a chicken, a wimp whose mother collected him on the babies' side of the road. A weird boy whose shoe they could put a frog in. A stupid little kid easily frightened by the tale of the murder at the Open. The perfect victim of a joke in which an anonymous letter warned him he was also about to be killed there. A little shit they could keep in a state of fear for the entire school year—two if possible, three if they were lucky.

"I know it was those kids," Victoria whispered, forcing herself to forget that the handwriting looked like an adult's.

Amador reread the letter, searching for some detail they might not have noticed.

"We can take this to the police." He looked up from the page at his wife. He stuck out his chin, an expression that, a long time ago, used to excite Victoria. "It's evidence."

Victoria was pacing up and down in front of him, rubbing one of her temples in a circular motion and imagining how she was going to make things right through the mothers of those kids. And if one or two kids who had nothing to do with it went down with the others, so be it. It was time those devils stopped messing with her son. Time to bring some order.

At her side, Amador continued to examine the letter—the back of it, the envelope, the inside of the envelope. His amateur CSI—the sound of the paper folding and unfolding again and again, the envelope opening and closing, the finger running over every line—all these sounds of an unskilled detective reverberated in Victoria's ears as if they came from a dreadful TV movie playing at full volume. Sounds that prevented her from hearing the lecture she intended to give to each of those perfect married couples who'd brought their twisted children into the world, capable of terrorizing a classmate and enjoying it.

"Amador! Stop. Please, stop. Stop that."

It had been those kids, she knew it. However much Amador examined the letter, the ink wasn't going to write the perpetrator's name. And Victoria preferred it that way. She didn't want her husband to study the handwriting any more. She didn't want him to realize it looked like an adult's. If he hadn't said so yet, perhaps it was because it didn't. If Amador didn't see it, she must be wrong. If Amador saw nothing unusual in the handwriting, it was because there was nothing unusual about it. If he stopped reading the damned letter, he would never realize. And then she could go to the mothers' houses and tell them that if their children messed with her son again, she would see them in court. Everyone knew about school bullies. If Amador didn't say anything about the handwriting belonging to a grown man, Victoria would make sure those mothers paid for what their children had done. Which was why Victoria clenched her fists when she sensed that Amador was about to say something she didn't want to hear.

"What I don't get is why they didn't write Leo's name on the envelope."

"Any kid can copy . . . ," she said back, without even listening to her husband.

While she spoke, she processed the new information.

"His friends . . . ," Amador went on, "his classmates, they know his name, right? If I was one of them, I'd have put Leo's name on it nice and clear. I would have written it this big on the envelope"—he measured it with his fingers—"so he knew the letter was for him."

Amador knew what he was saying, because he had once been one of them. He'd been a tyrant subjugating an innocent victim. A vague memory, in washed-out colors like the old Polaroids he kept in shoeboxes in the garage, projected the image in his mind of Alma Blanco under her desk. Leo's current teacher had been a classmate of Amador's in his first few years at the old school in Arenas, when the few children in the village, of various ages, were taught in the same classroom. The years had clouded his childhood memory of Alma, but Amador visualized the girl's hand gripping the table leg, white from the pressure. He remembered his classmates yelling at him to hit her with the ball again, even harder. Amador remembered kicking the ball. And Alma's scream.

It was just one of many such scenes repeated during their first few years at school. Until one day, in the middle of the fifth or sixth grade, Alma stopped turning up to class. As if the film of his memories had gotten jammed on an old Super 8 projector, the image of Alma terrified under the desk began to burn. But before it disappeared, for a second Amador saw Leo's face superimposed on the girl's. He heard him scream under the desk. And he saw the ball launched by Amador and four classmates hitting his son hard.

"What does it say, then?" asked Victoria, though she knew perfectly well—she'd read it a dozen times.

"'For a nine-year-old boy,'" Amador reread. "I don't know, Leo isn't even nine. What if it isn't for him? School finished a month ago. He hasn't seen his classmates since then. He doesn't speak to them outside school."

Victoria blew out through her nose. She remembered how her son had looked at her, downstairs in the living room, when she had asked him whether he had any of their phone numbers.

"He said he found it in his backpack. It could've been there a long time," she said, intent on maintaining the force of the accusation against his classmates. "And the date it mentions"—she swiveled her hand in the air—"the whatever it was of August next year . . . Leo will be nine then. It was someone who knows him," she concluded out loud.

"But there's something else that doesn't add up," Amador went on. "Isn't it a bit strange, his friends referring to him as a boy? They're children, too, right? It would only make sense to call him that if whoever wrote it was . . . Hang on a minute. I think this handwriting's an adult's."

Victoria stopped pacing up and down. She wanted to laugh at the gravity in her husband's voice. A headache erupted at the back of her head and spread to the left side before lodging itself in her eye socket. She sat down, defeated, and gave Amador a frightened look.

"So what the hell does all of this mean?"

This time it was Amador who shot to his feet. Arenas, a village of stone houses transformed into a collection of residential developments that formed a suburban bubble of green yards, Sunday barbecues, and smiling neighbors who still said good morning to one another, had suddenly become a rotten place where a lonely boy could be the target of a joke for one of those individuals with false smiles and perverted secret habits.

"Oh my God, what if someone's trying to blackmail us?" Victoria brought him back to reality. "I told you not to buy that expensive car."

Amador had to stop himself from yelling at his wife. It was she who had wanted to buy their enormous house in the most expensive part of town. It was she who boasted to her colleagues about the new car. Just as, for a while, she boasted about having the smartest son. If everyone in Arenas knew their finances were more than buoyant, it was because of Victoria's vanity. Because of her pride at the new status she acquired not thanks to her work as a lawyer specializing in intellectual property disputes but as the wife of Amador Cruz Jr. The idea that they were being blackmailed made sense, especially in the new, distorted version of Arenas in Amador's mind, but it wouldn't be because of the damned Aston Martin.

"I'm going to call the police, right now," Amador said out loud.

He rounded the bed without waiting for Victoria's opinion, and he kept talking so she would have no chance to reply. She followed her husband with her gaze, agreeing that calling the police was the most sensible thing to do.

"This guy's seriously stupid if he thinks he can't be identified by his handwriting in this day and age," Amador yelled from next to the bedside table as he held the receiver to his ear. "How many people are left-handed? One in ten?" He looked at the letter he still had in his hand. "Then finding him has just gotten ten times easier."

He dialed 112.

Victoria snatched the piece of paper from him just as he pressed the last digit. She examined the letter closely, as if it were the first time she'd read it. Sure enough, the handwriting was slanted slightly to the left. How hadn't she realized it before?

And it was right at the end of that thought that she made a terrible discovery.

Her face went cold. Her blood thickened, seeming to flow with difficulty. She felt a tingling sensation in both hands.

Beside her, a female voice emerged from the receiver that Amador was pressing against his ear.

Before Amador said anything, his wife's hand shot to the base of the telephone and pressed the button to cut off the call. Amador rested the phone on his shoulder. He felt a wave of anxiety when he saw the transformation of Victoria's face.

"Honey, Leo's left-handed," she said.

7.

AARÓN

Friday, May 19, 2000

Aarón walked through Aquatopia's parking lot.

On the ground, next to the concrete tire stop of one of the parking spaces, a cardboard cup with the Burger King logo on it was threatening to overflow. The rain had filled it with water to just above the edge. The plastic lid skewered with a chewed drinking straw was blowing away in the wind across the deserted parking lot. The sound of it bumping across the gravel lot made Aarón follow it with his eyes. When he could no longer hear it, he gave the paper cup a push with the toe of his shoe. It fell over, and its contents spilled onto the wet ground.

Aarón walked on toward the park's entrance. It was closed. Through the bars he saw several empty picnic tables and a row of soda machines, all of them switched off. Closer to him, two ticket booths had their shutters down. Aarón smelled chlorine.

He grabbed one of the bars and shook the gate. The drops of water from the passing storm, still sliding down the metal, soaked his arm. The hinges groaned. A thick chain wrapped around the lock rattled.

"Hello?" shouted Aarón.

There was total silence for a few seconds. Then he thought he heard something on the other side of the gate. He tilted his head to one side. The far-off sound gradually became a regular thud. Footsteps.

A short man with a trimmed beard suddenly appeared from behind the ticket booths. He was buttoning one of his shirt cuffs. He rearranged the neck on his jacket before reaching the gate.

"The park's closed," he said, raising both hands.

"Are you Samuel Partida?" Aarón asked.

"Depends who's asking."

"I'm"—he cleared his throat—"I'm Aarón. David's friend. We spoke on the phone two days ago. You told me to come today because you'd be less busy on a Friday."

Samuel rushed to the gate. "Of course, yes, sorry." He took out a set of keys from his pants pocket. "With the park opening in a month, we keep getting sales reps showing up wanting to set up stands, vending machines . . . ," he remarked while he opened the padlock on the chain. "It's always me they find, of course, but I'm just head of maintenance. The other stuff's nothing to do with me."

Samuel bent down, pulled bolts up from the ground, and opened the gate just enough to let Aarón in.

"Sorry to make you come here," he apologized, "but like I say, with the park opening for the new season soon, I don't have time for anything. Otherwise I'd have been delighted to invite you around for dinner." Samuel forced a smile. He glanced to the side just for an instant, long enough to think about how dark his house seemed now. "My wife works with the guy's aunt—your friend. David, isn't it? How is he?"

"David, yeah, we don't know much yet. He's still in the hospital."

"I've got to do a final round. Do you mind walking while we talk?" Samuel asked when he'd relocked the gate. "Otherwise I'll never finish. And I'm good and ready to go home."

He looked away again. This time he pictured his wife walking down the hall with a cup, always empty, in her hand.

"Come this way," he said, beckoning with his head. "So tell me, what is it you wanted to know about the robbery?"

He set off in a counterclockwise direction, one marked by a post with a picture of a bear holding an arrow. Aarón followed him. They passed a timber structure supporting a giant map of the park on their left and reached a trash can in the form of a hippopotamus. Samuel struck the animal's mouth, peered through the hatch, and shook the black bag inside to make the few things that were inside it fall to the bottom.

"Well . . . ," Aarón said.

Samuel smiled at him, nodding. Then he suddenly bent down and picked up a stone he'd found on the marked path. He threw it toward a landscaped area. It hit the ramp of one of the blue slides that ended in a round pool. It rolled down, making a plastic sound.

"Good thing they haven't just painted it," said Samuel. "They're coming on Monday to do it. Monday? Yeah, I think it's Monday. I don't even know what day it is anymore," he said, though he knew perfectly well the weekend was about to begin, two whole days at home. He could almost hear the clock in his living room slowly ticking.

"I read what you said in the newspaper," Aarón began. "Do you remember how the robbery happened, exactly?"

"Well, we're talking about 1971. I was nine. I don't remember everything, but you know, over the years I've filled in the gaps with things people told me."

Continuing on the path, they came to another trash can, this time in the shape of a frog. Samuel kept talking as he examined the trash bag.

"At the time, the Open wasn't a store, it was just a little gas station with two pumps. They filled you up and took payment in a repair shop, which is now the store. The American was very astute to convert that space into a store." He waved his hand in the air. "The few people who lived here had to go to the gas station if they wanted to travel to work in their cars. There was just a few of us in those days. My parents had recently moved to the village from Galicia. They came when they heard the watch factory was opening. They thought they were coming to the big city, and they ended up in a village almost as small as their own. But they had vision—look what Arenas has become."

Samuel gestured all around him, as if all the residential grandeur of the new Arenas was right there surrounding them. Instead, Aarón saw slides and empty pools. The fading evening sun, shining again after the passing storm, was reflected on the wet surfaces, giving them a golden glaze. There was something eerie about the emptiness of a water park closed to the public.

"My parents came around then, too," said Aarón, scanning the imposing incline of the Giga Splash. "I've lived here all my life. I studied at the university, and now I work in one of the pharmacies in the town."

"See? That only happens in Arenas. We've ended up with one of the best towns around. Me, I don't want to have anything to do with the big city," Samuel proclaimed as he adjusted his jacket. "As I was saying, there wasn't much at the gas station. They took your money in the repair shop. You can just imagine the haul the thief was going to make off with. It was the day of the famous blizzard. I'd never seen it snow like that in Arenas." Something strange happened in Samuel's eyes—he seemed to lose the thread of the conversation. "My wife and daughter love snow," he said.

Then his gaze looked normal again and he continued. "Come on, let's head to the restrooms. I have to check something." Samuel left the path and went on the grass. Aarón followed him. "I was in the gas station with my dad. He gave me a couple of bills so I could go in the repair shop with the owner and collect the change. I say the owner, but it must've been an employee. From what I learned later, the kid wasn't even thirty." Samuel turned the handle on the door to the men's restroom. It was locked. He brought out the set of keys again and opened it at the first attempt. "There was another guy in front of me when I went in. With a long overcoat on. The boy went behind the counter, and I kept back a little so he could see me. You can see I'm not very tall."

"Was there no one else inside?" asked Aarón.

Samuel started opening and closing all the faucets on the dozen or so sinks inside the restroom. No water came out of any of them.

"Well, yeah, that poor kid was there, of course. The one they killed. But I didn't even see him." Samuel seemed to discover his reflection in one of the mirrors. He looked at himself. "Did you know? He tried to shield me. And I didn't even notice him." He stood in silence for a few seconds and then suddenly continued. "Do me a favor, will you? Turn that valve that's above the door," he indicated. "The one on the right. Can you reach?"

Aarón spun around and stretched to reach the valve. He turned it. Samuel opened the faucet on one of the sinks again. He held his hand under it as if waiting for something to come out.

"Nothing. It's off at the water main," he explained. "Well that's a job for another day, I've put my shirt on now. Close that one again, if you don't mind," he said.

"You were saying a young guy tried to shield you," Aarón repeated, following Samuel's instruction.

"Oh, yeah." Samuel wiped his hands on his pants. "Let's go outside."

He locked the restroom door and they returned to the path that so many excited children had run up and down for so many summers.

"So, yeah," Samuel resumed, "the gentleman in front of me finished paying and turned to leave. It was right then that the"—he hesitated, trying to find the right word—"the whole thing started. The man in front of me, his eyes opened in an expression of fear I've never seen on anyone since."

But Samuel was lying. He had, in fact, seen another frightened expression of equal or greater magnitude. On the face of Laura, his wife. It happened the day he climbed out of the pool in the yard of their house with their daughter's blonde hair hanging over his left arm. Large maple leaves, dry from the fall, stuck to his chest. It was the day their home began to darken. And Laura began to wander around it in her dressing gown. It was the day the clocks started to make a lot of noise when they ticked.

"I turned my head," Samuel went on, pretending the small interruption had never happened, "to see what the man in the overcoat was so shocked about. But all I managed to see was a shadow moving quickly toward the counter. I'd be lying if I said I saw a gun. Then I felt a hard blow to my back that made me fall to the floor. I cut my chin open, see?" Samuel stopped and pointed at a scar that was visible among his beard hairs.

"Come on, it's getting late." He set off again. "It was the young guy who hit me in the back, the one I didn't even see when I walked in. They say he saved my life. But I'll tell you one thing: I don't think that thief meant to shoot a child. Who would do that? It was probably the young guy's movement that spooked him and made him fire. He didn't save my life—maybe I took his. God knows. But guilt's not something you can live with, is it?"

Samuel said his last sentence without quite believing it. He'd read it on a sticker from the help group he'd been going to for two years. A group that wasn't helping him, as intended, to banish an idea from his head: that if he'd listened to Laura and covered the pool when the summer was over, then the other Laura, the little one, three days short of blowing out the candles on her fourth birthday, would still be alive.

"For me," he continued, trying not to think about the child's cake they had kept in the refrigerator for more than six months, "the pain in my chin, the sound of a load of cans falling on the floor, and the sticky feeling of the oil that soaked my face . . . for me, all of that, and the two gunshots, happened at the same time."

Samuel left the path again, going up on the curb. "Come with me, I have to go to the pool at the back." They crossed another lawn and a wooden bridge and reached a shallow pool. Samuel continued: "After that, I remember my father lifting me up. He plugged the cut with his fingers and rushed me out of there. He laid me on the back seat of the car. Then the ambulances arrived. From the start, my father did everything he could to play down what happened, and I think that, luckily, he achieved it. You can tell, huh?" It was a rhetorical question. "I didn't see the young guy's body, either. I know his name was Roberto, and that the family still lives here. De la Maza was the surname. His mother, Celia, or Cecilia, came to see me a while after. She asked me to do something with my life that would make saving it worthwhile. She said this to a nine-year-old boy."

After skirting around the pool while he spoke, Samuel suddenly stood motionless. A puddle of green water had formed at the bottom. He observed it in silence.

"Would you mind picking up that leaf?" he asked Aarón without taking his eyes off the water.

"Sorry?"

"If you could pick up that leaf. Look. That leaf." He pointed at a maple leaf floating in the near-empty pool. "There's a net there."

Aarón waited for Samuel to tell him where, but he didn't, so he searched around. He found a metal pole on the ground, not far away from Samuel. Puzzled, Aarón caught the leaf in the net. Then he shook it over the grass to make it fall out.

"That's better," said Samuel. He remained hypnotized by the green puddle for a few more seconds. "Let's go. The park's opening in less than a month, and everything has to be ready."

"So there were five people there, including you," said Aarón, setting off after him.

"The young guy, the attendant, the man in front . . . ," Samuel counted, progressively lowering the volume of his voice. "Five, yeah," he said, showing five fingers. "The man in front of me turned out to be the local mayor. He died not long ago, as it happens. But he was over fifty back then, just imagine. If you told me I'd make it to eighty right now, I'd take it."

They had almost completed a lap of the park. Aarón saw another trash can, a turtle this time, and was about to stop. But Samuel carried on, ignoring the animal and its black bag.

"Look"—he indicated—"we've finished putting up this year's new slide. Did you go to the presentation in February?"

Aarón looked to his right and discovered a red staircase-shaped slide that wasn't very high.

"No, I don't go anymore. My mother used to take me when I was a kid."

"Oh, well, I love that day. Presenting the new slide of the year, with the mayor, all the children from the town . . . ," he said in a singsong voice, looking at the new attraction. "Come on, let's go to my office. It's there." They set off again toward a small concrete hut. Its exterior was decorated with pictures of palm trees. "I know they caught the murderer soon after. Apparently he had several robberies behind him. They said he was a Gypsy. He must've been pretty desperate to do something like that back then. You know what I mean." He paused. "Anyway, I barely saw the young attendant. But it was all in the next day's newspaper."

"Newspaper?" Aarón's voice shot up.

"Sure." Samuel pushed the door to what he called his office open and walked into a small room with a desk in the center and not much else. Two framed photographs were lying facedown. A third was still standing. It was a family scene of a beardless Samuel with a golden-haired wife and a blonde girl hugging his legs. "They mentioned the crime a couple of times, first when it happened and then when they caught the Gypsy."

"I don't suppose you have that newspaper, do you?"

"Sure, I have it," Samuel replied, "but it's at home." He pulled his shirtsleeve up to check his watch. "And it looks like I'm going to have to stay late tonight, too, as much as I wish I didn't," he grumbled, imagining the silhouette of his wife advancing through the hall. "Look, it's eight-thirty already, and I've still got a lot to do." Samuel sat at the desk, shifted some papers around. Aarón had the impression he did it randomly. "We're opening in a month, and everything has to be perfect. Come on," he said as he got up from the desk, "I'll show you out."

Aarón left the park as the sun was finally disappearing behind the sierra. The world remained full of light, but without shadows. The gate closed in front of him, the bars interposing themselves between his face and Samuel's. Some dry leaves became trapped at the bottom, between the gate and the ground.

"Would you mind getting them out?" Samuel asked, taking a step back.

Aarón kicked them away.

When no dry leaves remained, Samuel approached the gate to padlock it again.

"I'm going to lock up, I can't leave yet." He thought about the darkness of his house and his wife's dressing gown. "I have to do a final round."

Aarón frowned, but decided not to ask.

"The newspaper must be at home somewhere," Samuel added. "Come by here in a few days and I'll have it, for sure." He pulled the chain toward himself. Then Aarón saw him hesitate for a few seconds. "Why're you so interested in that robbery?"

For a moment, Aarón weighed whether it was sensible to say anything. "It's strange, but I think there could be some link between the two holdups. Two murders in the same place," he said, forgetting David was still alive, "in a place as peaceful as Arenas . . ."

"Two?" Samuel raised his eyebrows. "You're going to have to take a good look at that newspaper. From what I remember, it said Roberto was the third person to be killed there."

The plastic lid from the Burger King cup crossed the empty parking lot again. Aarón heard it bounce along the gravel.

8.

LEO

Tuesday, August 12, 2008

Victoria and Amador, sitting on the same side of the table, fixed their eyes on Leo when he walked into the kitchen. A quick glance enabled the boy to see that his mother's hands were resting on the red cover of his missing exercise book. The airmail envelope was dancing between his father's fingers.

"Sit down, we're going to talk about this." Victoria gestured at a chair with her chin.

Leo sat opposite his parents. Victoria turned the exercise book around. She opened it to a page marked with a yellow sticky note and moved it closer to Leo. Her elbows remained on the table, like the bellies of two cobras silently stalking their victims.

Amador took the well-thumbed letter out of the envelope. He placed it on the squared page, next to the formulation of a mathematical problem whose result Leo remembered. It was also obvious to him what they wanted to talk to him about. He held his father's gaze, ignoring the exercise book and letter.

On the night the envelope had appeared, about three weeks earlier, Leo had lain under the sheets on his bed and looked up at the stars shining on the ceiling. He listened to Amador come upstairs first—the board under the carpet only creaked in that way under his father's weight. Victoria came up later, with short, light steps that brushed the carpet. Leo heard her approach his bedroom door. There was silence when she pressed her cheek against the wood, and a faint click when she rested her hand on the door handle. Then the argument began. He could hear the scraps of sound that made it through two doors and a hall, and voices went up at unpredictable moments. Leo pulled the sheet over his head. He thought they had stopped yelling when he slipped into a dream as fragile as the surface of a soap bubble. But at some point, the bubble condensed into a drop that hit an imaginary floor, and Leo thought he could make out his mother's silhouette moving around his bedroom before disappearing into the oily figment of another dream. The next day, one of his three school exercise books was missing from his backpack. The red one. Now he knew where it was.

"What're we going to talk about?" he asked.

"Listen to me," said Amador, unsettled by the distrustful look his son gave him. "Look at your exercise book, Leo. Look at the letter. I know you can see it, too."

Leo didn't need to look at anything to understand what was happening. Humiliated in his own home, he preferred not to say anything and tried to get up.

His mother grabbed his wrist. "You're not going anywhere," she said.

He searched for his father's eyes without finding them—he was pretending to examine some irrelevant detail on the place mat. Linda was putting the final touches on a salad. When he started to feel his hand go numb, Leo looked at an indeterminate point between his mother's nose and mouth. He noticed the shine of the sweat on her top lip. Linda, out of focus in the background, came out of the kitchen, moving toward the garden, and closed the door behind her.

"Angel, you're going to have to help us out here," Victoria said without easing the pressure on his wrist. "Look at the handwriting on the letter and look at it on your exercise book. It's obvious you were trying to hide it, but there are things that can't be hidden." She wet her lips with a quick lick. When she continued to speak, her voice sounded like a teacher's. "The way the letter *S* starts and finishes is one of them. Leo, I need you to look at it and tell us the truth."

"Dad, it wasn't me."

His mother's fingers pressed harder.

"Leo, look at the *P*s, the *M*s and the *U*s," Victoria went on. "And it's not just us saying it. A colleague of Dad's thinks we're right. We've just been to speak to him." She turned to her husband. "Right, Amador?"

Amador sighed.

"The graphologist at his office," Victoria continued when her husband failed to look up. "Handwriting isn't a simple exam, but you, angel, you passed with flying colors. It took the man, what, ten seconds to confirm we were right?" Victoria pushed the letter and exercise book toward Leo. She held her face closer to her son's. Almost whispering, she said, "But you already know what graphology is, don't you, angel?"

The pressure on the wrist increased again.

"Sweetheart, we just want to help you."

Leo would have liked to burst out laughing at that statement. He had already learned to identify the new sickly-sweet tone his mother used to suggest joining a school sports team, or to tell him that he could count on them, something he was no longer so sure was true. If that day had been one of those rainy afternoons when his classmates dipped their hands into a muddy puddle to make a print on his white shirt, his parents would have been part of that savage group. Amador's hand would hit him on the back, and brown drops of mud would spatter the back of his head. His mother would then laugh at him, cheering the latest prank, along with the children. If his parents were capable of believing he was the note's author, that he could have made all of this up, then they were no different from the kids who tormented him at school.

Leo tried to pull his trapped hand away.

"It's the same handwriting, like it or not," his mother said before finally easing the pressure.

The blood tingled warm in Leo's dead hand, and he massaged the palm with his other thumb. A third, moist hand was printed on the glass tabletop. It slowly evaporated from the outside in.

"Leo, you're not going to hide from this. You're going to explain to us right now what it's all about," Victoria continued. "It's normal for kids like you . . . smart kids like you to get bored in class and let your imagination run wild. Maybe all of this is nothing more than . . ." She kept her mouth open for a few seconds, then turned to her husband. "And you can stop leaving me to deal with the boy by myself."

Amador didn't reply.

Leo took advantage of the silence to escape to his bedroom.

He shut himself in his room all afternoon, banishing from his mind any thoughts about what had happened with his parents. He didn't want anything to ruin that night. If the newspapers and the people he spoke to on the internet were right, the 2008 Perseids were going to be the most spectacular in recent times. The newspapers had announced that the meteor shower would begin on the night of August 12. In a few hours.

When it started to get dark, Leo pressed the button to raise the rolling shutters, opened the door onto his balcony, and positioned the telescope on the mark: an *X* formed from two strips of black tape. He and his father had calculated its position a few days ago. After checking the mark now, Leo clapped twice in quick succession, full of excitement. He looked up at the night sky and smiled, imagining what he would see later. It was going to be his first meteor shower. He had been waiting all summer for the event.

Downstairs, in the kitchen, Victoria and Amador were still arguing.

"He's not going to get away with it," she said. "We're going to have to punish him. Really punish him." One of her fists gently closed. "Wait"—she paused when it dawned on her—"isn't it tonight, that thing with the stars he's been looking forward to for so long?"

Amador remembered hugging his son tightly while they prepared the telescope, touched by his excitement. Now, hearing Victoria's idea, his heart tightened. But he didn't know how to refuse her. Not even when the look on his wife's face suggested she wasn't going to be the one who would confront Leo this time.

"Do I always have to be the bad guy?" she asked.

So it was Amador who opened Leo's bedroom door that night and, barely looking at his son, without saying a word, headed straight to the balcony.

"I've already checked the mark, it's in the right place!" Leo yelled from his bed, brimming with anticipation.

Amador looked at the X of black tape they'd stuck on the floor and felt his throat go dry as he lifted and folded up the telescope. Leo was observing him, gripping the frame of the balcony door and rubbing his bare feet against each other.

"Dad, don't . . ."

Acting as if he hadn't heard him, Amador went back into the room and pressed the switch that lowered the shutter automatically.

"I'm going to turn the power off so you can't open the shutter," he said.

Then he crossed the room and closed the door behind him.

In their bedroom, Amador threw the telescope hard onto the bed, where Victoria was sitting. He locked himself in the bathroom and turned on the faucet to refresh his face and neck before looking at himself in the mirror and saying, "Your son's completely normal. Everything will work itself out."

Leo spent the night lying on his bedroom floor, looking through the narrow gap he managed to create by forcing the shutter partly open and wedging it with an astronomy book. He looked up at the sky, imagining more than actually seeing the amazing dance of light and color that must have been taking place over Arenas on that moonless night, the night when Leo stopped trusting his parents. At some point during the spectacle, the dark figure of Pi dropped down from the roof and walked stealthily to the narrow gap through which his owner was trying to see what the cat could have seen had he looked up at the sky, but instead Pi opted to curl up and fall asleep.

"Look at the stars, Pi," Leo said. "Because you can."

After the incident with the telescope, Leo barely left the house for what remained of the summer. He visited Lake Arenas on the August 20 public holiday only to remain crouched on the towel under a tree until his mother ran out of patience. Victoria looked at him and then at the group of kids climbing up the weeping willow that grew on the shore. The most daring ones were launching themselves into the water from its branches. That day, when the whole town gathered to eat endless servings of churros and hot chocolate served in fragile plastic cups, Leo never left his solitary place in the shade of that tree. He didn't even take off his T-shirt. And on several occasions, Victoria felt a twinge in her stomach she had learned to recognize.

The summer ended and, with it, so did the ninety days Leo had enjoyed without listening to laughter at his expense. No recess going by, minute by minute, with nobody approaching to speak to him. No looks from his classmates on the other side of the road. And just like the minutes of recess, the days of the summer vacation had disappeared through the cracks of the automatic shutter that had prevented him from seeing the meteor shower. Days that were used up in the form of glowing dots that advanced from one side of the room that was his refuge to the other: from the wall of a new dawn full of possibilities to the opposite wall that marked the end of another day spent entirely among the pages of another book. From time to time, the excited voices of a group of kids banging sticks against the houses' heath-covered wire fencing had come in through his bedroom windows. Leo would peer out at the noisy muddle of color, laughter, and blue jeans that went past. For most of his schoolmates, it had been a summer of grazed knees from playing soccer until nightfall. Of wasp stings when they climbed out of the pool. Of Coke coming out through their noses during fits of laughter. Of occasional campouts in the backyard at someone's house. For Leo, they had been three months of reading, afternoons surfing the internet, and hours listening secretly to his parents' conversations.

On the last night of the summer vacation, Leo was wandering around the house with an empty stomach. He was trying to overcome the anxiety that the new school year brought. He and Linda were waiting for his parents to arrive before starting dinner. A wave of unease washed over Leo's slender body when he heard the key being inserted into the front door.

"Your *papás* are here," Linda said in her Salvadoran accent.

Leo sat down at the table.

His mother soon appeared. She headed to the refrigerator and served herself a glass of water overflowing with crushed ice. She looked at her son in the way she had looked at him since the argument at that same table, when she had trapped his hand with her fingernails. She approached him, gave him a kiss on the cheek. Then she asked him whether he'd packed his backpack and had his uniform ready for the next day.

"Yes, señora," Linda intervened. "It's hanging in the wardrobe. I left it there all nice and ironed."

Victoria didn't reply.

Amador walked into the room, ruffled his son's hair, and greeted Linda. "Whatever it is you're making, it smells great," he said.

He also wanted to know whether Leo was nervous about going back to school.

"I wish the summer would last a lot longer," the boy replied.

"Leo." Amador rested a warm hand on his son's when he sat down. "Your mother's decided we're going to give you back your telescope today," he lied. It had been difficult persuading Victoria that maybe they should change tack if they wanted answers from the child. "We're on your side. You know that, right, Commander?"

He looked at his wife in an invitation for her to continue.

"We're your parents, and we're going to do everything we can to understand what's happening to you," she proceeded. The ice clinked in her glass when she took a sip.

Amador felt his son's hand escape his.

"We know the meteor shower was very important to you," Victoria added, "but you must try to understand why we did it. You're going to have to help us with this. This isn't easy for us, either. And we know we're not communicating enough with you."

Leo was surprised at the effort they were both making to say everything in the plural.

"I don't care about the telescope anymore. I don't want it." He remembered peering under the balcony shutter, with Pi snoozing on the other side. "And you can keep thinking I wrote the letter."

Victoria tutted. She was about to speak when Leo got up from his chair.

"You don't need to tell me to go to my room without dinner. I'm not hungry."

Without giving them time to react, he left the kitchen and headed up to his bedroom. The folded telescope was on his bed. He understood why Dad had arrived in the kitchen after his mother.

He closed the door. From the wardrobe, he took out the two hangers his uniform was on. He felt cold sweat break out when he saw the gray pants and maroon tie. He placed it all on the desk and got into bed.

In the kitchen, Amador and Victoria finished eating in silence. Amador knew what his wife was going to say after taking a last bite from an apple.

"We have to take him to see Dr. Huertas."

He got up without answering. He took a packet of Oreos from the larder and headed to Leo's room. When he saw the telescope on the floor in front of the closed door, he could almost hear the words his son had said at the beginning of summer: *Dad, they're saying the meteor storm's going to be spectacular this year. Will you watch it with me?* Amador had to sit down on one of the steps.

9.

AARÓN

Andrea tapped him on the shoulder.

Aarón, sitting on the sidewalk at the university entrance, turned his head. A feeling of well-being enveloped him when Andrea's hair, hanging toward him from her head, brushed against his face. The smell of chamomile washed over his body and penetrated his skin in a way it had not for more than a week. He stood and got tangled in the strap of his bag, which ended up hanging from his waist as he looked at Andrea's eyes and mouth. He resisted the habitual urge to kiss her on the lips. He hugged her.

"Drea."

He said her name with an outbreath that caressed her neck. While the hug lasted, Andrea remembered one night, on Aarón's birthday. He'd taken all his clothes off in the living room to try on the Superman boxer shorts she'd given him half as a joke, and the contrast between the childlike underwear and masculine superhero pose he adopted had excited her.

The clumsy reunion made them smile. Andrea noticed how dry Aarón's lips were, surrounded by the untidy beard of a man who normally shaved the upper part of his cheeks and the fold of his neck to achieve a designer stubble look.

"Aarón." She held his jaw in her hands. "You're going to tell me what's happening, right now. It's me, OK? I need to know." She rounded off the authoritative request with a contained smile. "Also, I have a surprise." Her voice crackled with excitement, almost as if she were still his girlfriend. She bent to put her purse down on the ground and took out a blanket. It was brown, decorated with white flowers. It had once been thick and spongy, but now it was just a flattened length of fabric. "We're going to have dinner at the lake."

Aarón had to take a deep breath. It was the same blanket they had been lying on when, throwing himself in the lake and telling her to come in the water, he had declared his love for Andrea for the first time. The pleasant memory was interrupted by the image of David wishing Aarón luck before he got in the car that night.

"I'm not feeling too good . . . ," he said in an attempt to dissuade her.

"You're well enough for this, and that's that," she replied, suppressing a smile that escaped anyway. "How long has it been since we last spoke? Two weeks? Héctor told me you haven't been to see David. And I don't know how long your boss will be so understanding. He knows you're in a bad way—he understands the situation and all that—but sooner or later you're going to have to go into work. He can't cope by himself in the pharmacy. And one day he'll explode, you'll see. What is it you're doing stuck at home all day?"

"I'm not doing anything."

"Then it's time to do something." She rested a hand on his abdomen. "You can't shut yourself away and pretend this thing with David never happened. You're going to tell me what's going on with you, OK?" She prodded him twice with her index finger. "OK?"

Andrea managed to make Aarón smile. He took Andrea by the hand and they set off up the street. Both in short sleeves, they felt their skin cooling as the sun gradually disappeared. They breathed in the smell of freshly irrigated grass and the honeysuckle that grew on the fences around the houses that lined the road. Several kids passed in front of them on their bicycles, the playing cards attached to their front wheels making an engine sound. It was one of those afternoons that almost every inhabitant of Arenas claimed only existed in their town. It was the last Friday of May. Most of the students were heading home for the weekend and were running up the street in the direction of the American's store.

"See you on Monday, Professor!" three young men yelled to Andrea.

They strode past, containing their laughter and elbowing the one in the middle. They headed off toward the Open to buy their first beers of the night.

Sr. Palmer had returned to the store after nine days recovering in the hospital, two floors away from David's room. On the tenth night, he slept at home. On the morning of the eleventh day, he announced to the doctor that he intended to get back to work. *I've survived one robbery, what're the chances of anything similar happening again, in Arenas?* he asked the physician, while turning down sick leave that would have kept him at home for an entire month. When Sr. Palmer looked at his wife and raised an eyebrow to ask her what she thought about it, she said, *I just wanna go back to Kansas.* Each time his wife repeated that sentence, Sr. Palmer felt guilty that he hadn't been able to give her the children she had desired so much but had reluctantly given up because she wanted to be with him, the man who had made her laugh more than anyone else since she'd met him at the age of twenty. The man who'd persuaded her to find a new future in Europe. The man who sometimes thought he was unable to bear the sadness he felt when he saw the great effort she put into every new piece of needlework, a sweater for a neighbor's grandchild instead of her own. Sophisticated European grandchildren he promised her in Galena, who never came—because they didn't even have a son or a daughter—and who would have filled the usual silence of their home with the sound of children. Now that silence was broken only by the sound of the television they listened to at an increasingly high volume because, as time went by, however much they tried to hide it, Sr. and Sra. Palmer spoke to each other less and less.

"There's no change with David," said Andrea as they left the town's last surfaced road and headed down the dirt track that led to the park where the lake was.

"I know, I spoke to Héctor," he said. "I still can't face going."

They reached the shore of Lake Arenas still holding hands. It was dark now, with no moon yet. It was one of the largest artificial lakes in the region, a source of great pride for the Arenas Municipal Council. While they walked on the grass, an animal of some kind leapt into the water. The crickets fell silent for a few seconds before continuing their conversation.

Other couples had had the same idea. Their silhouettes were just visible and their movements could be sensed.

"Do you remember?" Aarón asked without expecting a reply.

Andrea spread the blanket out at the highest point, the place where the churros and hot chocolate were served up every August 20, the perfect vantage point from which to see the giant willow that grew on the shore.

When she'd finished laying out the blanket, Andrea slapped the ground, inviting Aarón to sit. "What's going on?"

From her purse, Andrea took out a couple of sandwiches she'd bought from the American's store in the afternoon.

"You know what's going on. David. Us . . . I think I have the right to be a little messed up, don't I?"

Andrea blew out through her nose. She wanted him to hear it.

"You're not the only one who's suffering, you know? The other day I had to go out in the middle of class to cry in the corridor." She looked straight ahead but didn't focus her gaze. "I saw two kids kissing in the back row and, well, do you remember?" She took Aarón's hand, an instinctive gesture that she didn't want to suppress. "And you haven't seen David in the hospital. His mother won't move from his side. Your mom's spending a lot of time with her. They both asked about you."

Aarón remembered his last conversation with his mother. Over the phone, she'd told him that what had happened to David had been an accident, that it had nothing to do with him and he had to stop being stupid. What his mother didn't know was that, after hanging up, Aarón had taken all his clothes off in the living room, headed absently to the bathroom, and stood under a cold shower. He stayed there even when his head and joints began to ache, glad to be able to focus on a physical pain and divert his thoughts from his guilt.

"I haven't spoken to anyone. Just Héctor," he said.

A masculine laugh, followed by a woman's shriek, reached them from not very far away.

"Aarón," said Andrea, "I know you went to see Samuel Partida."

He considered denying it or making up an excuse, but abandoned the idea.

"Samuel was the child who was in the Open," he began to explain. "Do you remember what the newspaper said? Samuel was the boy in that robbery that was so similar to David's."

"I know who he is. I read the papers, too, finally. I hate it when they use David's initials." The moon was beginning to appear in the east, as if it didn't want the waterslides to block out its surface. "But tell me why you've been to see Samuel and not David. The robbery that almost killed your friend happened two weeks ago, not thirty years ago." Then she paused before asking, "Is he the guy whose daughter drowned in the pool?"

Aarón remembered the family photo he'd seen in Samuel's hut at Aquatopia. The blonde girl hugging Samuel's legs. He nodded.

"I've been calling Héctor almost every day. They know I'm worried."

"Of course they know. And I know it, too. He's your best friend, how could you not be?" She seemed to spit the last words out. "But you have to go see him. You can't just stay at home." She stroked his beard. "You haven't even shaved."

Aarón blew out hard.

"And no more thinking this was your fault," Andrea added. "You can't punish yourself by thinking that." She pulled herself closer to him. "You can't blame yourself for something like this, do you hear me? The person who shot him, he's the guilty one."

"That's the thing," said Aarón. "It should have been me he shot."

"Look at me." She fixed her eyes on his. "Aarón, no one could've known what was going to happen. No one. None of it was your fault."

"I don't know how to explain it, but there's something . . . I don't think this was a coincidence. I went to see Samuel Partida because what happened to him and what happened to David are too similar." He was marking the rhythm of the words with his left hand. "They're two practically identical murders."

"Aarón, David hasn't died."

"I know. But they're so similar! It's almost as if . . . as if it was the same scene repeated in the same place."

Andrea rested her fingers on his lips to make him be quiet.

"I don't care if they're similar," she said. "All I care about is that David's in the hospital. And I want you to be all right. Stop trying to make sense of what happened. There is no sense in it. These things happen. One thing happened thirty years ago, and one thing happened now. Period."

"Are you sure?" He paused, aware of the impact his words would have. "Because it didn't just happen thirty years ago. It also happened in 1950. And a long time before that, in 1909. Samuel told me. Do you think it's a coincidence there've been four deaths . . . ?" He reacted when she gestured with her head. "All right, David isn't dead. But do you think it's a coincidence that three murders have been committed, in exactly the same spot, in a place like Arenas?"

"I don't understand."

"Wait," he said. "Look."

He took out the photocopies of the newspaper that Samuel had gotten for him. He left his sandwich on the blanket, still untouched. Andrea picked it up and bit into it, looking the other way before tackling the sea of black-and-white information that Aarón was now showing her.

"This part," he said, indicating the upper two-thirds of the first two pages, "is about what happened to Samuel. He already told me, more or less, and it was the same as it says here. A Gypsy went in to rob the gas station, another young guy wanted to protect a child, and . . . well, you know what happened, just like with David. But down here"—he brushed against her leg—"they say that the young guy, who was just twenty-one, was the third victim there. They say the place was a watch-maker's shop before, and that they robbed it twice."

"Before?" asked Andrea. "There was something in Arenas before the seventies?"

Aarón fixed his eyes on her.

"What?" she said. "It's an honest question. When my parents came here, it was just a bunch of houses in the middle of the countryside."

"Well, it already was that at the turn of the century. In fact, Arenas de la Despernada has existed as a village for a long time—as in, the fifteenth century," Aarón explained, as if it were a sin not to know it, when in reality he had been just as surprised to imagine life in the village any earlier than the fifties. "It was a mess after the Civil War, but before that, from 1900 or so, over a thousand people lived here. The first robbery they mention here happened in 1909!"

"And where did you say it was?" asked Andrea. "In a jewelry store? Was there really a jewelry store in Arenas in 1909?" Her disbelief made her voice more high pitched than usual.

"A watchmaker, yup," Aarón confirmed.

"A watchmaker? Maybe it has something to do with the watch factory on the highway, huh?"

Aarón placed his cell phone on the pages of the 1971 newspaper, to dimly illuminate it with the glowing screen, and read:

> It is not the first time this establishment, located on Arenas de la Despernada's main street, has witnessed violent acts rarely seen in such a small locality. The family that owns the premises, going by the name of Canal, decided to give up its previous business after the death of Antonio Canal, who died from a bullet wound behind his store's counter on January 29, 1950. The founder of the watchmaking business, Antonio's father, lost his life in similar circumstances on September 14, 1909. Two generations of the same family devastated by two robberies forty years apart, serving as a prelude to last night's events at the town's gas station.

Aarón stopped and looked at Andrea.

"Is it so strange they robbed a watchmaker twice in forty years?" she asked. "That's a long time. And it's not surprising that they attacked the store's owner, right? That's the person who's there. It still seems stranger to me that there was a watchmaker in Arenas at the beginning of the century. Seriously, you're fixating on this and seeing things that aren't there."

"Drea, this is important to me."

"And *you're* important to *me*." She grabbed the sheets of paper at the top and pulled. Aarón held on tight. "Tell me what difference it makes to us that a jewelry store was robbed almost a hundred years ago."

"Watchmaker."

"Whatever. What does it have to do with David?" She used the same tone she'd used the first time she asked him whether he'd been unfaithful with the intern who helped him at the pharmacy for a few months. "What does it have to do with David?" she persisted.

"I don't know. I have no idea what it means. But what should I do? Close my eyes to what I have in front of me? Four people have died . . ." He tutted and shook his head. "I mean, three people, in the same place, in a suburban paradise like Arenas."

Mentioning the town, he stretched out his arm in a theatrical gesture, encompassing the idyllic image the spring night offered them: couples frolicking and saying things into each other's ears for no reason other than to make their partners' skin react to their breath, on grass that was now a bed of moisture and desire. Like a pool of molten silver, the lake reflected the light from a moon that seemed to have been drawn with a compass.

"I don't know any more than you," Aarón went on, "but it can't be a coincidence. It's not possible. The same scene has happened four times in the same place. There has to be an explanation. And I'm not going to be able to relax until I find out what. Because I think I should've been the fourth, not David."

"Stop saying you should've—"

"No, Andrea, you stop telling me I had nothing to do with it," Aarón cut in. "Stop saying what everyone else is saying to me. Why was David at the Open that night? Because *I* asked him to go there. It's my fault. I don't care if my mother says it wasn't me who fired the gun, I still sent him there. And I know that, you know it, and his whole family is thinking it, however much they say otherwise. That robbery was going to happen at the Open that night. And I need to know why." His voice faltered in his throat and was reduced to a whisper. "I need an explanation."

"What for, Aarón? Will it save David?"

"No, Drea, of course it won't."

Suddenly, nothing made sense anymore. The sleepless nights tossing and turning in bed, thinking about how by now, he and David would have been preparing for their trip to Cuba. The hours spent reading Samuel Partida's cuttings again and again. The certainty that something more powerful than coincidence had led to all those people finding death in the same place. The headaches. The trembling. The hatred he felt toward himself for having unleashed the destruction of everything that was important in his life with a telephone call. The guilt. Biting a cloth and screaming until his throat hurt. The frantic search for a reason for this twist of fate. A reason that Andrea, with a simple question, had stripped of any significance. What if he did find an explanation? Would it save David's life?

"Of course it won't," he repeated in a low voice.

He wanted to hide next to her, close his eyes, and stop thinking.

But that was when a clear thought, as dazzling as the moonlight illuminating that perfect spring night in Arenas, lit up in his mind and glowed in front of his eyes.

"Not him," he said, or he thought he said. "The next one, maybe."

10.

LEO

Saturday, February 28, 2009

"Come on, grab your towel and get out." Victoria was waiting outside the car, her hand raised and her thumb on her key. "I'll leave you locked in there." She extended her finger, giving him one last chance.

Leo got out of the rear of the white BMW. He hung his towel over his shoulders, closed the door, and looked around him.

Victoria pointed at the colossal entrance in the distance, decorated with flags, where hordes of children were arriving with their parents.

"Come on, look how long the line's going to be."

Dozens of cars were parking, guided by the barely visible diagonal lines on the Aquatopia parking lot's gravel surface.

"Leo?" his mother insisted.

It was the last Saturday of February, the day when the park's organizers always presented each year's new attraction. With the onset of fall, one of the park's old slides was demolished, and they began to build a new project in its place. Resting on their bikes on the other side of the fence, the children followed the building work's progress through the winter. Months before the summer season, Aquatopia reopened its gates for a single day, an event that was almost as important as the August

20 celebrations in the town. Nobody wanted to miss the occasion. The mayor gathered all the town's residents to announce the new attraction's name. He also unveiled a large drawing showing how it would finally look. Every year, people doubted the work could be completed by June. Every year, the work was finished just in time.

"Why do we have to come today if someone can just tell us about it tomorrow?" Leo asked, walking behind his mother.

Leo had resisted the idea of going to the park from the outset, but he ended up agreeing to it for the same reason he had agreed in recent months to almost everything his parents had demanded of him. After what happened the summer before with the letter and telescope, Victoria and Amador had threatened to take him to see a psychologist. Leo couldn't allow that. Because he knew that Edgar, Slash, or one of the others would end up finding out. And that was the last thing Leo needed. To be considered an actual nutcase.

"Angel, some things have to be experienced," said Victoria. She put on the sunglasses she'd been wearing on top of her head and pursed her lips. "We're coming because today's the big day. I bet all your schoolmates are here."

She rested a hand on her son's back, and they headed toward the gate. The day had started sunny but cold. Even so, it was a tradition in Arenas to go to the new attraction's presentation wearing summer accessories. Most people were carrying towels. Some had rubber rings. The most daring stood in the line in swimwear and flip-flops. *At Aquatopia, it's always summer* was usually how the mayor ended his speech each year, as if it were the first time he'd said it.

Leo walked with his head down—he didn't want to bump into anyone he knew. After advancing a few paces, he discovered a cable snaking across the sand. He warned his mother, who was walking with her neck straight, like a wading bird, scrutinizing the crowd.

"There's a what?" she asked, before discovering the cable. "What the—?"

Wobbling on her heels, she dodged the restless viper of wire.

"Oh, it's the TV people. Come on, angel!" she yelled, waving a hand.

Victoria approached a young woman with swollen ankles who was brandishing a microphone in front of the visitors, her arm out behind her to give directions to a man with long hair gathered in a ponytail.

"Excuse me," said Victoria. "You can ask me a question if you like."

The reporter's attention was on the children who were milling around her. They were giving quick waves to the camera.

"We're not live, kids," she explained, before turning her neckless head to Victoria.

"I'm here with my son," said Victoria, indicating Leo, who had fallen several steps behind. "He's eight years old. There he is."

A redheaded woman with long hair and an erratic way of walking bumped into the post that Leo had become. She said sorry, searching for the face of this child who wouldn't take his eyes off the ground.

"Angel, come here, you're going to be on TV!" shouted Victoria. "Do you mind if I'm on with him? It'd be nice if my husband saw us. He's working this weekend, so he couldn't come today."

"Sure, no problem. It's a family occasion today," the young woman replied, giving her a bright smile.

Victoria mused that out-of-shape women like this reporter needed to be this friendly. She stretched the corners of her mouth to return the reporter's forced smile.

Leo dragged his feet on his way to his mother, raising little dust clouds with each step.

"Ready," Victoria confirmed before straightening her torso, throwing back her hair, and rearranging her jacket at the shoulders. "Will you ask a question, or should we just speak?"

Leo said that he didn't want to be on TV or answer any questions. He said it out loud, so the television people would hear him as well.

"But you're going to do it," Victoria said back, without taking her eyes from the reporter. "Just wait and see how envious your schoolmates are going to be. They're all going to want to talk to you."

His mother's right hand dropped like a pincer onto his shoulder. Leo felt his throat tighten. He could have cried with rage, but managed to contain the urge. The neckless reporter then signaled to the cameraman and held the microphone closer.

"Hello, young man, what's your name and how old are you?"

"My name's Leo," he said. "And I was born on June twelfth, 2000. You work it out."

Victoria must have detected the anger in her son's unfriendly voice, but decided to ignore it.

"We came to enjoy the park on such a great day like this"—she crouched down, then gradually straightened again as the reporter raised the microphone—"because we think Arenas is a great town, perfect for families, and we have to support our municipal council's campaigns. I'm a lawyer, and it won't do me any harm to have a day off to forget about the stress of work for a little while."

"And you, Leo, are you looking forward to finding out what the new slide will be this summer?" asked the reporter, turning her attention to the boy again.

"No. I'm only here because my mom wanted to bring me. She says I have to make friends." His mother's hand tensed on his shoulder, near his neck, without going so far as to squeeze.

"Oh, come on, I don't believe you!" joked the young woman. "You must have lots of friends, being as nice as you seem."

An invisible heat washed over Leo from above. The heat from his mother's gaze. Even if he ended up spending every afternoon of what remained of the school year shut away in a consultation room with a stranger, having to persuade himself there was something wrong with him, the look from his mother that he couldn't see but could feel was going to be the last one Leo allowed her to get away with.

"I'm a bit weird, that's the problem," he said.

The sentence appeared to escape from his mouth, but in reality, it came from the depths of his soul. When Victoria yelled his name, Leo savored it like a victory. The hand on his shoulder pressed down and forced him to turn around. His mother knelt to be able to look him in the eyes. For a moment it seemed as if she would scold him right there, but not a single word came from her mouth. Leo noticed a slight tremble in her chin.

Victoria stood, let him go. She approached the reporter. The TV woman had started to smile at Leo's unexpected response, but in the end, she had taken a step back to keep out of the telling-off.

Leo saw his mother exchange a few inaudible words with the young woman holding the microphone. He also saw her take two ten-euro bills from her purse. He deduced, correctly, what was happening.

"I'll give you one each," Victoria said with the money in her hand. Leo was just a waxwork statue behind her. "One for you, and one for you, if you promise me you won't broadcast this interview."

The reporter was accustomed to looks from women like this one, women who'd been the prettiest girls in class at school and still hadn't learned to hide the feeling of superiority that was painted across their faces when they found themselves in front of a woman who didn't fit the conventional standards of beauty, as she knew she didn't. For no other reason than this, she accepted the bills, before replying, "Lady, we're the local channel. All you had to do was ask and we wouldn't have aired it."

The reporter gave Victoria a fleeting smile, put the money in her pocket, then winked at Leo and turned away.

When Victoria returned to her son, she didn't even look at him.

"We're going home," she said into the air.

Then she remembered that Leo hadn't wanted to go to Aquatopia. That he was afraid of bumping into his classmates. She thought about how shyly he walked among people, his eyes on the ground. Victoria knelt in front of her son again and fixed her eyes on his.

"On second thought," she whispered, "let's stay."

They advanced toward the line where entire families were waiting to enter. They joined the end. In front of them, a baby smiled at them from its father's shoulder. The redheaded woman who'd bumped into Leo before passed them again. She brushed shoulders with Victoria on her way back to the parking lot.

"Tired of it already, that one," Victoria said with disdain.

Victoria shifted her weight from one foot to the other. She did it again a few seconds later. And then again. When she tutted, Leo knew what was going to happen. She grabbed him by the hand and pulled. They left the line.

"There must be someone we know up ahead so we don't have to stand in this stupid line."

They walked all the way to the entrance and then turned around to follow the line back. Victoria centered her attention on the parents' bored faces, avoiding the children's excited expressions. An announcement over the PA told them the park was about to open. The news was received with applause from those imagining the new attraction would surpass even the famous Giga Splash.

Many faces were familiar to Victoria. She recognized one of their neighbors, a short man with a perfectly trimmed beard, a smile fixed on his face. Victoria couldn't remember his name. She greeted him with a haughty chin gesture, accompanied by a slight arching of her eyebrows, nothing more than a forced expression of suburban courtesy.

Leo was recognized, too. He heard a girl's high-pitched voice repeat his name at least three times.

"Look, that girl wants to say hello," said Victoria. "How come you didn't tell us you had a girlfriend?"

Victoria held Leo's chin and turned his head toward the place where a girl with a freckled nose was waving. She was smiling, showing her tongue through the gap that a lost baby tooth had left.

Claudia sat three rows behind Leo in class. He spoke to her for the first time the day he helped her get up from the floor and rearrange her skirt. Some boys had tried to lift it, and in the struggle, she'd fallen onto her knees. Her glasses had been left hanging by one of their arms while the boys fled from the crime scene yelling things like *carrot-top* and *four-eyes*. Leo arrived in time to grab the glasses that were slipping from Claudia's sweaty skin. The girl got to her feet and looked at her palms and knees, which had been scraped on the floor. They were just grazed, but Claudia, her hair stuck to her face, ran off in tears to rat on the boys to the teacher without saying a word to Leo.

"Are you here with your mom?" Claudia asked when they approached.

The man holding her hand said a polite hello to Victoria.

"Yeah, she wanted to come," said Leo.

"Well, he did, too," Victoria explained to the man she assumed was the girl's father, gesturing at Leo with her eyes.

"There're a lot of kids from class here. We saw them join the line. It's *those* guys, you know," Claudia told Leo, stressing the word *those* in a way that he understood perfectly. "I've already told Dad I don't want to speak to them."

"And Dad only takes orders from his colonel," said Claudia's father, holding his hand to his forehead in a military salute that seemed ridiculous to Victoria. His hair was completely white despite his evident youth. "I told her to bring her friends, but this girl wants me all to herself."

"And where are *those* kids?" Victoria asked.

"Top secret," he replied, continuing the game of soldiers. "This corporal may not speak without his colonel's permission. And I wouldn't make her angry if I were you, because she's very bad-tempered." He was modulating his voice so that it sounded like a cartoon character's. His daughter was dying of laughter. Victoria didn't know where to look.

"Will you tell me, Leo's classmate? Claudia?"

"They got here after us," said the girl, swinging around her father's legs. "They're back there, in the line."

"You're not in the line?" the soldier dad asked, speaking like a normal person now. "You can join us here, if you want." He winked at Victoria.

"No, thanks, we're going to say hello to Leo's other classmates. I bet they're looking forward to seeing him," said Victoria.

That was when Leo separated himself from his mother and ran off, kicking grit against Victoria's ankles.

"Well, I'd better go see what's up with him," she said in a controlled way. Victoria had no intention of running and making a scene in front of everyone. So she started walking calmly after her son, who was now a dust cloud a long way ahead.

When she reached the BMW, she found Leo sitting by the front wheel. He was hiding his head between his knees and covering his ears with both hands.

"Come on, get up," she ordered.

Leo didn't react.

"Don't make me any madder."

Despite her urgent tone, Leo remained impassive.

"You're asking for it, Leo," she said, threateningly this time, kneeling beside him. "Don't ruin everything, we've had a few very good months."

She grabbed his arm. She had to shake him to make him raise his head, open his eyes, and look at her. Leo's face was covered in dust. His tears had made flesh-colored rivers.

"Angel, what've you done to yourself?" Victoria was suddenly frightened. She examined the boy's head, just behind the ears, with her fingers. "You're bleeding."

Leo began to tremble the way he had on the day he came down the stairs holding the airmail envelope.

"Tell me." Victoria swallowed in a final attempt to contain herself. "Tell me what's happening!" she finally screamed. Then she held the boy's face in both hands. She stretched her neck to look over the car in all directions.

The scream made Leo react. He breathed in sharply through his mouth. The taste of dust on his tongue was unpleasant. He coughed. He continued to breathe in a labored way until he managed to calm himself down. His eyes focused on his mother, as if he had just realized she was there. Victoria dried his mouth and eyes with the towel she had over her shoulders. She brushed the hair from his face, hooking it behind his ears. She waited for the boy to speak.

But Leo lowered his head, resting his chin on his chest. He could feel the warmth that the tires were still giving off on his back. He saw his mother's heel, free of its shoe. He saw her knee scrape against the sand on the ground, tearing her pantyhose. He saw one of her calf muscles tense.

"Speak to me, angel, what happened?" Her voice was trembling in her throat. Somehow, she lost her balance and the knee resting on the ground slipped. Tiny stones tore through the fabric and skin.

"Mom," Leo began to say.

"What is it? What—?"

"It happened again."

"What happened again?"

Victoria sat down. She didn't seem to notice the cut bleeding on her knee. She took his cheeks in the palms of her hands and used her thumbs to dry his eyelids. Leo felt the dirt on his face, Mom's fingers scraping against the grit. He smelled the warm orange-juice breath that came from between her lips. Comforted by the heat his mother's hands and body gave off, he said, "Mom, it happened again." He swallowed. "August fourteenth."

A sudden cold washed over his cheeks. His mother had snatched her hands away. He could no longer smell her breath. But he decided to go on.

"A woman . . . she came up to me . . . she had red hair." He sniffed, and a bittersweet mixture of flavors went down his throat. "She came up to me and . . . and she told me her name . . . I don't remember it . . . I don't remember her name, Mom. But she said the same thing as the letter." He contained a sob, and tears began to form at each corner of his eyes. "She said . . . the same date. And . . . and she ran off. Mom, she told me the same date . . . she repeated August fourth—"

The slap made him lower his head before he'd finished. He hunched his shoulders. His left ear was ringing. The pain of three furrows from Victoria's fingernails took a little longer to materialize. When he opened his eyes, he saw his mother with her face resting on her right hand. Agitated, she was looking at him, at the ground, and somewhere else. Her mouth was clamped shut, her chapped lips almost white. The sob that Leo had contained spilled from his throat.

Victoria's gaze then came to rest on him without her moving a muscle. She observed him for a few seconds that might have been several minutes.

She exploded. "A woman, huh?" Her voice was deep. "A redheaded woman came up to you and told you the same thing as the letter *you* wrote. Is that what you're telling me? Is that right?" She had lowered her voice but continued to speak more quickly than usual. "Great." She embellished the word with a clap. "Then let's go find her—she can't have gone far. Because I presume this woman can't fly. Or can she?" She paused and then added, "Or can she, angel? You're the one who's making it all up, so tell me if this woman can fly."

Victoria struggled to her feet. When she brushed off the dirt, she saw the hole in her pantyhose and the cut on her knee but ignored them. She tugged on her shirt's shoulders, adjusted the heels of her shoes, and repositioned the sunglasses that had danced on her head. She held her hand out in front of Leo. Seeing the boy impassive, looking up at her from near the tire, she grabbed him by the wrist and pulled. She opened the passenger door and forced him to get in the car before closing it. Victoria went back around the car and sat at the wheel. She removed her jacket and threw it onto the back seat. She started the vehicle without putting on her seat belt. A cloud of dust rose behind them when she accelerated.

"Come on, angel, look. Find her." Victoria did something with her left hand, and the front windows began to open automatically. "Tell me where she is."

They were driving back along the road that led into Aquatopia. Some straggling cars were still arriving for the event.

"Where is this woman?" Victoria moved her head from side to side. "Is it that old lady?" She gestured with her chin. "No, her hair's white. It's not her. Let's find a redhead. We're looking for a redhead!" she yelled.

Victoria stepped on the gas.

"Mom, please," said Leo.

"Come on, angel, I believe you." She was smiling hard to stress the irony with an exaggerated face that frightened Leo even more. "I believe everything you've told me. That's why I want to see this woman. Tell me where this woman is!" She took a deep breath to calm herself. She barely whispered her next words: "Your mother wants to speak to her."

Carlos Ferrero and Héctor Mirabal, who were out patrolling the peaceful streets of Arenas on that sunny February day, saw a white BMW enter a traffic circle too quickly.

"Aren't they going a little fast?" said Carlos.

"It wasn't that fast," replied Héctor, who finished chewing something and swallowed. "They're coming out of the water park. They probably didn't like the photo of the new attraction."

They both laughed, hoping the car would take the highway out of town. That way they could forget about the problem. There had been a time when Héctor had thought he would lose the ability to laugh. Now he took any opportunity he could. It was too nice a day to ruin it by fining some visitor from the city.

Victoria did take the highway that led out of the town. She pressed harder on the pedal.

"Angel, I can't hear you saying anything! Where the hell is this woman?" she yelled even louder, so that her voice could be heard over the thunder of the air coming in through the windows. Her hair was lashing against the roof and headrest. Her sunglasses fell between the door and seat. Her inflated shirt fluttered over her shoulders.

They drove for three or four kilometers. The speedometer needle turned sixty degrees. The engine protested with an irritating whirr. The steering wheel began to vibrate. Victoria wasn't paying attention to the gearshift.

Then, suddenly, she hit the brakes, without looking in the rearview mirror. The sound was like a herd of horses whinnying. The black rubber marks would take a long time to disappear from the pavement. Victoria steered the car and stopped on the shoulder, just before they reached the sign with which Arenas de la Despernada would have said goodbye to them. The elements had battered it until only the upper part of each letter was visible, as if the letters really were buried in *arenas*—sands.

Her hands gripped the top of the steering wheel. Her eyes were fixed on the road surface. Victoria asked her son to get out of the car.

"Are you going to leave me here?" Leo asked.

"I'm not going anywhere," she said, raising her voice. "What kind of mother do you think I am? But I need you to get out of the car. *Now.*"

The door didn't fully close when Leo got out in silence. Victoria stretched out her arm and pulled it shut. She hid her face in her hands.

Covered in dust, Leo broke out in a sweat on the road's shoulder. Three scratch marks flushed crimson on his cheek. Through the window, he saw his mother's shoulders shaking.

11.

AARÓN

On the plastic badge clipped to his shirt pocket, only the last letters of the surname *Canal* were readable, and all that remained of the initial that had once been followed by a period was a lower serif in a faded red tone.

"I've been wanting to trade this piece of shit for a new one for two years," Antonio admitted when he saw Aarón examining his ID. "I don't know why I bother wearing it. Everyone in this factory knows I'm in charge here. But what's that crap they say about leading by example? If I don't wear it, what're my workers going to do? Hey, it's not easy for me to carve out half an hour. I suggest you make the most of your time, kid. I'm good at keeping track of it."

Aarón glanced at Canal's wrists.

"Do you really think I want to wear one after making them for thirty years?"

The table they both sat at in one corner of the industrial warehouse that Antonio Canal used as an office was scattered with papers, screws of various sizes, circular and rectangular watch cases, hundreds of little hands contained in a pin box, and other watchmaking paraphernalia.

Behind the warehouse stood the watch factory. For a long time, it had been the only building on that forgotten part of the highway. But after the real-estate explosion in Arenas, a number of businesses had set up headquarters or branches near the factory, turning the area into one of the most active industrial zones in the northwest part of the Madrid region.

"I'm very grateful to you for—"

"Cut the crap. It's been a while since anyone called asking about my father. Or my grandfather. That's the only reason I invited you here." He gestured at somewhere behind Aarón. "Only the wall at the back of this factory belongs to Arenas, technically, and that's all I want to have to do with that town. It's ugly, that place, isn't it?" It wasn't a question. "Still, I provide jobs for fifty of you. It's more than the town's ever done for me. The HR manager's from there, and he keeps sneaking his people in." He took a sip of coffee from a disposable white plastic cup. "I'm going to have to have a word with that guy."

"They . . ." Aarón cleared his throat. "They brought us to the factory when I was at Arenas Elementary School. On a field trip." He banged a foot against the table when he tried to cross his legs. "Do they still come?"

"Heck, no!" exclaimed Antonio with a snort. "That was my mother's doing, may she rest in peace. She went back to Arenas every week to visit my father's grave. After everything that happened, she was still fond of the town. A saint. She was old, and it made her happy to see the schoolkids. When she died, I put a stop to that circus. My three kids are already more than I want to have anywhere near me. You can have one, if you want."

Aarón didn't know how to respond.

"For free."

He didn't even know whether he *should* respond.

"Seriously, he's yours."

They sat in silence for a few seconds. Aarón looked away. He discovered another part of the warehouse that seemed to be used for storing old machines.

"That part's no use to us anymore," Antonio explained. "The roof fell in"—he pointed upward with two thumbs—"and it killed a guy who'd only been at the factory two days." He slapped the table, and watch hands jumped out of the pin box. "With a wife and two kids. So damned sad. Lawyers, they have some uses. Now I have it all set up in the other warehouse. Much better. Look, a little distance between me and the workers doesn't do any harm."

He leaned back in his chair and took in the view as if, through his eyes, that filthy and chaotic industrial building was a cozy mountain refuge.

Aarón leaned forward, his elbows on the table. His proximity in this position enabled him to detect the smell of sweat that Antonio gave off.

"A few weeks ago, a friend of mine was shot," said Aarón. "It was in the same place where your father and grandfather . . . where they . . ."

"Where they were killed. And?" Antonio drained the plastic cup and threw it in the wastebasket. "Three points," he said.

"The robbery happened in the same place, on the same premises. It's a gas station now, the kind with a store." Aarón scratched his neck. His beard was beginning to itch. "It's owned by an American who—"

"I know the one. And I know what happened," Antonio interrupted. "Like I said, a lot of people from Arenas work here. I've heard them talking about it. It's incredible, it still surprises them, and they're still intent on forgetting. The 'curse of the Canals,' they used to call it. I guess they stopped calling it that when the next one was killed. Because they shot another guy there, did you know?"

"I know, in the seventies. And now David, my friend." Aarón rubbed his eyes hard. "Though he's not dead. He's in a coma, at the University Hospital."

He paused, expecting some words of sympathy, but none came.

"It seems strange that it's happened four times in the same place."

"Look, kid, I'd rather not think about it. I'm done with it. What happened with my father was traumatizing. It was fucked up. My mother sold the store, and we moved out of that shithole of a town."

His face lit up when he mentioned his mother. Now that he was smiling, he took the opportunity to use his little finger to extract some food remains from a back tooth. He observed the dark residue stuck to one side of his fingernail. He sucked it and the fragment disappeared into his mouth again.

"But my mother kept her chin up. She started with this factory. She'd worked with my father in the store and promised herself that she'd make the business work despite everything. She didn't just keep it going, she made it bigger."

Aarón was looking at the piece of food that was now stuck between two upper teeth. He imagined Antonio buying fruit salts at his pharmacy—experience told him this man suffered from acid reflux.

"Watches: if you can make one, you can make a thousand, if you know what I'm saying." He waited for confirmation from Aarón, who nodded out of obligation. "My grandfather made clocks of the best kind, with his hands. He put his heart and soul into it. But I mass produce them now. Most of the watches I make are for businesses that print their logo on them and then give them to their employees. A trinket."

"How long was it from"—Aarón cleared his throat again—"from what happened to your grandfather until your father?"

"Forty years, four months, and fifteen days. That's how well I remember it. My mother said it over and over in her prayers. All fucking day long. 'Oh God Almighty,' the poor woman would say, 'you only gave my good man forty years, four months, and fifteen days.' A saint, my mother was."

"I don't understand, what do you—?"

"You don't understand what, kid? One day they killed my grandfather and, all that time later, they killed my father." With alternating hands, he hit the table twice, marking points slightly farther apart than his shoulders. "And that was how long my father lived for. He was born on the day they killed my grandfather, see?" When he finished saying it, he looked at the first hand he'd marked a point with.

"I had no idea. So your grandfather never met his own son?"

"Nope."

Antonio took a deep breath through his nose and blew the air out through his mouth. Aarón didn't want to identify the new smell he detected.

"My grandfather was in the store, seeing to some customers. Just imagine what the village was like in 1909." He did some kind of mental calculation and then continued. "Fuck me, almost a hundred years ago. I don't know if they even had streetlights."

"They did. They installed electric lighting in the village in 1905," Aarón replied.

Antonio opened his eyes wide.

"I've been reading some stuff," explained Aarón.

"Back then, my family was always fighting with the owners of a bakery. Arguing over which business was the oldest in the village. And it was my grandfather's watchmaking shop, I'd bet my life on it." Antonio held up an open hand as if swearing an oath. "There were three customers. One was a kid who must have been scared shitless. I should know. Someone informed my grandfather that his wife was about to give birth to their tenth child, but he stayed to finish up at the store. By the tenth you don't bother running. Well, in those days, not even for the first. Children were a woman's business, as it should be."

Aarón thought it was a joke, but Antonio didn't smile, so he remained impassive.

"Then the bastard who ended up killing him came in. According to my family, he threatened my grandfather with a knife. The blade was the size of an arm. He wanted the most valuable watches. He was no fool. Like I said, my grandfather made real watches—there was a lot of money in that store. A lot." Antonio leaned forward. "What? You're going to write down what I say now?"

Aarón had taken a notebook out from his bag. "Do you mind?" He remembered the day of his conversation with Samuel Partida. How, after leaving Aquatopia, he'd run back to the car and noted the details of Roberto's murder in handwriting even worse than a doctor's, the kind they complained about so often at the pharmacy. He had struggled to write as quickly as his mind was going, seized by one of the fits of racing thoughts he was unable to control. Nor did the fact he was sitting at the wheel help, his elbow hitting the door with each new line. This time he had decided to note everything down on the spot.

Antonio looked at the notebook for a few seconds and gave his permission with a nod.

"He stabbed him right there. My grandmother was left waiting for him at home. It wasn't my grandfather who came knocking on the door two hours later. It was another old man from the village. He informed my grandmother of her husband's death before the boy, my father, had even cried for the first time. So no, my grandfather never met his son. I was luckier. At least I knew mine." Antonio lowered the volume of his voice. "Not for long, but enough to remember his face."

"You said there were three customers when they robbed your grandfather?" asked Aarón.

"Yeah, that's what I said. I believe there were three."

"Five people in total, including the man with the knife and your grandfather." Aarón repeated the information in a murmur while he noted it down. "One of them a child."

"Now you're going to tell me you want to hear about my father, I bet."

"Please."

"Then I'm going to need another coffee. But it won't buy you any more time. Pray the machine behaves itself."

Antonio propelled his stomach forward and up, forcing the rest of his body to follow. He walked to the opposite corner of the room. He was silhouetted against the light pouring in at a diagonal angle from the dirty windows at the top of the walls, reflected by the dust particles. He pulled up his pants at the buckle twice on his way to the machine, and a third time on his way back. The contraption behaved itself, but Canal's weary pace made Aarón's wait longer.

"I didn't offer you one. But you wouldn't have wanted it, I tell you. I wouldn't recommend it—it's water and rat shit. I'd bet my life it's these coffees giving me acid reflux all night." He rubbed his belly. "Let's see." He blew out, rested both hands on the table, and slumped into the chair. "The story of how my father was killed."

"I'm sorry to make you remember it."

"I told you to cut the crap. Most of all, don't tell me you're sorry. It was some other bastard who killed my father. The world's full of them, isn't it? A thieving piece of shit who couldn't even do his job properly. He paid a big price for it—he never got out of jail. He had no one to blame but himself. And I'm glad." Antonio convulsed in a series of coughs, the last of which sounded choked with mucus. He turned his face without bothering to hide it and spat something thick into the wastebasket, onto the white plastic cup. "I don't know why I stopped smoking. It's only made me worse." He took a long draw on his second coffee, which might well have been his tenth. "The guy rotted in jail. I hope his mother was still alive then so she suffered like mine did. Poor woman. Sometimes she told my father it worried her that he was still working in the same store where my grandfather was killed. But he always replied by asking her what chance there was that the same thing would happen again in the same place. And now we're on death number four, right?"

"My friend isn't dead, he's still—"

"Like a death zone on a highway, a shitload of people biting the big one in the same place. Fuck, it makes your hairs stand on end." He ran the palm of his hand down his sweaty arm. "My mother warned him," he continued, "but in the forties a man didn't pay attention to his old lady. Well, what the fuck am I saying? I don't pay any attention to mine, either."

"I was under the impression that this happened in 1950," Aarón corrected him.

"January the twenty-ninth, 1950, belongs more to the forties than the fifties, kid. It takes more than a month for people to shake the weight of ten years off. Like I was saying, my mother was scared. But we were happy in Arenas. Until that winter's day." He drummed on the table with his fingers. "My father ran the business with the values that had made the Canal family famous in the village for years. Dedication and decency. He sold watches, but he also fixed them. I still remember him, bent over his workbench all those nights. And me by his side. I liked being with him in the store. I remember the smell of wood and enamel. But I got bored a long time before him. Time is the most important thing people have, he always told me. Then he would concentrate on his work again, on some local's watch."

Antonio's voice had quieted again. Aarón carried on writing without saying anything.

"That night, he'd already closed. Two people were left in the store, but my father had turned off the light in the display window. Arenas had a dozen or so stores by then. A man tapped on the glass and showed my father a watch. A classic Perrelet. Fuck me, how could he not open the door for that?" He laughed, and Aarón did the same without understanding the reference. "Inside, while he was heading back behind the counter, the criminal grabbed one of the men who were in the store, a shepherd friend of my father's. He threatened to blow his head off with the revolver he'd pulled from nowhere. That was something he *did* do well, the bastard, like in the movies." Antonio raised his arm and extended two fingers to imitate a gun.

"The shepherd kept his mouth shut. The other man, built like a wardrobe—he worked in the fruit store or something like that, I don't know—he put his arms up like a little girl. My father offered the crook all the money he had. It was a lot of dough, almost a whole week's worth. The thief told him to put it in a bag with as many watches as he could fit. He did as he was told. Then the gunman let go of the shepherd, pushed him behind the counter against my father and the fruit seller or whatever he was, and tried to escape. Everything could have ended like that. If only it had. But things took a turn. After letting the thief in, my father had locked the door. He did it in the evenings. You know, with my mother always telling him it was a dangerous place . . ."

Antonio spoke with his eyes out of focus, as if images of what happened were projected somewhere behind Aarón.

"The guy with the gun kicked the door a couple of times before losing his cool and yelling at my father to intimidate him. My father put his hands in his pockets, searching for the key. He had it on a key ring with a bunch of them. When he managed to pull it out, the thief snatched it from his hands. My father was trembling. They were both trembling."

Antonio clenched his fist.

"The bastard was aiming the gun at him and yelling to not mess with him, don't take him for a fool, that kind of thing. He kept screaming while he tried every fucking key. Then the Guardia Civil showed up. They weren't even there because of the robbery—they had no fucking idea, of course. But they were going down the street and my father screamed. That was his mistake. The thief, cornered, started throwing insults at my father. It was after one of those insults that he fired. He hit him in the eye. He gunned him down right there, locked in, with the Guardia Civil officers on the other side and the stack of keys on the floor. And he remained locked up forever. From the store to jail, until he died. I think they killed him, too. I only hope his mother was still alive when it happened."

For a few seconds, the hard look from before returned to Antonio's face. Aarón was afraid he'd realize the half hour was up. To his surprise, Canal lay back even farther in the chair and continued his story.

"The second member of the Canal family killed in the same place. The people of Arenas started talking about 'the curse of the Canals,' and my mother sold the establishment. It was empty for a long time, until someone bought it to set up a gas station. Before the American. As far as I was concerned, Arenas no longer existed. 'The curse of the Canals,' they said. The curse of Arenas, more like."

"There were only two people in the store, aside from your father? The shepherd and the fruit seller? Only four in all?"

Sitting with his notebook in his hand, Aarón suddenly felt ridiculous. He was so unrecognizable to himself that he wished he could disappear right then. He imagined himself shaving. Tearing up the newspapers, photocopies, and cuttings so he would stop searching for parallels and putting together theories that ended up seeming stupid. Like the theory that there were always five people present at the tragic scene repeated in the same place at random intervals, one of them a child. Antonio Canal had just made it clear that there had only been four characters in the scene in 1950. None of them a boy. Goodbye stupid number-five theory.

"I didn't say there were four of us. I watched my father get killed."

Aarón had to make an effort not to stammer. "Are you saying that . . . you were there?"

"It'd be hard to remember it in such detail if I hadn't been. I was sitting at the front of the store, and I stayed behind the gunman when he came in. My father winked at me from the cash register. Like he had the situation under control." Antonio lowered his head and looked at the circles he was drawing on the table with his fingers. "But it's stupid going over it again and again." He blinked hard, like someone waking up. "And look, you got a lot more than half an hour out of me. I'm good at keeping track, don't think I didn't realize."

He followed his stomach upward again until he was on his feet. The chair creaked, as if sighing with relief.

"I'm off to see the workers. You can't trust these Arenas folks. Could neither of those guys have done anything to overpower the murderer? You don't know how big that fruit seller was. Anyway. You know where the door is."

"Just one last thing," said Aarón, getting up. He was left standing with his hand in the air when Antonio failed to offer his. "How old were you then?"

"Nine. I was nine years, three months, and two days old. My father taught me to make watches. But I learned something much more important from my mother: to value and keep track of time," he said.

He walked off without looking back at Aarón.

"Kid," Antonio yelled at one point, "your town stinks."

12.

ANDREA

Friday, February 27, 2009

Andrea took off her T-shirt and undid her bra. The cool air soothed the folds under her breasts and her armpits. If she'd driven a little farther, she would have found a better guesthouse to stop at—she might even have reached Arenas—but after driving for eight hours almost nonstop, the need for a bath and a bed had used up her patience. In any case, she didn't want to spend the night in the town. She stretched her back and neck until they crunched, then slumped on a soft bed whose sheets she knew she wouldn't get under. Her cell phone began to ring.

She looked at the screen and sighed when she read the name Emilio.

"You go away and all you leave me is a note?" he said. "Tell me you haven't left me forever, at least." Andrea heard the jocular tone in her husband's words. "You left the radio on and your breakfast on the table."

"I know, sorry for leaving like this. But my mom called me this morning," she lied, "to ask when she could come see us. I decided to surprise her. It's only fair that I go see her in Arenas once in a while, don't you think? I always make her come to us. And you know how much she hates being in the same city as my dad."

"It was a good idea, Andrea." She had forbidden him from calling her Drea since the first time he'd tried. "It was overdue. Sooner or later you had to go back."

Andrea couldn't stand Emilio when he was so sympathetic. His reaction to any situation was always the same affectation of normality and understanding. She felt like shouting at him that her mother didn't even know she was coming. But Emilio, the man she met when she went for an interview with a Spanish architecture studio in Toulouse—they were both going for the same job, which went to him—had been the only ray of light in the agonizing darkness that had hung over her life in the years after what happened with Aarón. Whether they were in bed or sharing a glass of wine, Emilio never made her feel what Aarón had been able to make her feel with a simple movement of his bottom lip. But he had saved her life when she fled Arenas to seek refuge at her father's house in France. Her father had taken her in as if she were still the seven-year-old girl he had left gripping the doorjamb one day, crying on the porch while her mother tried to coax her back in with a glass of soda. She had watched her father leave the house, not understanding why Mom was unable to forgive Dad.

"Thanks for being so understanding," Andrea said in spite of herself, as she always did when she realized she would forever be indebted to Emilio.

"But did you have to take the car? It's almost eight hundred kilometers. If you'd caught a flight in the afternoon, you'd be there by now."

Andrea didn't know how to respond. Or how to explain to him why the arrival of the year 2009 had terrified her. Or why, one morning like any other of that year, just as she was about to take a bite of her toast while the radio predicted a cold weekend, she had to get up, get in the car, and drive to Arenas. Except it wasn't a morning like any other, because the next day was the last Saturday of February. And Andrea knew that all the town's children would be at Aquatopia.

"I wanted to go back the same way I came. By land," she improvised.

"That's great, then," said Emilio.

Andrea noticed a bitter taste in her mouth.

"Let's talk tomorrow. I really need a shower," she managed to say. Now that she was so near Arenas, she was having to make a huge effort to silence the avalanche of memories that hammered her forehead almost like something physical. She wasn't going to be able to say another word.

"All right, but you drive carefully," Emilio advised, "and call me when you arrive. I love you."

He hung up without waiting for a reply, so he didn't hear the groan that emerged from Andrea's stomach, like the grunting sound a tennis player makes hitting the ball.

When Andrea awoke the next day, she wasn't sure whether she had slept. She walked out of the guesthouse into a sunny Saturday morning without even looking in the mirror, and climbed into her car. Gripping the steering wheel, she pressed her nose against her left shoulder and sniffed. In the end, she hadn't showered. *Then take your T-shirt off. I'd love to see you driving in a bra*, she imagined Aarón's voice saying. Emilio never said that kind of thing.

Andrea started the car.

Less than an hour later, the old Canal watch factory appeared on her left. The freshly painted lines on the highway had already shown her that nine years was long enough for a person to feel like a stranger in the town that had been her home, but it was the broken letters hanging from the factory's sign that rekindled the most recent memories she had of Arenas. Awful memories that flashed in her mind and that, so long ago, almost canceled out all her years of happiness in the town. It had been a time of little desire to eat or to live, a time that made her run away from Arenas before events ended up poisoning everything that connected her to it.

She hit the gas to stop herself from running away, now unable to remember any of the powerful reasons that, the previous morning, had prompted her to leave her breakfast on the table, write a note to Emilio, and drive off, leaving the radio on. Just after the factory, on the right side this time, appeared the sign that marked the entrance to Arenas de la Despernada. Her foot eased its pressure on the accelerator unconsciously. Andrea lowered the windows and enjoyed the sudden blast of cold air. She needed to distract herself from her thoughts with physical sensations. She also needed to repeat to herself why she was there.

"You're going to find that boy. You're going to tell him what Aarón wanted to tell him. And then you're going to leave. After that, you don't want to have anything more to do with it," she said. "You're doing it for Aarón. And for yourself. Because otherwise, you'd go crazy if anything really did happen. Not that it will."

The car in front braked, and Andrea had to do the same. The line of traffic reached all the way to that part of the highway, five hundred meters from the exit that led to the water park.

"Everyone'll be at the Aqua. The whole town," she persuaded herself. "He'll be there," she said in a sigh.

She looked around her at the town, each blink evoking memories and images of the various places she saw. In the distance, she discovered the outlines of several new residential developments that had been at the planning stage when she left. Before she could stop herself, her eyes came to rest on the three-story building where Aarón's apartment had been. Just thinking about him, about the last time she opened the door to that apartment, made her dizzy.

Andrea reached the exit for the park. But she left it on her right and accelerated hard. She had to do something first.

University Hospital welcomed her with a blast of the usual smell of disinfectant and medication. In the distance she saw an old man limping, flanked by two men dressed in green. There was nobody waiting to be seen at the reception desk. She walked over the aseptic marble floors to the low counter. Behind it she found a man with a face that was all cheekbones, his head shaved to mask his bald patch.

"Good morning, how can I help you?" he asked after ending a call that Andrea presumed to be personal from the way he had wrapped the receiver's spiral cable around his fingers.

He looked her up and down, and Andrea considered whether he had checked out her bust. Embarrassed, she remained silent, not knowing what to say. She had turned up at the hospital without a story ready, with no excuse or explanation for the question she was about to ask.

"Hello . . ." She pinched the skin on her neck and wished she had been wearing a necklace she could twist around her fingers. "I was wondering . . ." She looked away so she wouldn't see the disbelief that would be painted across the man's face. "I need . . ." She looked up and straight at his eyes. "Could you tell me, sir, if a child was born in this hospital on a specific day?" she blurted, just like that, accepting that the eight-hour drive and her struggle to remain sane had been reduced to this stupid question.

"And what's in it for me?" the receptionist said back. He wet his bottom lip and leaned forward. "And don't call me sir. I've worked here for ten years and, believe me, I've seen it all. A guy once grabbed my neck and almost managed to punch me. But that doesn't make me a person of authority." He looked from side to side, held a hand beside his mouth, and whispered, "Even my administrator's diploma is false." He rounded off the sentence with a wink.

Andrea responded with a nervous smile.

"As for your request, I don't know if I can." After a pause that Andrea thought theatrical, he said, "But do you know what? It'd take longer to call the supervisor—if he's even there and hasn't gone to the water park—ask for formal permission, make you sign a form, because there'll definitely be something to sign . . ." He was gesticulating with his right hand, rotating it nonstop, and Andrea understood how wrong she had been to assume he'd been trying to hit on her. "You know what I'm saying, right? It's going to be much easier and quicker for all of us if you tell me what it is you want to know and I tell you if I have it on file. Then you'll keep quiet, and I'll keep quiet, too. The perfect crime. If you want, you can show me some ID, so it seems official, and we'll leave it at that." He tilted his head. "Are you from around here, from Arenas?"

"Yeah. I was a professor at the university for a few years. Now I live abroad." She showed him her driver's license.

"From Arenas? Then you've put my mind at rest. We're all nice people here." He smiled and examined the license. "Wow, you looked good with blonde hair." He ran his forefinger over her name. "Andrea. So now that we know it's a family affair, tell me, what was it you needed to know?"

"Well"—she lowered her voice—"I want to check whether a boy was born here on May twelfth, 2000."

"Don't tell me: you're not sure when you should be giving a gift to a friend's son. It happens to me all the time. I'm always forgetting dates. Luckily, my friends aren't the parenting types, so I only forget their own birthdays."

While the man spoke, he typed a short word into a computer under the counter. The name on the badge clipped to the pocket of his white coat was Miguel. Andrea watched him look at various areas of the screen, clicking the left mouse button at seemingly random intervals.

"Year, 2000 . . . ," he murmured, "month, May . . ." He made a sound with his lips. "Nope, there's nothing." He kept his eyes fixed on the screen. Something changed in the furrows on his brow. "In fact"— his voice sounded deeper now, and he spoke more slowly—"there were no births until . . ." His forehead smoothed out completely, his eyes suggesting a discovery.

He gave Andrea a look in which all trace of friendliness had gone.

"I'm going to ask you to leave now," he said.

Andrea didn't object. She wanted to get out of the hospital anyway. Get out of Arenas. Miguel had just made it clear that Aarón had been wrong about everything. Incapable of waiting for it to fully open, she struck the automatic door with her arm.

Inside, Miguel looked back at the screen. In lime green on a background of dark green were the results of the search he'd just made at the stranger's request. And then he connected the question with the man with the burst blood vessel in his eye. The only assault he'd suffered at that desk. The same date and the same question. The same question and the same anxiety. The sincere concern in their eyes. The results were the particulars of the only baby born in University Hospital from May to June 2000. Miguel didn't want to look at the name under the flashing cursor: Leonardo Cruz.

Reading the name reminded him of the story that madman had told him. Something about a warning. A boy. Something about August 2009. A month in a year that sounded a long way off when the man with the bloody eye had mentioned it, but which would arrive this summer. It was August of this year. Miguel bit his fingernails, pensive. He put his hands over his face, reaching a decision. What did he have to lose? Nothing. And what could he gain? A child's life. Without much thought, he opened the computer's word processor and began to type.

Right away, the idea seemed absurd. He left the sentence half-written. Even so, he clicked on the option to print. He read the unfinished text and shook his head. He wanted to throw the piece of paper in the trash. Instead, he searched for an envelope in the drawers under the counter. He found a long white one with no hospital logos or marks on it. Now he typed the name Leonardo Cruz into the word processor. He placed the envelope in the printer. When it had almost finished printing, the envelope became jammed. Miguel pulled on it. A corner tore off, trapped in the contraption's roller. He looked back at the cursor on the screen. It was flashing in lime green at the beginning of the Cruz family's address.

The idea really was absurd.

Miguel stuffed the page into the envelope with the missing corner and placed it on a pile of documents to be filed.

Half an hour later, Andrea was parking the car at Aquatopia.

"What am I doing?" she asked the empty car. "This makes no sense. You were wrong about everything . . ."

When she got out of the vehicle, she felt the cold on her cheeks. She walked through the crowds toward the line at the entrance. She wandered about, changing direction several times to avoid encountering familiar faces. She fled from a cameraman and a woman with a microphone but observed the children that flocked around them. She searched among them for a certain aura. She bumped into one and tried to see his face. Then she walked along the line to the main gate. And decided she had done enough. She returned to the car.

"What am I doing?" she repeated, more to the steering wheel than to herself.

Tears slid down her cheeks, from the wrinkles that had appeared around her eyes in recent years to the corner of a mouth that didn't smile as it had in the past. With the salty taste of sadness in her throat, she heard the accelerated footsteps of a boy running to a BMW parked behind her. Through the rearview mirror, she saw him sit down by the front wheel and cover his face in a red towel he had hanging from his neck.

Andrea got out of the car. She didn't care that she had left the keys in the ignition and her purse on the passenger seat. She approached the boy, who was covered in sweat and dust.

"Hello?" Her voice trembled.

The boy had his head down.

Andrea waited for a few seconds. Her heart accelerated as she knelt in front of him. She held her hand to his shoulder. There was a spark of static electricity when she touched him.

"Are you here by yourself?" Andrea asked. "Aren't you with your parents?"

"I don't have a mom," the boy replied.

And looked up abruptly at Andrea.

The boy frowned, keeping one eye more open than the other. The expression was unmistakable. A shiver that Andrea had not felt for a long time ran down her body.

The boy felt it, too. Like an electric shock. A wave of well-being washed over him for an instant. Then it turned into anxiety. He began to tremble and shake his head. He covered his ears with his hands.

"Why're you frightened?" Andrea asked.

The child kicked his legs, raising a cloud of dust that enveloped them. He looked Andrea in the eyes.

"Hang on a minute," she said. An icy sweat covered her. "Do you already know something about August fourteenth?" The boy kept kicking. Andrea rested her knees on his ankles to contain him. "Tell me whether you know," she ordered. The dust scraped her throat, and she coughed.

"The letter . . . ," Leo moaned. "I know . . . August fourteenth."

"But that's impossible. How . . . ?"

She left the question unfinished because at that moment she accepted what she had to do. The boy was aware of the date. That was all she had come to do in the town she had not wanted to ever return to. And now she had confirmed it. The boy had been warned.

She saw a figure approaching them in the distance. A woman. It must have been the child's mother, so Andrea got up, climbed into her car, and accelerated. She escaped Arenas for the second time.

"You're not going to take me with you down this rabbit hole, Aarón!" she yelled aloud.

But soon afterward, as she drove, she lost control of her right foot. She stepped on the brake.

She could not run away again.

Nor face this alone.

She struggled to engage the reverse gear. She returned to the main street and headed back into town. When the outline of the house she was searching for appeared at the end of the road, she took a deep breath.

She stopped the car at the bottom of the steps that led to the porch. She climbed the stairs while she gathered her hair into a ponytail. She'd dyed it red to distance herself even more from the Andrea who no longer existed. She rubbed her face with both hands.

She rang the bell.

When the elderly woman with blue eyes opened the door, nine years of questions without answers were reflected in her face. Andrea couldn't speak. She just let herself weep, and hugged her.

"I've been wanting to see you again," said the woman. "And so has he."

13.

AARÓN

Tuesday, May 30, 2000

He picked up the white cup he and Andrea had bought at Ikea. A dark circular mark was printed on one of the photocopies of the newspaper that Samuel Partida had sent him. Never had one of his fits of racing thoughts lasted so long, driving him to exhaustion, and he would need a large dose of caffeine if he was going to be able to get all the loose ends down on paper.

Sitting at the table located up against the window in his apartment's living room, Aarón separated four blank pages from the stack he had in the drawer to his right. He took a sip of the cold coffee, rearranged them into a landscape orientation, and headed each of them with the dates when the four robberies had taken place:

September 14, 1909
January 29, 1950
February 3, 1971
May 12, 2000

The last date was exactly eighteen days ago. He underlined the years, and in a box to one side he indicated whether the scene had been at the watchmaker's shop, the old gas station, or the American's store. Beside his laptop, with its edges worn from use, was the notebook where he'd recorded his conversations with Samuel Partida and Antonio Canal. He also had the newspaper Andrea had borrowed from the super and never returned to him. At first, he'd thought it would also be possible to obtain cuttings from 1950 or even 1909. He'd imagined that the town's library would have an archive of periodicals going back a hundred years that he could access page by page on a screen, but the face Gloria the librarian had made when he asked made it clear he was wrong.

"If there's anything to be found, it'll be in here," he said.

He spread out the pages on the table as if they were pieces of a puzzle for which he had no picture as reference. Because it didn't even exist. Seeing the four dates, and each blank page representing a scene he had imagined so many times in recent weeks, was like staring at his own thoughts.

He drew five circles on each piece of paper.

"The people," he said out loud. After drawing the twentieth circle, he drew a line on each page separating one of the circles from the rest. "And the counter."

An image from his childhood, of him lying on the rug in his bedroom and joining the dots in one of his puzzle books, appeared in the nonexistent place where memories are projected.

"Connect the dots, Aarón," he murmured.

He scanned his handwritten notes in the notebook and tore out seven pages. He took the page with the 1909 date heading and held his pen ready. He knew it was Antonio Canal's grandfather who had died that year. He wrote his name inside one of the circles, the one on the side where the counter was. To differentiate him from his son and grandson, who had the same name, he followed it with the Roman numeral *I*. Underneath, he wrote the word *Victim*. He looked at the notebook pages again. He read diagonally, in the way one reads something one has already read, and returned to the piece of paper on which the crime was depicted to write the word *Boy* below one of the other circles. *One was a kid who must have been scared shitless*, he remembered, hearing Antonio's voice echo in the watch factory. Under another circle, he wrote the word *Killer*. In the absence of any more information on the other two people, he labeled them *Witness 1* and *Witness 2*. He went back over the notes from his conversation with Antonio Canal, confirmed there was nothing else on that first robbery, and returned the piece of paper to its original position.

"What's the point of this?" he asked. "I don't know," he replied to himself.

He picked up the page headed with the date in 1950. He filled out the circles in the same way. *Antonio Canal II* in one—the one at the counter again—and under it the word *Victim*. *It was some other bastard who killed my father*, Antonio had said. Aarón also wrote *Boy* below a second circle, adding the child's name, and *Killer* below a third. This time, he could be more specific with the two witnesses: *Shepherd* and *Fruit seller*. Glancing back at the notes, Aarón was able to complete the scene. By the deceased's name, he wrote his age: *40 years old*. He thought about the woman who had lamented her husband's death for the rest of her life, recounting the exact number of days and months he had lived. He also knew the age of the child, whom he'd named *Antonio Canal III*. He was nine at the time. *I watched my father being killed.* He found the place where he'd noted one of the watchmaker's last sentences and saw that he had written down the months and days that, like his mother, the younger Canal had committed to memory. The speed at which he'd noted the numbers made them illegible, but he didn't think it would prove to be important. He wrote *9 years old* next to the circle.

The boys are always nine, he thought.

He looked at the page, which was much more complete than the one with the earlier date.

He scratched his neck, and the beard crunched under his fingernails. He felt a stab of hunger but decided to ignore it. He couldn't remember when he'd last eaten. Or whether it had been day or night the last time he woke up. Or how long it had been since he'd spoken to Andrea. Or Héctor. Or his mother.

He moved on to 1971. To complete the reconstruction of that year's robbery, he had information from his conversation with Samuel Partida and from the newspapers. Mechanically now, he wrote *Victim*, *Boy*, and *Killer* under three circles. He completed them with the names *Roberto de la Maza* (the young man who was shot), *Samuel Partida* (the boy), and *Antonio Mercado* (the one who fired the gun). He also knew all their ages. The boy was nine, Roberto had just turned twenty-one, and the murderer was forty. He wrote *Witness* under the other two circles, and this time he was able to add their initials, which appeared in the newspaper: *L.M.* and *G.C.*

He proceeded in the same way with the piece of paper for May 12, 2000. He was struck by memories of Andrea getting out of the car, David offering to take the medicine to the American's store, himself wetting his face in front of the mirror and covering the floor in water, Héctor shaking his head at the hospital entrance . . . This time he was able to write the names and ages of all five people involved. When Andrea visited David in the hospital the day after the robbery, the Mirabal family already had all this information. She had given Aarón the details over the telephone, and they were both surprised to discover that Sr. Palmer, who appeared much older, was only fifty-three.

Aarón wrote the name of the boy who had witnessed the latest robbery, Andrés Cañizares, on the paper.

"Nine years old, of course," he said out loud as he wrote down the age of the boy who had witnessed the latest robbery. The detail made his stomach turn over.

He also wrote the names and ages of the would-be thief and the man who helped David and made the call to the police on his cell phone. He paused for a few seconds before writing *David Mirabal*. His left hand then wrote the word *Victim*, as he had named all the previous ones, but he quickly crossed it out.

He crossed it out with all the force with which the echo of guilt reverberated in his temples.

Aarón laid out the four pages on the table, like an unfinished tic-tac-toe grid. He examined them with his chin resting on his thumbs, pressing his jaw until it hurt. A warm gust of air blew through the open window. He wiped the sweat from his forehead. Staring at his graphic representation of the events, he felt a sudden shiver run down his back.

An imaginary Andrea appeared by his side. Aarón could almost smell the chamomile. She placed a hand on his shoulder and, voicelessly, said to him, *What's this got to do with David?*

"I don't know, for fuck's sake," he blurted at the table.

He covered his face with his hands, separating his fingers to look at the four diagrams, the collection of circles. The dates. The names. It was absurd. But a sudden feeling of certainty gripped his stomach again. Without needing an explanation, he marked the circles that represented the victims with a large *X*.

"Yes, David, you, too."

He didn't expect to find a hidden inverted pentagram or some paranormal explanation out of a horror novel, but it enabled him to see more clearly what he already knew. Five circles, representing five people, in each robbery. Four *X*s representing the victims. And there was always a boy at the scene, always age nine.

"I've known this for days. I didn't have to do all of this to realize that . . . Hang on a second."

His eyes moved toward the circles belonging to Antonio Canal II in 1950, Antonio Mercado in 1971, and the man with the cell phone in 2000. Beside all of them, his rushed hand had written the same thing: *40 years old*. His heart accelerated. He searched among the ages he'd noted down.

"I'm missing more than half—I didn't think . . . ," he began to say, but he stopped when he saw two instances of the number 21. It was the age of the thief who shot David. The same as Roberto de la Maza, killed in 1971. "Are the five people all of the same ages?"

Aarón studied the four pieces of paper again. He'd written the ages of all the people in the 2000 robbery. But none in the 1909 one.

"But I have three for 1971," he said, "and they're the same as 2000."

He searched among the newspaper cuttings and photocopies. Using his forefinger, he went back over the reconstruction of the events that year. He stopped at the initials of the two witnesses. He confirmed that he'd added them randomly to the two empty circles: *L.M.* in the one representing the gas station attendant, and *G.C.* in the remaining one. He snatched up his notebook and checked his notes from his conversation with Samuel Partida. He remembered Samuel telling him something about the man he'd had in front of him. *Man in front. Overcoat. Town mayor at time. Died recently* he managed to read among the scribbles he'd made in the car, forcing himself to remember.

He entered *Arenas de la Despernada mayor death* into the search engine on his laptop. He had to scroll through several pages of results before he found what he was looking for: a short announcement, from a year and a half earlier, of the death of Gabriel Calderón, *the former mayor of the town of Arenas de la Despernada, Province of Madrid.* Aarón glanced at the initials and confirmed they were the same. *Born on November 1, 1917*, he read on, and stopped. With his usual speed in making calculations, he wrote down *53 years old* by the *G.C.* circle in 1971. He smiled when he verified that Sr. Palmer was the same age on the day of the most recent robbery.

Now there were four ages repeated between these two events. Looking back at the notebook, he rediscovered Samuel's description of the cashier: *Young, under 30*, he had written.

"Twenty-nine, perhaps?" Aarón sang softly into the silence of his apartment, absorbed in his diagrams. "Like my friend David, and like me?"

He would have frightened himself had he been able to see himself, in his underpants, with sweat dripping down his cheeks into the irregular bushiness of his beard, while he wrote *29* beside the last empty circle in 1971.

"Connect the dots, Aarón."

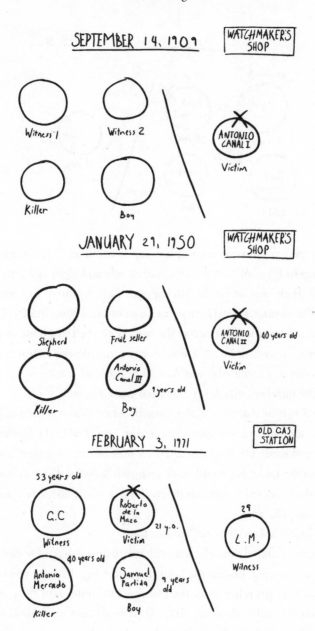

SEPTEMBER 14, 1909   WATCHMAKER'S SHOP

Witness 1   Witness 2   ANTONIO CANAL I
                                      Victim
Killer   Boy

JANUARY 29, 1950   WATCHMAKER'S SHOP

Shepherd   Fruit seller   ANTONIO CANAL II   40 years old
                                      Victim
Killer   Antonio Canal III
              9 years old
              Boy

FEBRUARY 3, 1971   OLD GAS STATION

53 years old
G.C   Roberto de la Maza   29
Witness   Victim 21 y.o.   L.M.
                                      Witness
40 years old
Antonio Mercado   Samuel Partida
Killer   9 years old
              Boy

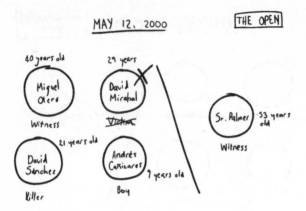

He picked up the two complete pages, one in each hand, and held them up in front of his eyes. He looked left and right twice to make certain. There was no doubt. All the ages were repeated. But not their roles. The murderer was twenty-one years old in 2000. The 1971 murderer was forty, the same age as the man with the cell phone in 2000. The young attendant in 1971 was twenty-nine, like the victim in 2000. The victim in a coma who was Aarón's best friend.

"The numbers match up, but what does it mean?"

And just at that climactic moment, when Aarón sensed he'd discovered something important, the certainty vanished again, leaving him empty and weak. His fingers eased their pressure on the pages, and they fell onto the table. He could smell chamomile again. *What does all this mean?* the inner voice that was determined to sound like Andrea asked. *Will it save David?*

"I know it won't," he replied out loud.

Aarón slumped onto the sofa, exhausted and hungry. He closed his eyes to try to sleep, but for the hour he spent lying there, he was unable to disconnect his mind from the names and numbers on the pieces of paper on the table. Thinking about food made him nauseated, and he knew this was a definite sign he had to eat.

Getting up, he felt his back freeze when a gust of air hit his sweat-soaked T-shirt. He lifted his toes as the cold air from the refrigerator reached them. Andrea had always laughed at the way his big toes went up when he was barefoot. He took out a box of chicken breasts in breadcrumbs that only needed six minutes in the microwave. It made him miss Andrea so much that he no longer knew whether it really was hunger that was making him feel empty. Because he remembered her in the enormous T-shirt, one shoulder uncovered, the lock of hair falling onto her face, her fingers covered in breadcrumbs and beaten egg, preparing breaded chicken breasts—homemade, not frozen—like she did almost every Saturday they spent together in that apartment. *How could I not make my favorite boy his favorite dish?* she would say, blowing air out of the side of her mouth to separate the hair from her face before presenting her cheek in expectation of Aarón's grateful kiss. He would take the opportunity to hold her from behind, feel his member press between her buttocks, and ask her what movie they would watch that night. Even a million microwave ovens like the one that was now defrosting and badly cooking Aarón's dinner couldn't produce the magical warmth of those nights with Andrea. At that moment, he missed her more than anything in the world. His longing for freedom had suddenly lost all its meaning. His urge to discover another world away from Andrea, his fear of becoming a father with her, no longer made sense.

"It's all my fault," he said to the chicken fillets as he took out the hot plate.

He returned to the pile of papers and, with a quick glance, remembered all the coincidences.

"I have to call Antonio Canal. This guy has to give me some more details—his family members' ages, at least."

Ideas began to swirl in the depths of his mind. *I'd say it starts behind my eyes and spreads to the rest of my head from there. They're ideas I don't have to think about to understand them*, he would have told a psychologist asking him to describe his racing thoughts. Aarón picked up a pen to do some calculations. He remembered asking Antonio how long the interval between the two robberies at the watchmaker's shop had been. He smiled over the papers, because that question had been more pertinent than he could have imagined.

He searched the internet for the number for the Canal watch factory. The guy didn't seem to have grasped the importance of having a website yet, so Aarón turned to an old copy of the Yellow Pages he found under the kitchen sink. He started dialing the number. When he reached the sixth digit, his gaze came to rest on the clock on the microwave.

It was 5:24 a.m.

He hung up.

He hugged himself when his back went cold again. He looked at the floor, at his bare legs and feet. His stomach tightened, and this time it hurt. He thought of Andrea. He approached the table, and seeing the papers made him dizzy. He picked up a square chicken breast and bit into it—he didn't recognize any flavor that resembled the ones she made. He ate without appetite. He started on the next one.

And he preferred not to wonder what was happening to him.

After several minutes during which he believed he hadn't thought about anything, he found it impossible to swallow the last mouthful. He felt the excitement in his stomach again.

"How did I not realize?" he whispered into the air.

Turning his head, he looked at the *February 3, 1971* he'd written in large letters on one of the pieces of paper. He slapped his forehead.

His laughter sounded deranged.

14.

LEO

Friday, March 20, 2009

The first drop of water on a rainy spring day hit Pi on the muzzle. Leo watched the cat close his eyes, then lower his head and rub it with his right paw. When more drops formed tiny crystal jewels on the black fur of his back, he untangled himself from his owner's legs and ran to the porch. He lay on the mat with a white cat printed on it, himself in negative.

"Linda, have dinner ready when we get back," Leo heard his mother say before the door slammed shut. "What the hell? For God's sake, Pi, get out of the way." The cat was unperturbed. "Your father's on his way!" she yelled to Leo as her heels crunched along the gravel driveway. "Get in the car, you're going to get soaked."

Leo was sitting on one of the stone pillars at the perimeter of the Cruz family's front yard. He looked up at the sky. Raindrops hit his eyelids and his bare knees between the socks and shorts of his uniform.

The four blinkers on the BMW flashed simultaneously, accompanied by a low-pitched whistle, when Victoria pressed the key button.

Leo headed through the yard toward the car. He was dragging his space backpack by one of the straps. The letters in the words *Space Commander*, which had been so prominent before, were now illegible. *How much did you say it cost?* Victoria had asked during dinner one time in front of Leo, despite it having been a birthday present from Amador. *Isn't it pretty worn for a backpack that's only a year old?* Leo himself had jumped in to respond. *It's just that I wear it as much as possible. It's no surprise it's worn. And the lack of gravity affects it, too.* Victoria didn't understand why Amador had to contain his laughter.

Leo climbed into the back seat of the car on the right side. Victoria occupied the passenger seat. She put the key in the ignition, leaving it ready for Amador. The key ring hung down like a pendulum. She grabbed hold of her rectangular purse, her fingernails tapping against one another, waiting impatiently for Amador to appear. He was returning from a business trip. When Victoria informed him over the phone that the psychologist had confirmed the boy's appointment, Amador promised he'd return in time to accompany the boy.

Victoria opened her purse.

"Here, angel, this is for you, for agreeing to come."

Leo took the Lisa Simpson PEZ dispenser after the second time she shook it. Leo activated the device and sucked on some candy.

A taxi appeared at the end of the gravel driveway. Victoria buckled her seat belt. Amador got out and said goodbye to someone with a tap of his knuckles on the taxi's rear window. When he got in the BMW and went to leave his briefcase and jacket on Victoria's lap, she gestured at the back seat with her eyebrows.

"Hi, son," he said to Leo when he turned around. "Ready?"

Leo shook his head, hiding behind his mother's headrest. Amador wanted to smile to soothe him, but didn't know whether he had managed it. The image of his son made him remember the Leo of two years ago.

They had driven to a little town on the Costa del Sol to pick up the cat that a former colleague of Victoria's was giving them, which they would later name Pi. For the duration of the six-hour journey, they listened to the songs Amador had programmed on the car stereo. *Is the singer going to die?* Leo had asked, listening to the lyrics in one of them. *Wow, I see you're making the most of your English lessons,* Amador had replied. *But no, son, it's just the lyrics. The person dying is the character in the song, which is why he's saying goodbye to all the people he loves,* he had explained in relation to the Terry Jacks hit. Leo had bitten his bottom lip and added, *Dad, what do you think happens when we die? Do we reincarnate?* When Amador heard the question, the sensitivity and depth of his seven-year-old son's thoughts made him feel dizzy. Because it wasn't what you'd expect from such a young boy. And because Amador had been taught that being different is not usually a good thing.

As a young man, when he was determined to start at the Department of Mathematics instead of studying law as his father wanted, Amador Cruz Sr.'s look of disappointment had been enough to banish the idea of studying sciences from his mind. So what could have been an excellent career as a mathematics professor at the private university they were to open years later in Arenas was reduced to a habit of solving the sudoku puzzle in the Sunday paper. Amador had completed his law degree. And on his return from gaining his master's in San Francisco, his father had used his influence to get him through the door at the same international law firm where his father had worked all his life. Amador was already a partner at the firm when he met Victoria Cuevas, the woman his father had wanted to see him marry and who sure enough became his wife, to her delight and to his father's. Neither of them knew how Amador had given up the woman who could have been the love of his life, a young Mexican writer, all curves and dreams of success, with whom he had been madly in love in San Francisco. He said goodbye to her at the airport despite their plans for a future that never came, in which Amador was a professor at the private university in Arenas and María was a successful author of romance novels.

That was why, during that trip to the Costa del Sol, in the seven-year-old boy who spoke of fate, reincarnation, and successive lives, Amador saw the courage of someone who dared to be different. The courage he had never had. The courage of someone who sat by the side of a soccer field with a three-hundred-page book on his knees while his classmates imitated him by knotting their ties in the same impeccable way as he did or holding their hands over one side of their faces to mock the patch he had to wear when he was diagnosed with a lazy eye. A boy, his son, whom he loved at that moment more than ever, seeing in him the improved version of himself.

"Amador, what're you doing?" Victoria tore him from his thoughts. "We have to be there in ten minutes."

Amador put aside his memories of his father, of Pi, and of the trip to Estepona, and grabbed the steering wheel with his left hand. He held his right hand out toward his wife.

"They're already in the ignition," she said.

"Hi, honey," he replied, without looking at her. "Why're we going in this car?"

"The other one's at the repair shop," said Victoria. "Anyway, where were you intending to put your son? In the trunk?"

"Leo doesn't mind bunching his legs up if it means he can go in an Aston Martin. Isn't that right, champ?" he asked, though he knew Leo wasn't interested in cars.

He started the engine and stepped on the gas.

They left their neighborhood without saying a single word.

"We're going to get stuck in the student traffic as they come out," Amador said when they reached the road that led to Arenas's main street. "You've brought the letter, right?" he added, turning toward his wife.

A fixed stare was her only response.

"Just great, Victoria." He hit the brakes and let his hand drop onto the gearshift. "It's all we have."

"Today's just to meet each other. We'll have plenty of time for everything," she said in her defense.

"And what if Leo doesn't want to talk? How're we going to explain about the letter?" he whispered. "Or the redheaded woman?"

"I didn't manage to see the woman," said Victoria, projecting her voice toward the back seat. "How strange, huh?" She waited for a response from Leo. "He'll have to tell Dr. Huertas all by himself. Because that woman was real, right, angel?" she asked. "And she had a really fast car," she concluded.

Leo saw his father pinching his mother's leg.

When Amador had arrived home the Saturday Leo and Victoria had gone to Aquatopia, Leo was already in bed. He'd listened to the gravel crunch under the car's approaching wheels. Then he must have fallen asleep, because he didn't hear his father's footsteps approaching the house. When his bedroom door slowly opened, Leo turned on the light.

"You're still awake," Amador had said.

Leo didn't answer. His father sat on the bed, by Leo's waist. Leo covered his face with the sheet, on which the robot WALL·E was looking up at the sky with inquisitive eyes.

"Do you want to tell me what happened?"

Leo shook his head. He turned over, pressing himself against the wall.

"Come on, son." Amador shook Leo by the leg. "We've had a few very good months. What's this about now? You know this episode's going to force us to take you to that place where you don't want to go."

"I know," he replied. "You don't believe me, either."

"So what should I believe? You haven't told me anything about what happened."

"She's told you already. And you think I'm making it up again."

"Leo, do me a favor. Look at me," his father said. "Look at me, son."

Leo sat up until his back was resting against the wall.

"Leo, who did this?"

Amador stroked the scratches on Leo's cheek, angry when he guessed who had done it to him.

"Did a woman really come up to you and repeat the same thing the letter said?" he asked.

Leo looked away. He didn't answer.

"In any case, son, all Dr. Huertas is going to do is help us." Leo hid back under the robot picture. Seeing the boy go into a sulk, Amador added, "Understood, Commander. Sleep, and we'll talk tomorrow."

Leo remained silent.

"I'm going to turn the light off now. I love you, Leo." Amador kissed the crown of his head, which poked out from under the sheet near the pincers that WALL·E had as hands.

Amador had gotten up carefully and walked toward the door guided only by the greenish glow from the alarm clock on the bedside table. He was so absorbed in his thoughts, thinking that Victoria had some explaining to do about the scratches Leo had on his face, that he didn't hear his son murmur, *I love you too, Dad.* Perhaps he only said it to the sheet. Or perhaps Leo had only thought the phrase at the onset of the deep sleep he was wrapped in that Saturday night when the dust from the parking lot was nothing more than a bad memory on his skin.

As if he hadn't heard his mother's joke about how fast the redheaded woman's car was, Leo grabbed the front seats to pull himself forward.

He peered through the space between the two headrests. The traffic lights turned green, as did the color of the puddles on the pavement. Amador accelerated. They entered the main street with the traffic still flowing. In five minutes they would be at the clinic.

"Dad," Leo said in a serene voice, "do you remember our trip to the beach when we went to get Pi?"

Amador smiled. He searched for his son's eyes in the rearview mirror, picturing the sunlit road that had brought them together for six hundred kilometers and perhaps forever.

"Do you remember the song we listened to? The one I really liked."

"Sure," Amador replied to the mirror. "Of course I do."

Victoria frowned and looked out at the street.

"Will you put it on for me?" Leo asked.

The question touched Amador. He looked at Victoria. Absorbed in what was outside, she was moving her head from side to side. He could hear the sound of her fingernails as the one on her forefinger hooked onto the one on her thumb, released it, then hooked it again.

"We went in the old car. I don't know if I'll have it here."

"But it's the same CD changer," Leo pointed out. "You put it in this car when you bought a new one, didn't you? Your sports car already had one."

Amador turned on the stereo and skipped through the tracks on the discs.

"We're almost there, anyway," Victoria intervened. "There's no time. Later, on the way home."

Sure enough, the doorway where Dr. Huertas had put up a plaque, engraved at the town's jewelry store, appeared on the right. Amador found a place to park just outside the entrance. He maneuvered while reading the song titles that were flashing up in bright blue digits on the radio's screen.

The first chords of "Seasons in the Sun" began to play seconds before Amador finished parking the car. Leo smiled at his father via the rearview mirror. Amador winked at him. Victoria unbuckled her seat belt and stretched her hand, with her index finger extended, toward the radio's on-off button. Amador reached her in time to stop her, grabbing her wrist.

"We're going to be late, there's no time to—"

The pressure from Amador's fingers increased. Victoria shook her arm to free herself. She straightened her skirt and got out of the car, slamming the door behind her. She crossed the sidewalk with little leaps, holding her purse over her head, until she was able to take shelter in the doorway. From there, she looked back at the car, tutted, and looked off into the distance.

Inside, Amador and Leo sat back in their seats, reliving their trip.

"Ready," Leo said when the song had ended.

The nail on Victoria's index finger cracked near the flesh. She ignored the pain and gestured forward with her chin.

"Look, son, the license plate up ahead is a palindromic number," she said, projecting her voice to the back seat. "Maybe it's a coded message."

"Don't do that to him," Amador snapped.

Leo was resting his face on the car's rear window. The glow from the traffic light keeping them stationary colored it red.

Victoria switched hands and made a new pair of fingernails click. She continued to look ahead, at the palindromic license plate on the van advancing down Arenas's damp main street, which was crowded at that time of day with students' cars. She tutted, she sighed much more loudly than she would have had she been alone in the car, she shuffled in her seat. She rearranged her skirt and undid another button on her jacket. She glanced at Leo in the rearview mirror. He was clutching the PEZ dispenser in his left hand. For a second, Victoria was touched by the sight of the reddish remains of the candy on her son's lips.

"So? Doesn't it tell you anything, that license plate? Who knows, angel? Why don't you take a good look? Maybe if you rearrange the numbers somehow it means"—she started moving her hands in an agitated way—"I don't know, maybe it means . . ." Before she finished the sentence, Amador shook his head, his knuckles turning white on the steering wheel. "Maybe they're telling us the date of your death."

Amador hit the brakes hard.

They all lurched forward.

Victoria reached for the dashboard to stop herself. There was a stab of pain in her forefinger. Her husband stared at her in silence. Then he searched for Leo in the reflection in the rearview mirror.

"That's certainly not going to help him," Amador whispered.

"I can't understand what you're saying if you speak so quietly," Victoria snapped back, engrossed in her fingernails again. "I can't hear you. And I don't think Leo can, either. Isn't that right, angel?"

"Of course I heard," said the boy, his voice garbled by the candy in his mouth. "And Dad, the psychologist won't be able to help me, either."

"Dr. Huertas couldn't do much with you giving yes and no answers to all his questions," said Amador. "You came across as a rude boy. When you've been going to him for a month, we'll see what he says." He turned to his wife again. "How could you have forgotten to bring the letter?"

As ever, the traffic subsided at the end of the main street.

Before long, Amador stopped the car in front of their garage, the gravel crunching under the tires. An intermittent warning sound indicating an open door beeped until Victoria slammed it shut and began walking across the yard. Dodging Pi on the doormat, she opened the front door with her key. Linda came running through the living room.

"Even the cat gives me a better welcome than you," Victoria said. "Didn't you hear us arrive?"

"I'm sorry, señora, I was upstairs making Leo's bed."

"He'll be going to his room early tonight." Victoria didn't look at her. "He won't be needing dinner."

She crossed the living room toward the kitchen. She served herself a glass of water, filling it to the brim with crushed ice from the refrigerator's dispenser. She chewed before drinking.

Amador took longer than necessary to turn off the car's lights, put the hand brake on, inspect the glove compartment, and tidy some CDs that were already tidy. He wanted to give Leo the chance to say something. But Leo said nothing. When his father opened the child lock from the front, he got out of the car, dragging his backpack by one of the straps. The same backpack the letter had appeared in.

Leo placed a hand over his head in an ineffective imitation of an umbrella and headed toward the house. He broke into a run when he saw Pi sitting on the mat. He knelt beside the cat and extracted the last PEZ from the dispenser.

"You believe me, don't you?" he said.

Pi sniffed the candy. He pushed it with his muzzle until it fell to the ground. He examined it there while Leo smiled for the first time that day.

"Don't give the cat sugar," Amador said as he went through the door. In the downstairs bathroom, near the kitchen, he turned on the faucet to refresh his forehead and neck before looking at himself in the mirror and saying, "Your son's completely normal. Everything will work itself out." He heard Victoria saying something to Linda in the dry tone she also used with her son more and more often.

"Are you coming in?" Leo winked at Pi. "Come on, Pi, come on. You'll get wet out here."

A little push with his foot was enough to make the cat leap from the mat to the rug inside. The door slammed when it closed, helped by Leo and the draft created between the entrance to the house and the kitchen window. Leo took off his shoes and headed to the stairs. His feet appreciated the soft feel of the carpet that ran up the wooden steps. He hated his school shoes.

In his bedroom, Leo left his backpack, jacket, tie, and the rest of his uniform in a pile by the desk.

He didn't turn on the light.

He looked up at the ceiling. At the stars glowing in the dark. *That must be a black hole*, Dad had improvised when he affixed the last sticker in their unfinished Cassiopeia. He wished his father could do the same now: make up some reason that would explain the messages, the letter, and what happened with the redheaded woman, instead of getting angry and taking him to a doctor against his will.

Footsteps approached his bedroom.

"Dinner's on the table," Amador told him, "and it smells good."

Leo finished undressing. He tidied the pile he'd made by the desk and put on the yellow pajamas that Linda had left on his pillow. Wearing lion-paw slippers, he headed downstairs.

When he reached the kitchen, Victoria removed his plate from the table. She gestured at Linda to take it and put it in the refrigerator.

"There'll be no dinner tonight," she said.

Amador tried to say something but gave up. Instead, he headed to the refrigerator, poured a glass of milk, took a packet of Oreos from a drawer—moving Linda out of his way—and gave it to Leo.

Victoria slammed her cutlery onto her plate. Linda lowered her head.

Leo turned around and retraced his steps back to his room. He left the milk and cookies on the desk. Downstairs, his parents were arguing again.

Two hours later, Leo was asleep under an incomplete starry sky while his parents' backs did not even touch in a marital bed that grew ever colder and wider.

Only Pi, who was walking on the damp roof in the early hours, saw the approaching silhouette that stopped for a few seconds at the front gate, by the mailbox, and then walked on with a nervous gait.

15.

AARÓN

Thursday, June 8, 2000

When Andrea saw Aarón's name on her cell phone screen, she recognized the excitement of the first few times he had called her house. *Shall we go for a drive and listen to the radio in the car?* the nineteen-year-old Aarón had asked, to which she had responded with a stifled giggle, turning her back to her mother, who would later warn her not to trust Aarón because he would end up leaving her. According to her, all men were as bad as Andrea's father.

Angry that she had allowed herself to feel like she was in love again, Andrea took the call. Around her, descriptive-geometry students were leaving the classroom, filling it with shouting, comments on the professor, and the constant sound of chairs screeching on the floor. She rubbed out what she had written on the blackboard during the lecture, kicking up more chalk than usual.

"Drea." Aarón's voice sounded excited. "Drea, I'm at home. You have to see this."

Half an hour later, Andrea arrived at Aarón's apartment.

She opened the door with her key.

"I did it without thinking. I guess I should knock now," she said apologetically.

Aarón looked at her from the table in the living room. He jumped up with some papers in his hand and went to hug her. She felt his breath near her hair, searching for the chamomile smell he liked so much.

"Are you crazy?" he said. "This is still your home."

Andrea turned her face away when she thought he was going to kiss her. Aarón took her hand and led her to the table. He sat her in a chair opposite his and pressed her legs together with his.

"I'm sure of it. I'm right."

Aarón smelled of bed. His neck was red from his growing beard.

"Everything I imagined. It's true. And there's something we can do with it."

He spoke with excitement in his voice, almost euphoric.

"Did you really call for this?"

"It's not just talk now. Everything fits. This was no coincidence."

Without giving her time to react, Aarón untangled his legs from hers, turned in his chair, set the papers he had in his hand on the table, quickly moved his fingers between them, and arranged them in an order that Andrea thought premeditated. When he got up, Andrea saw stains on his red jogging pants.

"Come on, look," he said from above. "Stand up."

Andrea got to her feet as if in slow motion. She looked at Aarón with wide eyes. Concentrating on the pages on the table, he was biting his bottom lip. He was smiling. Andrea wanted to scream at him. She wondered why she didn't—scream at him with all her might. Like she did three days after Aarón admitted to her that he'd slept with Rebeca. Like she did that night when she woke up in the early hours, with him sleeping beside her, and hit him with all her fury, cursing him for humiliating her. Kicks and punches that didn't stop until he woke and realized what was happening. Aarón had grabbed

Andrea by the wrists then and lain on top of her to immobilize her with his body weight. Their naked bodies brushed against each other on an especially hot night in Arenas, and Aarón asked for forgiveness with words and caresses. They made love in a way that both of them remembered later on many occasions, Andrea doing so with a sharp pain in her heart that she kept to herself, because she had sworn that she would forgive him, with no bitterness.

"I can't see anything," Andrea said now.

The long late-spring evenings in Arenas meant that night fell without one's eyes immediately realizing it. Through the window, the stars had begun to shine and the world was navy blue. Aarón turned on the desk lamp. A circle of light appeared on the table. Andrea ran her eyes over the newspaper cuttings, the numbers, the pages torn from the notebook, the names.

"What is all this, Aarón?"

"You mean it's not obvious? And here I thought that, arranged like this, it'd be clear at first glance."

Andrea moved her lips but said nothing.

"I see it so clearly now, I don't know how I could have missed it," he said. "Even when I spoke to Samuel Partida for the first time, the February third, 1971, thing didn't register." He paused and pointed at Andrea. "And you didn't notice it, either. Don't start telling me you realized the first time I told you, that night at the lake," he reproached her.

"What is it I'm supposed to realize?" she asked. She thought about it for a moment. "Oh, OK, your birthday. So what?"

"You can't imagine," he said. He held the palms of his hands toward the table, without resting them on it. "All right, maybe it's a coincidence I was born that day. The same day as David. It's more than curious, but all right, let's say it's just a coincidence. But there's something else. I told you I went to see Antonio, right?"

"You haven't called me for two weeks," Andrea replied.

Aarón blinked with an expression of genuine surprise. He cleared his throat before continuing.

"Well, I went to the watch factory on the highway. The one in the industrial zone. I spoke to the owner. He's the son and grandson of the people who had the store here, in Arenas, years ago. Both of them were killed—do you remember the newspaper?" He waited for her to nod. "They were both killed in the same place, in the store."

"Where the American's store is."

"The Open, yeah. And do you know what happened the day they killed the watch factory owner's grandfather?" He answered the question without giving her the chance to respond. "His father was born. And then he was himself killed in the watchmaker's store on January twenty-ninth, 1950." He stabbed at one of the pages with his forefinger. "Andrea, Roberto de la Maza was born that day."

"I don't know who Roberto de la Maza is," said Andrea. "What're you talking about?"

"Roberto de la Maza, the one who was killed in 1971. In the robbery Samuel Partida told me about. He was killed at the gas station on the day I was born," he explained in a higher than usual pitch.

"Stop." Andrea hooked her hair behind her ears. "Wait a second. You've lost me. It's too much information."

Aarón burst out laughing, amazed that she wasn't following him. Two weeks ago, he certainly did have too much information to process. Now it all seemed incredibly coherent. He stopped laughing when she pushed her chair away with a violent movement of her legs, headed to the sofa, and slumped down with crossed arms.

Aarón went to her. He lifted her chin with two fingers.

"Drea, you have to see it. You have to tell me you believe what I'm saying, because I can see it, and it's real. All the dates match. You don't have to understand anything, forget the details"—he gestured at the table—"but trust in what I'm telling you. The Canals, Roberto,

David . . . they were all born on the day the previous victim was killed."

After saying that, he felt relief.

But Andrea's expression was unchanged.

"Aarón, what're you talking about? Can you hear yourself?"

"No," he replied, raising his voice. "I want *you* to hear me. What I've found, it's simple mathematics: one's born when the previous one dies."

"And I *am* hearing you. But I don't understand anything you're saying. It makes no sense."

Andrea got up and headed to the bathroom, closing the door behind her. Leaning on the sink, she looked at herself in the mirror. *Everyone grieves in their own way. Let him have his,* Ruth had said to her one night from the foot of the bed in which her son was still lying faceup, breathing with the same cadence he'd been breathing with for almost a month, in the half-light of the hospital room that was gradually becoming her new home. *Just tell him no one blames him for anything,* Ruth had added as she pulled the blanket up to David's chin, rested her hands on his chest, and gave Andrea a smile filled with hope. *Good night. And thanks for coming. I'm going to sleep here tonight again. With David.* That night, Andrea had kissed Ruth on the cheek and decided she would allow Aarón to take the time he needed. If he wanted to blame himself, then so be it. If he wanted to drive himself to exhaustion searching for an explanation for what happened, then so be it.

"Drea?" he asked from outside the bathroom. "Come on, you have to help me—"

But Andrea covered her ears and didn't hear the rest of the sentence. When she took away her hands, Aarón was knocking on the door.

"What, Aarón? What?"

"There's more, much more," he said.

Andrea sighed. She left the water running while she gathered the strength to paint a smile across her face.

"Come on," she said as she went out. She took Aarón's face in her hands. "Finish telling me."

She turned off the bathroom light. The apartment was only dimly lit again, from the desk lamp. A sudden draft ruffled the papers. Aarón took several pages from the table, and they sat on the sofa again. Andrea thought about Dr. Huertas, the local psychologist who'd become a friend of her mother's after the two years of therapy she underwent when Andrea's father left.

Encouraged by Andrea's smile, Aarón said, "Antonio told me himself when I met him. His father was born on the same day his grandfather was killed. I could've deduced then that it was something that was repeated. But it took me a while longer. I had to find out more dates, the dates when almost everyone was born or died."

"You got them from the newspapers?"

"Yeah, from the newspapers. I also spoke to Canal again, and called some other people in the town." Aarón gestured with his eyebrows in a way Andrea didn't recognize. "And in the cemetery, of course."

"Don't tell me you went . . ."

"Where would you have gone?"

Andrea rubbed her lips. She nodded in an exaggerated way without saying anything.

"When I checked the dates, it became clear. That number of coincidences can't just happen by chance." He held one of her hands and stroked it with his thumb. "You asked me one night if all of this would help me save David. It won't, of course." His thumb stopped. "But it might save the next one. What do you see here?"

He laid out the four pieces of paper as well as he could on the sofa and their legs. Andrea looked at all the circles, the *X*s marking one circle under each date. She shook her head.

"Look," he said. He pointed at the four instances of the word *Boy*. "There's always a boy. A different boy. But always age nine. That gave me the first clue. Then I saw that it's not just the kid who's the same age in each robbery. Drea, it's incredible, but all five people, all fucking five of them are like characters that're repeated in the same scene, with different people each time. The twenty people who've been involved in these robberies are always—every time—of the same ages." He looked at the pages and at her. At her and at the pages. "Do you think it can be a coincidence?"

Andrea fixed her eyes on those of an Aarón she didn't recognize.

"And the boy's age doesn't just match in years." He leapt up to the table, rummaged through some papers, and returned to the sofa with his notebook. "It matches in years, months, and days."

Aarón thought of Antonio Canal, or more specifically his mother—and the way she measured time—while flicking through the pages with his thumb, a cloud of figures, ink, and obsession in front of Andrea's eyes.

"The boy who witnesses the murders is always age nine years, three months, and two days. Always. He was the same age on all four occasions: Samuel was, Antonio was, the Cañizares grandson was . . ." He fell silent. He ground his teeth inside his closed mouth. "Do you know what that means?" His jaw muscles stood out. "That we know how old the boy will be next time it happens. And if we count from May twelfth . . ."

"May twelfth? When David was shot?" Andrea blurted. It came out sounding more disdainful than intended. "What next time?"

"It's obvious: this is going to happen a fifth time. And this time it's going to be the boy who gets killed. He's the only one who hasn't been killed yet."

"Aarón, I don't—"

"There're always five people." He raised his voice now. "Each time, the victim is a different age. The fifty-three-year-old guy who died was Antonio's grandfather, then the forty-year-old was his father. Roberto was twenty-one and . . ."

"Don't say it, Aarón. Don't you dare say it," Andrea pleaded.

"And David was shot, and he's twenty-nine." Andrea felt saliva spatter her. Aarón clenched his teeth. "Exactly the same age as me. Because I should've been killed at that moment. I should've been the fourth because that's what was predetermined." He sucked in air to regain his breath. "It was predetermined from the day I was born. And seeing as how I'm not going to be able to save him—as you've told me so many times—I'll have to make do with saving the boy, because this will happen a fifth time, and this time he'll be the one who gets killed. And, Drea, if the day comes when a child dies at the Open and I haven't done everything possible to prevent it, knowing what I—"

He stopped dead to take in air again before continuing.

But he didn't continue.

He lowered the finger he'd been pointing back and forth between the papers and Andrea. It was the first time he'd said everything out loud. And it sounded strange.

"And how do you intend to save him?" Andrea asked.

For a few seconds, Aarón was certain she'd said he was crazy. That the guilt had made him crack. That the boy was nothing more than an invention of his mind to substitute for the friend he hadn't been able to save in the real world. But Andrea hadn't said that. Andrea had asked him how he was going to save the boy. And that meant the boy existed and she believed him.

"By counting the days," he said. "If this boy's going to be nine years, three months, and two days old on the day of the next robbery, all we have to do is count from the day when David was shot. I can figure out when it's going to happen, Drea." He smiled. "We can know when it's going to happen next time."

Another piece of paper appeared on their legs, among the other four. It was headed with a date she only glimpsed out of the corner of her eye. Enough to see that it was sometime in 2009.

"I guess the scene will be the American's store again," she said.

"It wouldn't make sense for it to happen anywhere else."

"And do you also know why this is happening here, to you, to us?"

"I don't know, Drea. But I can't ignore what I'm seeing. This"—he lifted one of the pages—"this is real."

Andrea swallowed and thought of Dr. Huertas again. She tried to maintain a half smile. Aarón's eyes seemed unfamiliar.

"Also, since the next victim is born when the previous one dies," he went on, scratching his beard, "this boy's already born. He was born on the night David was shot, May twelfth this year." He bared his teeth without smiling. "I can go to the hospital to check. I can warn the boy's parents today, Andrea."

Aarón took hold of her wrists and moved so close to her that Andrea could see the dry skin under his beard.

"I"—he breathed through his mouth—"can save"—he wet his lips with his tongue—"his life."

He continued to grip her wrists.

"But you're not going to," she said.

"What do you mean I'm not . . . ?"

Andrea freed her hands. She gathered up all the pieces of paper between them. She made a small pile, tidying the corners with a teacher's skill. She folded the five pages in half. She cut her finger on the edge of one of them and put it in her mouth to suck it. She placed the notebook on top of the pile, got up, and slammed it all down on the table, on the laptop.

"Because you're not. Because I'm not going to let you go to the hospital." Now it was her pointing a finger. "Look at the state of you. I am not going to let you go there to inquire about a child you don't know, or tell some poor parents their newborn's going to be killed in less than ten years, based on a load of nonsense." She waved her hands around to make everything seem more chaotic. "On a bunch of numbers and weird stories about reincarnation. For God's sake, Aarón, do you realize what you're saying?"

"I didn't say anything about reincarnation," he replied from the sofa.

"Well, that's what it sounds like. 'One's born when the previous one dies.'" Her mouth spoke for her, and the mimicking tone came out without intending it. "I'm sorry," she said. "Aarón, look at yourself . . . you're not well. And I want to help you." She approached and held one of his ears. "Will you let me?" She scratched his scalp.

"You haven't believed anything I've said." He shook his head to free himself of Andrea's hand.

"No." She took a deep breath. "No, I don't believe you. I didn't even understand you." She glanced involuntarily at a shelf, on the corner of which sat the stone from the lake. "And I'm going to do everything I can to forget this conversation. Because I don't care. And I don't care because David's dying while you and I are talking. And he's the one who needs your help. Not a . . . a boy from the future," she improvised, "who you don't even know exists."

"Well, it's very easy to find out whether the 'boy from the future'"—Aarón's mimicking *was* intentional—"exists or not."

He didn't say anything else. He crossed his legs in Andrea's direction and hooked his hands around his knees.

"Aarón, you're not going to do it."

"Try to stop me."

Aarón was swinging his right leg back and forth, pivoting it on his left knee. When he stretched his foot, his ankle clicked.

The sound repulsed Andrea.

"Fuck you," she said. Without even thinking about it, she picked up the papers she'd just deposited on the laptop and threw them in his face.

The edge of one of the pages scratched the cornea of Aarón's left eye. Blood began to pool from the corner of the eye to the iris, while the upper eyelid contracted involuntarily, causing stabs of pain. Tears blurred his vision.

"Don't go," Aarón said, without seeing Andrea for what would have been the last time.

When the door closed, another kind of tears filled his eyes.

16.

LEO

Saturday, March 21, 2009

The morning caught Pi sleeping on the roof, from which he'd watched the silhouette approach the entrance to the Cruz house and walk on with a nervous gait. The sun had returned strong. The smell of the moisture escaping from the slate tiles the cat was resting on seeped through the half-open balcony door of Leo's room. It was his bare feet that woke first in the sun's heat, raising an alarm that made Leo open his eyes and retract his legs into the disappearing shade on his bed.

"Your *papás* are having breakfast in the garden," Linda said when he appeared at the kitchen door. "They're having toast."

She stroked Leo's cheek and smiled. She seemed to want to say something to him, but when Victoria walked into the kitchen, she stopped herself.

"There you are. I was on my way to get you up," Victoria said. She was carrying a champagne glass of orange juice. "Come on, angel, we're outside, in the garden."

The sprinklers welcomed Leo with a whistle when they emerged from the ground to spray semicircles of water on grass that was still moist from the night. Amador was reading the newspaper.

"With all the rain we had yesterday, we should turn them off," said Victoria, sitting at the table. She put on sunglasses and wrinkled her nose at the garden. She followed one of the sprinklers with her gaze, turning her head like a dog hypnotized by a car's windshield wipers.

"It's almost going to be harder to deprogram it and then program it again," Amador replied as he took a sip of his coffee, without looking up from the newspaper. "It doesn't matter. With this sun it'll dry out in no time."

After returning his cup to the table, he closed the paper and navigated through the pages with his thumbs, looking at the top corner of each. He took one out and folded it in half. He placed it in front of Leo, beside a plate with two pieces of jam-covered toast on it.

"Good morning, Commander. Here, a pen." He took it out of his shirt pocket and placed it on top of the sudoku puzzle.

"How long do you think it'll take me this time?" Leo asked.

Beside him, Linda was spooning cocoa powder into a cup. With a nod, Leo indicated that he wanted one more. She scooped up a mountainous last spoonful and they both smiled. Then Linda poured warm milk on top of it, knowing that if the señora saw her she would be the one who was told off.

"If you take longer than three minutes, it's because you're losing your powers."

"Angel, have breakfast first," Victoria interrupted. "You can play later. You must be starving after not wanting any dinner last night."

Leo pushed his cup away and picked up the pen. Bent over the table, he rested his forehead in his right hand and started to write numbers on the newspaper that he would then cross out or go over more firmly. He wrote some outside the grid and some inside. From time to time he stared at one of the empty boxes before adding a number to it with confidence. Finally, he ran the pen over each row, moving his lips slightly, and then dropped it. He slapped the table as if hitting the button in a TV game show.

Amador reviewed Leo's work. He raised his eyebrows at Leo before inserting the page back into the rest of the newspaper.

"Come on, time for breakfast," he said. "The jam's delicious."

Leo gulped down some hot chocolate. He enjoyed the fleeting happiness the smell of cocoa made him feel. The same thing happened with chamomile. With a brown moustache painted on his top lip, he bit into his toast. He tasted the freshness of the peach on both sides of his tongue.

"I see you're in a better mood today," Victoria cut in. "Did you sleep well?"

Leo nodded, though it was a lie. He struggled to swallow his second mouthful.

"Angel"—Victoria lifted her sunglasses and rested them on top of her head—"yesterday was just the first day. Your attitude of not wanting to speak to the psychologist makes things diff—"

"Victoria," Amador stopped her. "Leave it. Let him finish his breakfast."

"It just makes things difficult," she finished saying. She lowered her sunglasses and drummed her fingers on the table.

Linda reappeared, silent as ever. She placed their daily pile of correspondence on the table. Sticking out from between the large yellow envelope of *National Geographic*—which continued to be sent to Amador because he never found the time to unsubscribe—and the Venca catalog that was addressed to Victoria and always ended up in the trash, unopened, was the blue-and-red edge of an airmail envelope.

They all saw it, but none of them said a word.

Victoria took off her glasses. She looked at the boy. Then at her husband. She picked up the envelope with her eyes fixed on Leo, searching the boy's expression for something other than the fear that had made his entire body go tense. Victoria took a deep breath and looked at the envelope.

She remained silent for a short while.

"It's for you," she said. She threw the envelope at Amador with a flick of her wrist. "Who the hell's writing to you from San Francisco?"

"San Francisco?" he asked.

Amador took the envelope. His hands were cold. To make light of it and avoid raising suspicion, he opened it right there. It was a photo. The same one as always. Of the coffee shop on Lombard Street where he met María, the Mexican writer he decided to leave behind. Just that. Not a single written word.

"It's nothing, a postcard from my grad-school roommate," Amador lied. "He's getting married this summer," he improvised.

He returned the photograph to the envelope before Victoria asked anything else. Later he would retrieve it from the back pocket of his pants and rip it up, letting the pieces fall into the trash and shaking the contents to hide them under the remnants of their toast from breakfast, just as he was intent on keeping the memory of that romance under a pile of unfulfilled dreams. María was still trying to keep Amador from forgetting. And she did so by sending him the same photo of the same coffee shop every year.

He turned his attention to Leo. "Don't worry, son. It was nothing, see?"

Leo noticed something different in his father's voice.

"No," said Victoria, "Leo wasn't worried. He already knew that letter wasn't for him, right? You didn't write it, so it couldn't have been another . . . what should we call it? Another . . . death warning?"

Pi appeared from nowhere—a dark shadow that suddenly landed on the table to one side of Leo. He skidded on the tablecloth. The cups vibrated on the saucers. Victoria's glass, still half-full of orange juice, wobbled on its circular base and toppled over. It emptied its contents onto Victoria's blouse. She held one hand to her chest and hit Pi on the muzzle with the other. He returned to the ground with a deep meow and an even more abrupt movement that created chaos on the table.

"Leo!" yelled Victoria. "Linda!"

The housekeeper was already at the table, trying to bring the disaster under control. Leo and Amador helped her. Victoria, a few steps away, stuck a napkin in a glass of water and rubbed the mark on her blouse. They stacked the plates, with the breadcrusts piled on top. Linda gathered the tablecloth by folding its edges into the middle. Amador dropped two glasses when he tried to pick them up with his fingers. Linda told him not to worry.

"Leo will help me," she said. "Won't you? Come with me to the kitchen," she instructed him. "Let your *papás* enjoy their morning off."

Victoria, busy with her sartorial emergency, didn't intervene in the conversation. Amador, who really did want to enjoy his morning off, allowed Leo to help Linda with the dishes. After two trips, the table was clear, and Victoria and Amador went back to their morning pastimes. He read the national newspapers while remembering María's white shirt slowly leaving a breast uncovered as she chopped onions. Victoria observed the garden while mulling over the previous day's meeting with Dr. Huertas.

In the kitchen, Leo left the cereal box on the breakfast bar, fascinated by the optical illusion on the back that made a spiral appear to move by itself. When Linda saw his intention to return to his parents, she blocked the boy's path and closed the kitchen door behind her. Drying her hands on the pink apron that matched the rest of her uniform, she looked from side to side before speaking.

"Come with me," she whispered.

She took Leo's hand and guided him down to the basement. It was where her bedroom was. The smell of detergent and ironed clothes enveloped him. Linda's room was an improvised, windowless area partitioned from the laundry room. It had a single bed, a chest of drawers, and a wardrobe. It amused Leo to see two uniforms identical to the one Linda was wearing right then—he remembered a funny comic strip showing Batman's wardrobe. Over the bed's headboard, nailed to the wall, he saw photos of Linda on a beach with two little girls younger than him, another photo of a man in military uniform, and a sticker with a blue-and-white flag on it.

"Is that El Salvador's flag?" he asked.

Linda released his hand and sat him on her bed. She gathered her smooth, black hair behind her ears. Her dark cheeks seemed fleshier when seen from up close.

"Leo, look, I saw what happened with your *papás* and that letter you found last summer. And I don't like seeing you sad. Or that they're making you see a doctor." She paused for a moment. "I don't know if I did the right thing," she said.

From under her apron she took out a long, white envelope.

"I found it in the mailbox this morning with the other mail. It says it's for you."

Leo took the envelope. In printed letters this time, someone had clearly written his name:

LEONARDO CRUZ

A cold sweat painted terror all the way down his spine. He tried to remember if the redheaded woman had addressed him by name.

"Don't open it," Linda said.

But Leo had already taken out the piece of paper he found inside.

> *Someone wants to warn you that something bad will happen in August 2009. I don't remember the day. I don't know anything else. Tell this to an adult or your parents. I can't do anything else. I can't risk*

That was it. A few typed lines, interrupted in the middle of a sentence, printed on an ordinary sheet of paper. Leo let his hands drop to his knees. The paper and the envelope fell onto the floor.

When he looked at Linda, she saw fear and sadness in his expression. It was the same look her youngest daughter had given her the day Linda said goodbye to her at the airport, unable to explain to her why she had to go so far away. Linda held Leo tight. When he began to tremble, she shushed him involuntarily in the way only a mother knows how to do, though not all mothers.

The scream came loud from the kitchen. "Leo! Where the hell are you?"

The kitchen door opened over their heads.

"Leo?" said Victoria to the stairway before beginning to come down. She was angry. Her voice and the sound of her heels made it obvious. "Linda?"

Leo separated himself from Linda's warmth with great difficulty. He went down on his knees, retrieving the letter and stuffing it into the envelope. He realized now that a corner was missing. Linda started smoothing down the sheets and plumping the pillow.

When Victoria appeared at the door, Leo pointed at the photos that Linda had over the bed's headboard.

"Is this El Salvador's flag?" he asked her again, ignoring the emotions that were trying to choke his voice.

"Yeah," replied Linda, "that's right." She thought of her daughters again when she recognized the fear in the boy's eyes. She sensed Victoria's presence behind her.

"Sorry to interrupt the geography lesson." Victoria walked into the room, touching the ceiling with her hand, as if the lack of space oppressed her or she thought it was going to fall in on her. "May I ask what you're doing here?"

"I wanted to know what—"

"Linda's flag," Victoria cut in, looking around. "Sure. But neither you nor I need to be in the service area." She took Leo by the arm. "Come on, I want you to see what your cat's done now."

Leo gave Linda one last look, then followed his mother up to the kitchen. The three corners of the envelope, hidden in his pajama pants and held up by the elastic, dug into his belly and groin.

They crossed the kitchen, heading for the garden. Leo felt his mother's cold hand dragging him behind her. His heart was pounding in his chest, danger burned between his legs, and fear froze him inside. He wanted to scream and cry, but he had no intention of doing it in front of her.

If Victoria had looked at her son's face and not at the living-room floor, she would have seen how pale it was and how his gaze was absent, as if he was unable to focus on the reality he had in front of him. But Victoria remained oblivious as she yelled at Leo, showing him the trail of chocolaty milk pawprints that Pi had left behind when he fled the crime scene into the living room and across the white Persian rug.

Her voice was muffled in Leo's ears, her gesticulations slowed through the filter of panic that, this time, he did not allow his parents to see. Leo rode out the scolding like he did the shower of insults that could rain on him at any moment at school, then looked up at his mother.

"I'm sorry," he said. "I'll have a word with Pi."

"About that," Victoria said. She went back out into the garden to join Amador, who was still sitting in the same place and had watched the events with his lips pressed tightly together. "Your father and I"— she rested both hands on her husband's shoulders—"we thought maybe we should give that cat to someone else."

Leo ran to his room, without stopping when he heard Dad yell his name. Pi joined him at some point on the way. He closed the door and positioned a chair between the floor and the handle, though it wasn't necessary because no one tried to come in. He slumped onto the bed, which was now completely exposed to the midday sun. Pi leapt up beside him and rested his head on Leo's stomach.

"Wait," he said to the animal.

He took the envelope out from his pajama pants. His trembling hands made the paper rustle, as if blown by the wind. He ran his finger over the edge of the missing corner. He read his name again. It was blurred. He had to blink to clear his eyes of tears. On the first envelope, the airmail one, there had been no name. He couldn't remember the redheaded woman saying one, either. She had certainly been surprised to discover that Leo already knew what might happen on August 14, which meant she hadn't known anything about the first letter. Leo reread the contents of the one he now had in his hands. Its author didn't know the exact date, which the person who wrote the first message and the redheaded woman did know. While all three warned him of the same thing, they seemed to contain different quantities of information.

"How many people are trying to warn me?"

He felt the hairs stand on end all over his body. Tears finally overflowed from his eyes.

Leo began to tear the letter into increasingly small pieces. They were scattered all over him and Pi. He tried to calm himself down by telling himself that, despite what Dad, Mom, and the psychologist said, all of this was really happening. He hadn't written the first letter. The redheaded woman existed, just as the dust in the Aquatopia parking lot that completely covered him that morning existed. And this message had reached him because Linda had found it in the mailbox, which meant that someone, a real person, had left it there, because it had no stamp, postage, or address. He squeezed Pi tight when he thought about what would happen if the warnings were correct.

They said August.

And it was already late March.

17.

AARÓN

Aarón was standing in front of the trash can in the kitchen. It was night outside.

In his hands he held the airline tickets to Cuba. David Mirabal's name appeared on one of them, Aarón Salvador's on the other. On both, the departure date. June 10. Today.

He recalled David having the idea to go on a trip to take his mind off the breakup with Andrea: *Do it, then, man. Tell her. Tell her everything you just said to me. That what happened with Rebeca might be a symptom, that you feel like you've missed out on a lot of things in the ten years you've been together. And that you're not ready to be a parent. If you're not ready, you're not ready. It's not something you can force. Let's ask for a week off and go somewhere. Anywhere. I don't know, Cuba. Just you and me. To celebrate your new life. Or cry together. Whatever you prefer.*

Aarón tore the tickets in half.

A tear burned at the corner of his eye.

The pieces fell into the garbage bag.

"It was my fault," he said to the empty apartment.

Then he turned and looked at the table piled with papers. There was only one way to alleviate the guilt.

He sat at the table and searched through the drawers. At the back of one of them, he found what he was looking for. He pulled out an envelope with a blue-and-red-striped rim. He placed it on the table near the pages Andrea had thrown in his face two days ago. He searched through the chaotic pile of papers and found the last one he had shown her. At the top, in large letters, he had written *August 14, 2009* on it.

"Exactly nine years, three months, and two days after David was shot on May twelfth," he said out loud, "the date I have to warn the 'boy from the future' about." He mimicked the way Andrea had said it. "To prevent what must not happen from happening." He smiled at the piece of paper with confidence. "And if I really have gone crazy like Drea thinks, and all these numbers mean nothing, then no one's going to die at the Open, there's nothing to worry about, and this letter can't do any real harm."

He searched for a pen on the table. He found a blue ballpoint stuck in the spiral spine of a notebook. He held it in his left hand, swiveling it on his thumb.

"There's a lot to be gained," he went on, "and not much to lose. Right, David?" He said his friend's name without wincing.

He picked up a fresh sheet of paper.

He didn't need Andrea to tell him that inquiring at the hospital could go badly. They might not give him the information about the birth. And if he could locate the boy's parents, in all likelihood they would call the police as soon as he told them what he'd discovered. He wasn't worried about that. He had close ties to the local police in Arenas. And he would try again later on. But if Aarón didn't have a sufficiently long *later on* to speak to the boy himself—the idea that he had cheated fate was beginning to frighten him—then the letter would have to work. A letter he intended to give to Sr. Palmer, the man who knew the town better than anyone else. The man in whose store the boy would die.

"But the American won't be at that robbery," he blurted out to the empty room. "Do you think I don't know? He'll be over sixty that year, and that age isn't part of the scene." He shook his head, as if stating fundamental truths. "But he'll have time to deliver my letter." He stretched out his arms so that they were parallel with the table, and examined the paper. "My backup plan."

Everything seemed perfectly clear, almost startling. He felt a shiver at the bottom of his back while he wrote:

> *I don't wish to frighten you, but it's impossible to explain any other way. Please, do not go to the gas station in Arenas. The American's store. Do not go there on August 14, 2009. I don't want to scare you, but it could be the day of your death. Don't go. I'm sorry, I had to warn you.*

He folded the piece of paper in half twice and then inserted it in the envelope. When he licked the glue, the sour taste made him screw up his nose. Then he turned it around and wrote:

FOR A NINE-YEAR-OLD BOY

That night, Aarón slept as he had not slept for a long time.

When he turned to his right after going through the automatic doors of the American's store, the excessive cold welcomed him. A shiver ran down his back, similar to the one he had felt the previous night before writing the letter. The sole of one of his sneakers squeaked on the floor. The Open was almost empty. A pregnant woman was walking toward the door, holding on to her husband's arm. The three of them exchanged a friendly suburban greeting.

Sr. Palmer was watching the television that was hidden under the counter. The sound was deafening. The device he had to wear over his left ear didn't work very well even when turned to maximum volume. Until Aarón slammed his hand onto the counter, the American didn't notice his presence. He screwed up his eyebrows for a second, then smiled when he recognized the face. He picked up the remote control and turned down the volume on the TV.

"Ah, it's good to see you here again." He coughed, as if he still smoked, to make his voice clear. "What's up, run out of pizzas and frozen chicken, huh? That stuff isn't food." He leaned toward Aarón. "What happened to your eye?"

"I don't know, it must've happened while I was asleep. I woke up like this," he lied.

"Well, you don't look good. Andrea was here the other day, and I told her to take care of you. How are you? I know David's still the same. How're you holding up? His brother came by recently. He was with that other guy, Carlos, the one who's always with him. And do you know what they bought? Donuts. Cops buying donuts. I don't know why I left Kansas if everything's going to be the same."

Aarón knew Sr. Palmer was trying to be funny to cheer him up, but he hadn't managed it.

"I . . . ," he said. His smile was forced.

"Let your girl take care of you. Women know how. Listen to what I'm saying, I've been alive twice as long as you. Look at mine. I was in the store on the night of the shooting, too, and here I am again." Sr. Palmer thought of his wife, sitting with her knitting in her hands, a sweater for the grandchild of a friend and not for her own.

"Drea and I . . . ," Aarón began to explain, but he broke off.

"A man's nothing without a woman by his side. When're you going back to work? Tomorrow's Monday. It's time. I've already sent my wife to the pharmacy twice. You know I can't leave the store, and she doesn't like going out much . . ."

"Don't worry, I'll bring your medication tomorrow. We have an agreement, right?" Aarón said, referring to the free gasoline the American offered him as payment for his extracurricular work.

"I wasn't saying it just because of that. It'll do you good to get back to work. This store's what keeps me going."

"I've been a little, you know, switched off . . . but I want to get back to normal as soon as possible." Aarón looked from side to side.

They fell silent. All they could hear was the constant purr of the refrigerators. The American thought about putting his hand on Aarón's. He didn't. Just as sometimes at dinner he didn't put his hand on his wife's as it rested on the table next to a bowl of onion soup, though God knew he was dying to do so. Instead, he smiled. Aarón looked at the floor, obviously embarrassed. Then he turned to the entrance. There was nobody in view. He fixed his eyes on Sr. Palmer's. The American sensed something was not right.

"Listen," Aarón began, "I'm going to ask you . . . I need you to do me a favor."

He pulled an envelope from the back pocket of his jeans and deposited it on the counter.

It had been a while since Sr. Palmer had seen an airmail envelope. He remembered the letters he used to write years ago, telling his parents in Galena how lovely and how different Europe was. Letters of several pages full of promises of success and dreams of forming a large family in the Old World. Sr. Palmer observed his own hands over the counter, more wrinkly than one would expect for someone his age. And he sighed when he thought of his wife.

Aarón looked back at the Open's main door. A motorcycle crossed the street with an irritating whirr. He also looked at the other side of the store, as if hunting for some secret entrance an accidental witness could sneak through. He wet his lips and deepened his gaze.

"This letter." He held it at the height of their eyes. "I need you to give it to someone."

"Sure, Aarón, everyone in the town uses me for that. *Jeez*," he said in English, "you were scaring me. Look, the other day, the wife of one of the Moreno brothers left some suitcases here. They're her husband's. She kicked him out. And she didn't even wait for the man to get—"

"No," Aarón cut in. "This is important. More important than that. I can explain it or we can leave it as it is. I don't know whether you'd rather know or not."

Aarón was inviting him to decide between the red pill and the blue pill. Sr. Palmer didn't understand. He just nodded, waiting for him to finish speaking.

"You know me," Aarón said. "You've known me for a long time. You know I don't go around making strange stuff up. You know that."

The American nodded again. It was true. Although, all of a sudden, he knew why Andrea had seemed so worried about Aarón the last time he saw her, with a defeated look in her eyes hidden behind the hair she left hanging over her face.

"Perfect," Aarón went on. "Because I'm not making anything up this time, either. I want that to be clear. I want you to look at me and listen to what I'm going to say. Because I have to warn you"—he glanced back at the automatic doors again—"that someone's going to rob the store again."

Sr. Palmer tapped his hearing aid.

"Leave that," said Aarón. "You heard perfectly. There's going to be another shooting here."

"Bullshit!" the American burst out after a few seconds. "Aarón, you know I have a weak . . ." He gestured at his heart instead of naming it. "If this is some kind of joke . . ."

"A joke? Come on, man, would I play a joke on you, knowing your heart condition?"

"Aarón, I don't know what's going on with you—"

"You trust me, don't you?" said Aarón, showing his best face. "I know you do. That's why I'm going to ask you to keep this letter. See what it says here?" He ran his finger over the addressee. "It says it's for a nine-year-old boy. Do you know why? Because it's possible—well, I'm certain—that this store's going to be robbed again. It's happened a lot of times before. Four times. Did you know?"

Sr. Palmer nodded. He recalled Aarón as a boy, holding his mother's hand—she had been a polite young woman with thick lips and generous hips. As if it were only a few days ago, he remembered her kneeling on the floor in the store, her skirt above her knees, to clean Aarón's mouth with her sleeve, because he'd eaten some candy without paying. He also remembered how she apologized and offered him money that more than covered whatever candy Aarón could possibly have ingested, with a timid smile and a firm look, and how she left the store, pulling on the boy and the door handle long before the door was automatic. The Aarón with the unkempt beard that he now had in front of him was the same kid who'd turned up at the store with fake ID to buy beers for himself and his girlfriend, the Andrea who was already beautiful then. The same kid who'd walked triumphantly out of the store with the cans under his arm, an adult for the first time in his life, certain that he'd managed to fool the American, though the American knew he was seventeen because he had watched him grow up, had seen him since he made his mouth sticky with stolen candy. The same kid who'd kissed his girlfriend at the Open's door, a revolving one at the time, celebrating the beers with a kiss that was silhouetted against the orangey sun of a fading evening in Arenas, making the most perfect image of adolescent love and a summer full of possibilities Sr. Palmer would ever see.

"Well, if you knew about the previous robberies," said Aarón, bringing him out of his daze, "you must see that it can happen again. It's logical, don't you think? The problem is that, next time, it's going to be a child who gets shot."

Aarón didn't sugarcoat his words, refusing to diminish the gravity of a sentence that references a child, death, and shooting.

The American distrusted the device over his ear again. He shook his head and went around the counter to come closer to Aarón. As clumsy as he had always been when it came to showing affection, he considered hugging the boy, but all he did was grab his arm at the elbow.

"Aarón." He shook him, making him drop the envelope. "What're you talking about? Are you all right? If it's because of David, I know he's going to get better. The other day one of the nurses' sisters was here, and she—"

"Wait," Aarón interrupted. "Tell me, what day were you born on?" Aarón knew his age—it had been published in the newspaper and had surprised the entire town. Fifty-three, the same age as one of the people in each previous robbery. "Tell me. It's just to confirm some things, some stuff. Tell me the date."

"But what—"

"What day were you born on?" he repeated in an exaggerated, weary tone.

"March tenth, 1947," said Sr. Palmer. "What does that have to do with anything?"

As quick as he had always been with calculations, something sang out of tune in Aarón's head. *It can't be—his date of birth doesn't . . .* But he didn't finish the thought. Suddenly, he felt uncomfortable. He picked up the envelope again and pressed it into the American's hands, squeezing them in his own. Sr. Palmer seemed uncomfortable being in close physical proximity.

"Do you remember when I bought my first beers here? You knew. You knew I wasn't old enough. And I thought I'd fooled you. I was so proud of my moustache. That's why this town loves you so much. Do you think anyone else would've sold them to me? I don't think so." Aarón lowered his voice and leaned forward. "Pretend you believe me again. Just trust me. Keep this letter. Please. You'll probably never need it. I'll take care of this whole business. But keep it. And don't read it. That way you won't be complicit in what it says. Don't worry, I promise you it says something good. Something"—he searched for the right word—"something important. In all likelihood you'll never have to deliver it."

His voice was reduced to a whistle.

Sr. Palmer had to hold his ear to Aarón's lips to hear him.

"And if the day comes when you have to do it," he went on, "well, I guess . . . you'll just know." Aarón fell silent while he listened to words in his head: *One's born when the previous one dies.* Then he added, "The boy might remind you of David."

Sr. Palmer's face became distorted.

He pulled his hands away and returned behind the counter. He was holding the crumpled envelope in his fist. He stuffed it under a pile of papers in a gap between the counter and one of the walls.

Aarón smiled at him.

"Take care of yourself," Sr. Palmer said.

Without waiting for a response, he picked up the remote control and turned the volume right up. He stared at the TV screen. He'd heard enough.

Aarón thanked him, but the American shook his head.

"And give your wife a kiss from me," Aarón added. Slapping the counter, with an involuntary smile on his face and an unknown emotion in his stomach, he headed for the exit.

He welcomed the heat of the street—the air-conditioning was always excessive in the Open. As he headed along the sidewalk, his eyes down to avoid the sun, he bumped into the pregnant woman he'd seen earlier in the store. There was a spark of static electricity when he touched her belly to apologize.

"I'm so sorry."

The woman looked at him with disdain, her top lip curling up to show her gum. Aarón pulled his hands away as if they burned. He apologized again and headed toward his car.

"Why don't you watch where you're going next time!" the husband yelled at him. Then he turned around, placing a hand on his wife's belly. "Are you two all right, Victoria?"

18.

LEO

Friday, June 19, 2009

On the last day of school, Leo came out with his shoes in his hand. He'd stuck his socks, made into a ball, inside one of them. He walked barefoot, feeling the ground's heat. His teacher, Alma Blanco, noticed the black dirt on the soles of his feet. She was seeing out the year watching the children from the window of an empty classroom. Since her own childhood, the end of the school year had always given her a good feeling. At the school gate, groups of children of all ages filled the afternoon with screams, laughter, goodbyes, and the year's last passes with a soccer ball.

Leo walked on with the rest of the schoolmates. He was looking down at the ground. Some kids stopped to watch him—he saw their shoes approach, come to a halt, and go away again. Edgar's, Slash's, Jay's, and whoever else's. He crossed the front playground in the direction of the street, where he always waited for Mom. On the sidewalk opposite the American's store.

"Everyone to the Open!" someone yelled. "Slash is going to do his end-of-year special."

The pack changed direction. Several pupils passed in front of Leo, urged on by Slash, who continued to announce the performance with the self-assurance of a circus act. Hurrying mothers and women dressed in uniforms similar to Linda's were pulling away children who kicked out in protest at having to leave.

"Get out of the way, dumbass," they said to him.

There were more collisions. More chidings.

Then a hand grabbed his wrist and pulled it down.

"Leo," said the voice. "Leo, it's Claudia."

She stumbled forward when one of the eager spectators pushed her.

"Hi," Leo responded.

"Why . . . ?" Claudia was looking at the shoes he was holding in one hand, but she didn't finish the question.

"Are you going to the Open?" he asked. "Everyone's going, look."

Jay passed between them, running away from someone who was chasing him. He struck Claudia's shoulder, and her glasses almost fell off. Leo recalled her sitting on the floor, her skirt up to her waist.

"Slash is going to do the thing with the Mentos and Coke again. He says the foam's going to go higher than ever this year. He says his dad brought him some Mentos from China. Apparently, they put gun-powder in them there to make them taste better."

"No way. They can't put gunpowder in candy."

"Who knows? It's what he said. Are you coming?"

"I never go to the Open." Leo looked at his bare toes, moving them up and down.

Claudia opened her mouth to say something. A short distance away, her friends had started to sing. Intermittent giggles accompanied the melody. Claudia narrowed her eyes at them.

"See you after the summer," she said. "Or maybe we'll see each other at the Aqua again. My dad's taking me this Sunday. I still haven't tried the slide we saw in February."

She ran to her friends and put her hand over one of their mouths. The four of them looked at Leo and then exploded with laughter.

The human current dragged Leo to the traffic light the parent-teacher association had fought so hard for and the crosswalk they demanded be repainted twice a year. As it almost always was, the green pedestrian light was flashing. The gang of kids crossed the road, driven by the lure of another endless summer ahead of them. The sidewalk's paving stones burned under Leo's feet. He put his hand in one of his shoes. They were still soaked. He heard his name called several times. Some boys were imitating pistols with their hands. He was dealt a blow with an open hand on the back of his neck. He gripped the straps on his space backpack and imagined himself being propelled toward the moon. With his eyes still fixed on the ground, he wished his mother would hurry up and arrive.

The pack began to dissolve on Leo's side of the white stripes. The stragglers crossed the street at top speed. One boy with a voice that changed in pitch, on the verge of adolescence, lay on the pavement and crossed both lanes by rolling over and over, yelling nonsensical military orders. A ball traveled from one side to the other without bouncing, landing on the roof of an SUV parked by the sidewalk. The last to cross, a boy smaller than Leo, was holding his arms out parallel to the ground, imitating an airplane's wings. A projectile must have reached him, because something glanced off his right arm. Then the noise was more distant. The grass at the entrance to the Open, to one side of the gas pumps, was just fifty paces away from Leo, but it was far enough for the noise to sound muffled and less threatening. The automatic doors were opening and closing at the frenetic pace of the torrent of overexcited kids flowing in and out. Some of them just stuck a foot in, then returned to their group to hug their classmates and celebrate the victory of having tricked the mechanism. Others were shirtless and play-fighting. The girls watched them in little groups. The rest were competing to see who could spit the farthest or form the most strangely colored puddle with their saliva after chewing an assortment of gummy candy. Leo could make out Claudia, who was licking an ice pop. Slash was wearing his tie around his head. His nose was unmistakable. He was parading around with a cap in his hand, making the others put coins in it. He yelled at one of the smallest kids, the one who'd crossed the street aboard a fighter plane.

Leo felt sorry for the old storekeeper, for what he'd have to put up with that afternoon. He thought about the man who hadn't charged him for the stolen candy when he and his father went to buy milk one evening last summer. A cold sweat covered Leo when he remembered the strange feeling of recognition he'd experienced that night, when he exchanged looks with the old man.

It was the night the first letter appeared.

Leo felt he needed to go to the Open, to speak to the old man, but he couldn't cross the street barefoot. Everyone would look at him. Or they'd do worse than just look. Edgar and Slash were at the entrance to the store. The ground was burning. Leo lifted his feet alternately, first the left, then the right, as if he needed to pee. He moved onto the strip of shade cast by the traffic light and squeezed his feet into the narrow black band on the sidewalk.

He waited.

He heard a click when the pedestrian traffic light turned red.

He saw Edgar enter the store, cheered on by the small group that had formed at the door. He came out a minute later with a bottle to each side of his body. The others yelled, laughed, clapped.

The traffic light changed again.

Leo thought about the fine scabs that had formed on the three scratch marks his mother's slap had left on his cheek. He thought about Pi sleeping on the other side of his balcony door while the Arenas sky lit up in a shower of fire over their heads. He thought about another year spent finding the most secluded seat on which to sit and eat alone in the cafeteria. Another year waiting for his mother every afternoon on this side of the street, alone. With this last thought, his foot took a step forward before he had made the decision to do it. When the right foot followed the left one, Leo knew there was no turning back. He squeezed one of the backpack straps hard.

He trod on the paintwork of the first white stripe. It was just as hot. The shapeless mass of his classmates pulsated in the distance, like the monster in that old film he had watched with his father without his mother knowing. He stepped onto the second white stripe, imagining himself crossing a hanging bridge over a river. If he stepped outside the timber boards, outside the white stripes, he would plummet into the void.

Someone yelled. "Hey, look! The nutcase!"

There was a silence. Then the laughter broke out again. Slash signaled to Edgar and Jay. They ran toward the crosswalk and cheered Leo on as if he were an athlete on the final stretch of a big race.

Leo looked down. He made himself think about the old man. About the airmail envelope. About the corners of the other envelope, the one Linda had handed to him, digging into his groin. About his mother's ever-emptier eyes. He needed an explanation. And the old man might know something.

"What's up?" Slash yelled at him. "You want to be normal now?"

"Well, going to a shrink's not very normal, nutcase." This time it was Edgar speaking, imitating a baby's babbling. "This place isn't for you. The wusses get picked up by their mommies on the other side."

Leo reached the end of the bridge. Pain shot from his big toe to his ankle when Slash stamped on his foot.

"Are you going to cry?" Slash's face appeared down below, his long black curls hanging toward the ground. On his chin was the scar that had made him a hero years ago, since the now-distant first day of school.

Leo turned his head away.

"I said, are you going to cry?" he repeated, louder.

Another shot of pain surged through Leo's foot.

"Pah!" Slash spat out. "He's no fun even for this. Let's go."

The feet disappeared.

Leo crossed the gas-pump area. He lengthened his stride to avoid treading in a puddle of gasoline and wobbled as he regained his balance. He heard more laughter. He recognized Claudia's pink socks when they approached, together with the feet of some other children. Then they returned to the main group to make comments.

"Where's he going?"

"What's he doing?"

"Is it true he's carrying his shoes in his hand because . . . ?"

"Edgar and Slash take it too far with him."

"Once, Edgar . . ."

"It's just that he's a little weird."

"He's always by himself."

Three boys blocked his path, their fingers outstretched to form pistols.

"Bam, bam!" they yelled. "Remember what happened in the Open!"

Then, as if they'd practiced it, they took turns exclaiming a syllable.

"Nut!"

"Case!"

"Nut!"

"Case!"

The blast of cold air froze the sweat on Leo's face. His feet welcomed the coolness of the Open's polished floor. The doors closed behind him as he walked toward the counter, thinking of the old man, his heart thumping in his chest. But on the other side of it, there was a slender salesclerk. It wasn't the same man as before. He was watching the chaos outside the store with a worried look while he organized several packs of batteries in a cardboard box.

Leo placed his shoes on top of the counter.

"And what do you want? I said enough already," the man said with a serious expression, as if fearing the kids were going to start looting the store. "And get those shoes off there."

Leo picked them up and apologized with his eyes. The new clerk peered over the counter and looked at Leo's bare feet, his big toes sticking up.

"What're you doing barefoot, son?" he asked.

Leo looked back at his classmates.

"Them? They did something to you?" The man's voice rose in pitch by at least an octave. "Was it them?"

Leo nodded.

"What is it they did to you?"

"They shoved me in the toilet."

"Oh, sure." The salesclerk couldn't contain his laughter.

Leo maintained his gaze. Then he looked down again.

The salesclerk's smile faded.

Edgar and Slash had held Leo by his shoulders. Jay and another kid had forced his legs into the toilet bowl. *Let's see if you get flushed down and don't come back next year!* Edgar had screeched at Leo while he pressed the button and the first current of cold water soaked his shoes. *He doesn't fit. A rat that doesn't fit. When my mom got rid of the bird, the toilet sucked it down right away*, Slash added. They kept pushing him down and pressing the flush button in the absurd hope that the piping would suck him away, while his arms began to hurt from the pressure.

"I was looking for the older gentleman that works here," Leo said.

"Older like me, or older like an old man?" The salesclerk wrinkled up his face by squeezing it with a hand on each side. He made Leo smile.

"Like an old man." Leo passed a hand over his head and added, "With white hair."

"Do you mean Sr. Palmer?"

Leo shrugged.

"Do these seem like normal batteries to you, or are they the small ones?" asked the salesclerk, holding one of the packs out to him.

"The small ones. It says 'triple A' there."

The salesclerk looked at the packet and picked up another. He compared them, straining his eyes.

"Yeah, it must be him." He threw the batteries back toward the cash register, as if he no longer cared about them. "But he doesn't work here anymore. It's got to be more than a month since he sold the business. He left it exactly as it was, with the neon sign and everything. I reckon it's going to be 'the American's store' for a very long time." He used the epithet with some disdain, aware he wasn't going to be able to fight against three decades of habit. "And I don't know whether I made a good investment yet." He looked around and sighed. "Forty years for this . . . You make sure you study, OK? You look smart—by the time you're my age you could be president."

"Does the gentleman live in town?" Leo asked.

"His house is here, but he isn't. He's gone."

"He's gone?" Leo repeated. Then he understood. "Oh, he's gone." His voice faded.

"No, it's not that. Did you think . . . ?" The new storekeeper ran his finger across his throat. "It's nothing like that."

He turned toward the window to eye the gang of kids. One of the boys was kneeling, handling something on the ground.

"The old man must be in seventh heaven. He came to Europe to get rich with the store . . . and in the end he managed to do it. Not in the way he expected, but he managed it. A blind guy comes here every day selling lottery tickets. Sr. Palmer bought one every weekday. Well, look."

The storekeeper reached under the cash register. When he brought his hand out, he was holding a packet of glow stars. Leo thought of his ceiling.

"Not that." He stuck his hand under again until he found what he was searching for. "Look at this pile of old lottery tickets he had stashed under here. He even collected them. They're all here." He flicked through a wad of tickets held together with a rubber band, making it sound like a pack of cards. "Except the winning one, of course. He took that one, of course, the lucky bastard. Thirty years working here, do the math."

"Seven thousand, eight hundred tickets," Leo said right away.

The storekeeper raised his eyebrows.

"I'm good with numbers."

"He had to win in the end. Thirty years buying them is a long time. I don't know how much he won, but enough to stop working. So he's gone back to the United States."

When Sr. Palmer returned home that night, he had sat on the sofa to watch the late-night news with his wife as if nothing had happened. *What's with the smile?* she asked him. With his heart racing and stomach in a flutter, Sr. Palmer waited patiently for the newscaster to announce winning numbers in the various draws. Then he took the ticket out from his shirt pocket and unfolded it in front of his wife's eyes. He promised they would use the prize money to do whatever she wanted, and nothing else. Sra. Palmer took less than a second to decide: *I just wanna go back to Kansas.*

The new storekeeper smelled the bundle of old losing tickets and returned them to their place under the counter.

"So now you know," he said to Leo. "If you see that guy in the street, tell your mom to buy a ticket off him—he brings good luck." The storekeeper thought for a few seconds. Then he opened the cash register and took out a euro. "Or even better, buy it yourself."

He offered Leo the coin.

Leo shook his head.

"Come on, that way, with all the money you win, you'll be able to buy some new shoes." He leaned toward Leo and whispered. "And the kids who did that to you, they'll see who has the last laugh."

"I bet they'll still be laughing," said Leo.

"You keep it. Things will change one day, you'll see."

Leo thanked him. He picked up his shoes and held the coin in his fingers. He gave a little leap to reposition the backpack on his shoulders, smiled at the man, and headed back toward the door. Now the heat outside seemed appealing. The storekeeper looked out through the glass again to check on the kids. He blew out with a whistle when he saw a white BMW stop at one of the gas pumps.

"One day," he said, "one day."

The automatic doors opened to allow Leo through.

He stepped onto the hot pavement and recognized his mother's car, parked by one of the pumps. He sighed with relief, but her face hardened when she looked him up and down, discovering his bare feet. He felt ashamed.

That was when he felt the jet hit his face. The foam went up his nose and into his throat. His nostrils burned. He coughed. He struggled to keep breathing. A sweet taste flooded his tongue. His eyelids were stuck together. His left eye, the one the pressurized soda had hit, began to pulsate in spasms of pain. When the liquid entered his ears, it sounded like a rodent digging into his brain.

He opened his mouth to try to breathe.

The second jet went down his throat. It reached his stomach like a punch. He retched violently, expelling a large amount of liquid outward. It wasn't like vomiting—the liquid simply flowed through his body, first in, then out.

When he was able to open his eyes, he saw Edgar laughing on the ground. Two empty bottles of Coca-Cola Light were spinning beside him. Slash was also laughing. And Claudia. She was chewing the now-bare stick of her lemon ice pop. She pointed at him, along with her friends. The braces in one of their mouths flashed as they reflected the sunlight.

The hot air soon started drying out the soda. Leo's face felt shriveled. Sticky. His white shirt had turned brown. His shoes slipped through his fingers and fell to the ground. A new wave of laughter sounded muffled in his blocked-up ears. He also dropped the coin he'd just been given. It rolled on the pavement.

When he dared look at his mother again, he saw her cover her mouth with her hand.

Leo headed to the car without bothering to dodge the puddles of gasoline, allowing his bare feet to be submerged in the liquid.

"You're not intending to get in here like that, I hope," Victoria said when he opened one of the rear doors. "Look at you, you're covered in . . . and your feet . . . Go on the sidewalk. I'll drive alongside you. But put your shoes on or you'll cut yourself."

On the last day of school, Leo went home on foot beside his mother's car. He gripped the passenger door with his left hand, his soaked shirt sticking to his body. The unpleasant feeling of his shoes sodden with water, Coca-Cola, and gasoline irritated him at each step.

When they arrived home, Leo went straight to the bathroom to wash, then shut himself in his bedroom. He immersed himself in his astronomy book. But more than reading, what he was doing was escaping.

He was still reading when night fell. His stomach was rumbling, and he decided to go out to ask permission to eat. He wasn't sure his mother would allow it. As he removed his chair from the door, the telephone rang.

Victoria took the call on the cordless handset in the living room on the fourth ring.

"Hello?" she asked, just as Leo reached the bottom of the stairs. "Hello?" she repeated.

There was just emptiness at the other end of the line.

She said hello a third time before hanging up.

"Now you come down, huh?" she said to Leo.

"I'm hungry, Mom. Can I have some dinner?"

There was something in his voice that moved her.

The telephone rang again.

"Yes, hello." It wasn't a question this time, but an order. It had no effect. "Excuse me, who is this?"

Amador spoke from the kitchen. "What is it?"

"Nothing, they won't answer," she said, with the telephone still at her ear. Then she hung up. "Yes, angel, of course you can have dinner. What kind of mother do you think I am?"

Victoria headed to the kitchen while Leo was walking through the living room.

The telephone rang again.

"What the fuck?" Amador lost his temper. "Stay here," he instructed Victoria. "I'll get it—let's see if he has the balls to do it with a man."

Leo was by the telephone.

"Don't touch that!" Amador yelled at him. "OK, what is this?" he said when he picked up the handset. "I can see the number you're calling me from on the screen. It's been at least ten years since telephone pranks stopped working. Hang up—I'll call you," he added.

Amador was angry, but not afraid. He knew he was smarter than the other person. He hung up and searched for the most recent call received. He pressed the dial button. It was busy. The other person hadn't hung up yet.

"What the fuck is he doing?" He put the handset back in its charger. "And don't you go copying your father. Not a single swear word, you hear?"

He pinched Leo's chin. "Do you want to tell me what happened at school?"

Leo lowered his head.

As Amador returned to the kitchen, Victoria gestured to warn him that Leo had picked up the telephone.

"Hello?" he said into the void.

He heard nothing.

Until he heard something. Breathing.

"Leo?" said the voice. It pronounced the name in a strange way. "Are you Leo? Listen to me, Leo, I know you've already been warned about what might happen on August fourteenth. Don't go to the store. I'm going to try to make sure nothing happens. But you must not go. I'm—"

Leo returned the telephone to its base unit before the man could finish. He began to tremble. To blink in a strange way. Amador and Victoria knelt beside him. They shook him, trying to make him react. When Victoria recognized the look of terror in the boy's eyes—the same one they had seen the day he had come down the stairs with the envelope in his hands—she stood and went to the kitchen. She served herself a glass full of water and crushed ice from the refrigerator. She chewed before drinking.

In a telephone booth in town, a man headbutted the glass twice and then rested his forehead on the coin slot. He took hold of his crutches and positioned them under his arms, intending to leave. But then he picked up the telephone again, took a piece of paper out of his pocket, and dialed a number.

19.

AARÓN

Sunday, June 11, 2000

Aarón grabbed the steering wheel. He let go of it. He repeated the action several times before he was able to keep his hands on it. The car's interior smelled of hot plastic. He lowered the window, and in the side mirror he watched the man who was with the pregnant woman kneel down to kiss her belly. Beyond them, two workers in blue coveralls were working on something outside the school gate.

The steering wheel stopped burning under his fingers. Distracted, Aarón started in second gear, making the car shake violently. He laughed when the two wheels on the right side dropped down from the curb, making him hit his head on the roof. He went around the traffic circle at the end of the main road to take the highway that led to University Hospital.

"You always have to ask the American twice," he said.

Then he accelerated to double the legal speed.

He wanted to know the boy's name.

Several vehicles, including two ambulances, were scattered around the parking lot. Aarón parked next to a gray Renault. He looked at himself in the rearview mirror. He ran his hands through his hair, over his ears, like a nervous teenager preparing for a first date. With his fore-finger and thumb, he went over his dry lips in an attempt to tidy the irregular hairs of his unkempt beard. He smoothed down his eyebrows with three wild slaps.

"All right, enough, ready."

He got out of the car, forgetting to close the window. He was thinking about what he would say to the girl at the reception desk. He noticed his pharmacist's ID badge poking up from his jeans pocket.

One of the ambulances started up, without lights or its siren, and left the parking lot. A police car Aarón hadn't noticed before was vis-ible in the adjoining space. In a reflexive action that surprised him, he ducked behind his own car's hood. Maybe it was Héctor's car. Maybe Héctor was with David, the brother he now visited every day just to see him breathe. Crouching, Aarón strained his eyes. There was no one in the vehicle.

He zigzagged between the cars on his way to the entrance. It was a small hospital. From a distance, it almost looked like another residential complex, since it was made up of adjoining units of just two stories. The smell of disinfectant and medication received him as he stepped through the glass doors of the high-ceilinged entrance.

That smell transported him straight to the night of May 12, when he and Andrea had walked through the same doors to find Héctor shak-ing his head. No doubt containing a desire to scream at Aarón that it was all his fault. David was in this same hospital right now, but Aarón didn't have the strength to go to see him or face his mother, or Héctor, or anyone else. He scraped his knuckles against his jeans and felt the rigid pharmacist's ID badge. He remembered why he was there. A gray-haired lady was watching him with bored attention from some seats in a corridor to the right. Aarón smiled at her and headed toward reception.

"Because he didn't deserve you," said a young woman dressed in a white coat who had her back to him behind the low counter, her backside on the desk.

The man she was talking to seemed younger than Aarón but was showing signs of incipient balding. When he noticed Aarón arriving, he gestured at his colleague to instruct her to leave. The girl turned her head, bit her bottom lip when she saw Aarón, and said goodbye to Miguel—the name Aarón was able to read on the badge on his chest—with a silent pinch of his shoulder.

"Good afternoon, sir, how may I help you?" Sitting on a wheeled office chair, Miguel gripped the desk to pull himself toward it. He looked Aarón up and down, and when he spoke again his tone was less polite. "What can I do for you? Do you want someone to look at that eye?"

It took Aarón a moment to understand. Then he remembered the burst blood vessel Andrea had caused.

"No, it's nothing." He cleared his throat. "I'm from one of the local pharmacies, in Arenas. The most recent one to open, about six years ago. Do you know it?"

"Yeah, I think so," Miguel said, screwing up his face.

"We received an order this morning for some medication for a four-week-old child," he lied. "The mother was pretty upset."

Miguel nodded.

"The doctor's been to see her at home. It's just a light fever and some coughing and mucus," Aarón went on, "but you know what first-time mothers are like. And she's at home alone and can't leave the baby with anyone, so I offered to take her the medication that's been pre-scribed for the boy as soon as possible."

"Poor thing . . . ," said Miguel.

"And the worst thing is that we hung up before she gave me the address," Aarón improvised. Then he added, "And the phone I have at the pharmacy, it's one of the old-style ones—it doesn't identify the caller. My boss, he's old school."

Miguel maintained a serious look for a few seconds. Then he seemed to understand. His eyes and mouth opened at the same time.

"And how are you going to take that poor kid his medicine now?" he asked.

Seeing his tall tale work made Aarón want to smile. He contained himself and put on an expression of concern.

"That's why I came here," he replied. "The woman lives in Arenas, so the child must've been born here, for sure. What mother's going to want to travel to Madrid when she can have her baby right here, huh? I don't know whether you could check the hospital's birth records. The mother told me her son's four weeks old, so he must have been born on . . ." Aarón pretended to do some calculations, then added, "May twelfth."

Miguel also seemed to be calculating. He was looking at his right hand while touching the tips of his four fingers with his thumb.

"No," he concluded, "if today's Sunday, June eleventh, four Sundays ago was May fourteenth." He pressed his thumb hard against his ring finger, where his calculations must have ended up. "Yeah, it's May fourteenth."

Aarón felt an urge to twist those fingers.

"I don't think it was exactly four weeks," said Aarón, who had begun to pinch his thigh.

"Well, let's start on that day and work from there. What is it you needed to know?"

"The address," he blew out, "or the phone number. So I can take them the medicine."

Miguel diverted his eyes to Aarón's left hand, the one he was pinching his jeans with in a nervous way. Aarón saw something change in the furrows on his forehead.

"You were saying you're from . . ."

"A pharmacy in town." Aarón felt drops of sweat surface at the bottom of his back.

With all the confidence he was able to muster, he took the pharmacist's ID badge out from his pocket. He held it up. The receptionist took it from him and looked at both sides. The furrows on his forehead were beginning to look like question marks.

"All right," said Miguel. "I'll search for May fourteenth, then."

"In fact, I think the mother said he was born on May twelfth. That must be why I said that date just now," Aarón insisted. He wrote a twelve on the counter with his finger.

Miguel looked pensive for a few seconds. Aarón wanted to scream at him.

"OK, look, what I can do is look at an interval of one week. I don't—"

"I'm almost certain the mother said May twelfth," repeated Aarón.

"And I'm almost certain that if she'd said May twelfth, you would've told me that at the beginning instead of saying four weeks."

Aarón was afraid he'd been caught out.

"I'm going to search for the week from May seventh to fourteenth," Miguel decided. "And if you don't mind, I'm going to call the mother myself to confirm that her son's sick and that she placed an order with your pharmacy."

Aarón remained silent. There was only so much he could say before the receptionist became suspicious.

Miguel placed a pencil between his teeth and started typing on his computer. After pressing a few keys, he said, "Of course. I can't access that data. It's protected. I register the admissions here, but personal details are in the patient files. Only the doctors can access those. It makes sense, you know. I've been here less than a year—I guess they don't trust me yet." He rolled his eyes.

Aarón looked at the pencil, wet with saliva, that Miguel had left on the desk. He wasn't surprised the man's superiors didn't trust someone who chewed pencils like a child. He thought about picking it up. About the possibility of inflicting pain with its sharpened tip.

"Look," said Miguel, pointing at the screen of the computer, "I can see the admissions to the birthing center that week." He spoke while typing. "But when I click on the patient's name, it's going to ask me for a password and . . ." He broke off.

He looked at the screen from top to bottom. He moved the mouse. Aarón noticed Miguel trying to hide the sidelong glance he gave him before fixing his eyes on the monitor again.

"What is it?" Aarón wanted his voice to sound natural, but an agitated tone came through.

"There were no admissions that week."

"What do you mean, there . . . ? Yes, no, that's not possible."

"No child was born here all week. Not in this hospital."

"Is that even possible?" Aarón couldn't believe it.

"It must be possible, because I'm looking at a screen showing the relevant information and it's what happened. But it sure is strange."

"You're lying."

"And you're going to make me have to call security if you keep talking to me like that."

Aarón pinched his leg with the force he would have liked to use to twist Miguel's fingers. With the force he would have liked to grab the pencil soaked in drool and—

"He must have been born that day!" he yelled. "I told you to search for May twelfth, not the whole fucking week!"

He lost control of his fist and it struck the counter hard.

Miguel leaned back.

"Have you looked properly?" Aarón controlled the volume of his voice this time. He rubbed his chin with his right hand. His beard crackled under his fingers.

"What is it you want?"

"I want you to tell me the name of the boy who was born in this hospital on May twelfth."

He said the words in a continuous stream, squeezing the bridge of his nose with two fingers, between his eyes.

"There weren't—"

"He was born here. On May twelfth. I'm telling you he was born here!" He grabbed Miguel's arm to pull him. "They killed my friend, OK?"

"I don't—"

"Almost killed him!" Aarón closed his eyes like someone straining to remember something. "They almost killed him. A bullet in the back. And then the boy was born. The boy had to be born! It happened every previous time. I discovered it." He smiled. His voice had risen in pitch. "That's how it always happens. I can't be wrong!"

"I really am going to have to call security now," said Miguel, the words quivering in his throat. He reached slowly toward the telephone. "There's no mother, and there's no baby with a fever, is there?" he said.

Aarón grabbed Miguel's head from behind. He pulled violently to bring the receptionist's face closer to his.

The elderly woman got up from her seat and began to walk down the corridor as quickly as her hip would allow her. At the other end were two men dressed in green.

"Look"—Aarón spoke through his teeth—"I've put my life on hold to save a boy who was born on May twelfth and who someone's going to kill in nine years, three months, and two days. On August fourteenth, 2009, this boy is going to be shot unless I manage to warn him about what's going to happen. And not you, not ten of you, or Andrea, or anyone else is going to stop me from doing it. Do you hear me?"

Aarón fixed his eyes on the receptionist's, their noses almost touching. Miguel seemed unable to blink, and he fixed his attention on a corner of Aarón's eye.

"I'm going to save him, do you understand? I'm not going to be stopped by some hospital receptionist."

The muffled sound of rubber soles on the floor reached them. The two men in green were running toward the reception desk.

Aarón looked sideways without turning his head or reducing the pressure on Miguel's neck.

"I'm sorry," he whispered.

Then he let go. The footsteps were coming closer. He opened his mouth to say something but shook his head and escaped toward the door. As he ran away, dodging the cars in the parking lot again, he yelled something indecipherable to rid his mind of the image of David dying in a bed in that very hospital.

From the desk, Miguel heard the wheels screech on the hot pavement. His arms were stretched out, the weight of his body supported on the palms of his hands, his head sunk into his shoulders. One of the orderlies ran out to the parking lot, pursuing Aarón. The other approached the desk to make sure Miguel was all right.

"Yeah, I'm fine. He didn't do anything to me."

"There's a cop in the hospital."

"I'm OK, I just want"—he filled his lungs—"to breathe." He blew out all the air.

Minutes later, he was recounting his story to an off-duty officer of Arenas's local police service who was visiting his mother at the hospital. Miguel told him what he remembered while alternately massaging his arm and neck. He didn't mention what the maniac had said about a boy someone was going to kill, perhaps to avoid the matter turning into something bigger that would result in him having to spend several afternoons making statements at the police station. Perhaps because he had been frightened to recognize a hint of sanity in the lunatic's bloodshot gaze.

20.

LEO

When Leo woke up, with his book still open on his chest, he discovered Victoria standing next to him.

"How many times have I told you that you can't read in bed?"

Leo had picked up the book during the night, just after the alarm clock reached midnight. The glow of the four digits had bathed the room in a greenish light in the middle of the night that marked the beginning of August 14. And Leo had begun to tremble under the sheet. The cat, at the foot of the bed, had lifted his head, struggling against his eyelids to look at Leo. *Pi, promise me you won't let me go to the Open today, whatever happens,* Leo had said to him.

"Come on, come down to have breakfast and get dressed. We're going to spend the day at the lake," his mother said. "With your classmates."

Leo looked at the alarm clock.

He trembled again under the sheet.

When Victoria left the room after telling him to be ready in fifteen minutes, Leo got up and headed to the room his father used as an office. He slowly opened the door. His father was sitting in an armchair, his face hidden in his hands. A pair of enormous headphones covered his ears.

Leo simply stood there with his hands interlocked at his stomach. Looking at his father. Without knowing how to tell him he was frightened to death.

Victoria suddenly appeared and positioned herself behind her son. She rested her hands on his shoulders. Leo took a deep breath to gather his strength.

"Amador!" yelled Victoria. She rapped the open door with her knuckles. "Amador!"

He removed his hands from his face. When he saw his wife and son, he took off his headphones in a nervous way. Barely audible, *ranchera* escaped through them. Amador sat up in the armchair.

"What're you doing here?" He glanced from side to side.

"We're going now," said Victoria.

Leo saw something in the look his father gave her. A profound expression. Resignation. Consent. Then he looked down at Leo and farther down at his son's hands over his stomach, before lowering his eyes farther still to the floor, refusing to make eye contact with his son.

Leo wanted to say something. But didn't know what.

"What is it about that Mexican music you like so much?" Victoria asked.

Amador didn't respond. He put his headphones back on and closed his eyes.

"Are you still in your pajamas?" Victoria said to Leo. "We're leaving in ten minutes."

When they reached the lake, children were throwing themselves into the water from the weeping willow on the shore. As far as Arenas's children were concerned, the lake had never been an artificial one.

"Go on, go join them," Victoria said to Leo.

He remembered the sticky feeling of the soda on his face. He hadn't seen his classmates since the Coca-Cola incident on the last day of school. He walked away from his mother with a towel over his shoulders and the book he'd started reading the night before under his arm.

Leo lay facedown on the towel in the shade of a tree. He enjoyed the softness of the material and the mixture of grass, moisture, and detergent smells. The soap scent made him think of Linda. He opened *A Brief History of Time* to the page where he'd fallen asleep, and began reading.

He read for the entire day.

Until he found himself straining his eyes to decipher the words on the paper in the lack of light. He looked up and found that the lake was almost empty. The sun was going down. He blinked as if waking from a dream that had made him oblivious to what was going on around him. Fifteen meters—or a hundred kilometers—away, Victoria was laughing. She was talking to some woman she would later criticize at home.

Leo felt relieved when he thought the day would end like any other. Then the letters, the calls, and the redheaded woman's tears would be nothing more than memories of a nightmare that had gone on too long. It wouldn't be his last summer, and he would still have time to learn to enjoy the vacation. There would be more meteor showers. He'd missed last year's because of his parents' punishment, and this year's, which had taken place two days ago, had been ruined by unexpected cloud cover. If August 14 ended like any other day, Leo could still see a shooting star. His mother and father would think he had made up the story about the Open. And he would have to keep visiting Dr. Huertas after the summer. But the pain of his parents' lack of trust and the annoyance of the sessions with the psychologist were a price Leo was prepared to pay if August 14 ended like every previous day.

And it was about to.

A car's horn sounded in the distance, but immersed in his thoughts, Leo didn't hear it. It must have been his mother, ruffling his hair with her hand, who alerted him to the sound.

"Don't you hear it?" she said. "It's your father. He's here."

"Dad?"

"Yes, Dad. Come on, get dressed." Victoria looked at her son, still sitting in the clothes he'd arrived in. "Just grab your towel, let's go."

"Why's Dad here?" he asked without moving.

Something began to tighten in his chest. Leo remembered the strange look he'd seen on his father's face that morning. The resignation.

"We're going to the American's store," said Victoria. Her eyes remained fixed on Leo.

"Today?" he muttered, looking up at his mother from the towel, the word catching in his throat.

"Yes, *today*."

His lower lip gave way to the pressure from his teeth, and the tissue split open. He noticed his eyes were moist, and he also noticed water inside his nose. Just as he knew his mother had noticed it, too, though she was trying to hide it.

"Your father's waiting for us." Victoria turned around and began heading toward the park's entrance. "I know you're not stupid enough to run off," she said as she walked away.

Leo climbed into the car without saying anything to his father.

"Son, you have to understand," Amador said.

"It doesn't matter whether he understands," Victoria snapped. "It's what we're going to do."

Amador stopped the white BMW in front of the American's store, which had been unable to shed its nickname despite Sr. Palmer's departure.

A torrent of images passed through Leo's mind. It began behind his eyes and spread to the rest of his head. A stream of ideas he didn't need to think about to understand. Like an electrical current that didn't hurt but depleted him. In the back seat of the car, he kept his eyes wide open, fixed on his bare and bony knees. Then the whirl of thoughts ended, culminating in an idea that was as bright in his mind as the Open's yellow and violet neon, now reflected on the car's hood.

"It's my destiny," he murmured.

He stuck his face between the front headrests.

"Dad, the messages are real," he said in a trembling voice. "It's true. Who could've known I'd come here tonight? In the end, the warnings had the opposite effect, Dad. In the end, they've made me come to the place where I must not come."

He could barely pronounce the last word, impeded by his labored breathing.

"Don't talk—" Victoria cut in.

Leo raised his voice over his mother's.

"Dad." He felt the tears roll down his cheeks. "Dad, I'm scared."

He tried to contain himself. Then he gave in. He cried with his face in his hands, in the loud way children do. He kicked his legs. He punched the back of the front seat. Amador's hand went to his seat-belt button. Victoria grabbed it and stopped him from unbuckling.

"Leave him, he feels guilty," she said.

As she intended, Amador remembered the psychologist's words.

They listened to their son let it all out in the back seat until his throat was dry and he stopped sniffing. Amador would have liked to tear his own ears off. Leo took one last deep breath. He dried his eyes with the palms of his hands.

"Why are you making me do this?"

Amador turned his face toward the window, biting his left fist.

"Angel," said Victoria, "it's so you see that this whole thing about August fourteenth is just a fantasy. Dr. Huertas is supporting us in this. He almost gave up his vacation to be with you today. We told him it wasn't necessary. Do you realize the trouble you're causing?"

"He promised me he wouldn't speak to you without me there."

"Well"—Victoria turned her head to look at him—"I guess you're going to learn a lot of things today. You've always wanted to be a grown-up."

"I never . . ." He broke off.

There was a moment's silence.

"We're going to wait for you here." Amador didn't want to look at his son. He knew that, if he did, he might step on the accelerator and take him far away from this madness. To the beach, perhaps. Pi would surely like to see the place where he was born. "We'll be here the whole time. But you have to go by yourself, Commander. The ship's yours. Go in and out, that's all."

And what if he's telling the truth? Amador had ventured to ask the psychologist one afternoon in the consultation room, resting his elbows on the desk beside the red folder with Leo's name on it. Victoria had uncrossed her legs violently on the leather armchair and feigned one of her exaggerated laughs to invalidate the question as absurd. *Then you'd be wasting your time and money, because you'd need to be speaking to a parapsychologist*, the therapist had replied.

"Better still, stay inside for a few minutes and think about why you made all of this up," said Victoria. The nail on her forefinger clicked against her thumbnail.

"Victoria, please."

"Dad, I don't want to go."

"Son." Amador was still looking through the windshield. He wanted to stop feeling Leo's hand clutching his shoulder. "You have to go. Otherwise, all those afternoons at the therapist's will have been for nothing. Then we'll go home, eat cookies, and look through the telescope." He smiled as he imagined the scene. "Look, it's not cloudy like it was the other night anymore. We might still see a shooting star."

Amador heard the sound of the rear door opening. He closed his eyes.

At the other end of the parking lot, a man, crutches lying on the passenger seat, straightened up inside his car. Seeing the boy get out, he gripped the steering wheel and lifted his face toward the rearview mirror. He watched the boy approach the store.

Leo walked across the gas-pump area. As he had done two months ago, on the last day of school. He remembered the heat on the soles of his feet. His throat was sore from the strain of the sobs and his tears were now dry on his face. He had seen his father with his eyes closed inside the car. He wanted to turn around and scream at them that he hated them. He didn't.

The pavement turned yellow or violet as it reflected the light from the neon sign that Sr. Palmer had brought from Kansas. A mosquito exploded on the murderous fluorescent lamp that hung next to it. Leo held his breath.

Inside the BMW, it occurred to Amador that he would forever regret doing nothing to save his son's life, and his hand escaped to the door handle.

"Don't you dare," said Victoria.

Amador—ready to run after his son and hold him and tell him he was sorry, that it wasn't necessary for him to go through all this—lost the strength in his fingers. He let his hand drop until it was resting on his leg. He didn't want to look at his wife, preferring to keep her out of focus. The sound of her fingernails was all he needed to confirm her presence.

The car's radiator whined behind Leo, who breathed deep and smelled gasoline. A timid breeze crept under his shorts, between his T-shirt and body. The garment was filled with air for a few seconds and then hugged his body again when the wind that also swung the Open's luminous sign stopped blowing. He advanced at a slow but determined pace, his arms down beside him and barely moving. His parents would regret this. First the idea terrified him. Then he began to enjoy it. So much so that, for a second, he was no longer frightened of what might happen. They were going to discover the truth in the hardest possible way. They would know he hadn't written or made up any of the messages. And it would be too late to say sorry.

The man with the crutches saw the boy going too close to the store. He didn't want to wait any longer. He opened his car door, resting a crutch against the car to then use it to get up. He brought a leg out by pulling on it with his left hand. His agitated movements made his leg slip into the crutch, sending it flying a few paces.

"No, no, no," he said.

While he stretched to reach it on the pavement, he saw the boy outside the door in the left-hand side mirror. He yelled at him to stop, but the boy went in.

The cold air inside the store enveloped Leo, and he began to tremble. Then he ran like he had never run before.

Seeing him escape, the man with crutches gave a huge sigh and slumped back into the seat.

Amador also sighed, then smiled.

"Catch him!" screeched Victoria.

Amador's hand returned to the door handle, opened it. He shot out in pursuit of his son. Victoria also got out of the vehicle and followed her husband. She walked at an accelerated pace, without quite breaking into a run. The car was left with the two front doors open, the lights on, and a loud warning signal beeping intermittently.

Amador ran until he was able to reach out to grab the neck of his son's T-shirt, but leaned too far forward and ended up losing his balance, dragging Leo down with him.

"You're quick," Amador blew out, his knees still on the ground.

He kept hold of Leo by the T-shirt. He knelt so that they were at the same height. He tidied the boy's hair and rearranged his clothes.

"Listen to me."

Victoria's footsteps grew closer. Leo looked in her direction and his expression soured.

"We're going to do this, all right? We have to do it. If there really is someone in there who wants to hurt you, I'll be at the door." He paused, sucking air in three times to regain his breath. Then he looked toward Victoria to calculate the distance, how much time he had. "I'm not going to allow anything to happen to you. Leo, your father won't let anyone do anything to you, do you hear? Eh, Commander? Understood?"

Leo nodded.

"This will be good for you. When you come out of that store, you won't be afraid anymore."

"Angel, what the hell is wrong with you?" Victoria scolded him from twenty paces away.

"I promise," Amador whispered. "This time I'll take you to the door."

When Victoria arrived, she remained standing and crossed her arms. "Are you going in or do we have to make you?"

Leo looked down at the ground and then at his father. The three of them were under a streetlight, inside the orange circle it projected onto the pavement, contained within a luminous cone as if about to be abducted by an alien spaceship. A moth fluttered among them, drunk on light.

"If . . . if I was making it up, I wouldn't be afraid to go in," Leo said in an attempt to reason with them. He sniffed. "I wouldn't mind going in there. Dad, if I was making it up, I'd know nothing was going to happen to me."

Victoria bent down and tried to make eye contact with her husband. She raised her eyebrows.

"See?" she said. Then she turned to Leo. "If you'd gone in just like that, you would've had to admit we're right. It'd be obvious that you weren't afraid and that it was all an invention of yours. You needed to do this, all of this—crying in the car and trying to make a run for it—to make your story believable. You think you're so smart, but you're doing exactly what the psychologist said you would do. Every single step. One after the other." She marked the final words with her thumb and forefinger pressed together, as if holding an imaginary pencil.

Amador squeezed Leo's shoulders and repeated, "I'm coming with you to the door, all right?"

Without giving Victoria the chance to object, he took Leo's hand. They retraced the steps Leo had taken on his attempted escape, back to the Open. Victoria stood there for a moment with her arms crossed. She watched them walk off until they were two dark silhouettes that sometimes merged into one. She shook her head.

Back at the entrance to the Open, Amador squeezed his son's shoulder, which felt damp under his hand. The boy looked at him when he gave him a push. Amador nodded silently.

Slumped on the steering wheel, his face directed at the dashboard, and with a cell phone at his ear, the man with the crutches didn't see that the boy had returned in the company of his father.

Leo took a step forward.

The doors opened with a plastic squeak. At that moment, a tall young man, soaked in sweat and wearing jogging shorts, a maroon hoodie with the emblem of Noroeste University on it, and headphone wires around his neck walked into the store.

Leo followed him.

He heard the plastic squeak behind his back.

Outside, Victoria positioned herself beside her husband, standing to one side of the entrance.

Leo counted two people in the store in addition to himself and the young jogger. When he recognized the storekeeper from the last day of school, he upped the total to five.

The student in jogging shorts stopped at the drinks area and scanned the refrigerator. The storekeeper was flicking through the pages of a magazine open on the counter, without much interest, his chin resting on one hand. A man in a suit with white hair and a jacket hanging over his shoulder opened the freezer full of bags of ice. He started to pull one of them, which was stuck to the bag underneath it. Leo turned his head in both directions. He couldn't find the fifth person. He knew he had seen him.

A shiver ran down his spine.

He was certain he had seen a fat guy dressed in dark clothes. A gigantic T-shirt with sleeves that reached below the elbows. And sagging pants. Below his backside. That man was there when Leo had come in. He scoured the store again.

The storekeeper looked up when the man in the suit dropped a load of ice cubes on the floor. The plastic bag had torn when he yanked it out. Then he looked at Leo, farther away. He raised a hand and waved. The movement caught Leo by surprise and startled him.

The storekeeper looked down at Leo's feet and held his thumb up in a sign of approval when he saw that, this time, he had his shoes on. But Leo didn't respond—he just moved his head from side to side.

The storekeeper retracted his thumb, puzzled.

"Excuse me a second," he said to the student in the sweatshirt, who'd approached with a sports drink in his hand.

When the storekeeper came out from behind the counter, the man in the gigantic T-shirt with the sleeves below the elbows emerged from somewhere. His enormous frame appeared like a black shadow in front of him. Leo was hidden behind it.

Then the storekeeper heard the boy scream, but he couldn't see anything.

Outside, the man with the crutches also heard the boy's scream. He felt his chest tighten, cutting off his breathing. He looked up at the rearview mirror. His cell phone slipped from his hands before he could manage to make contact. He looked back at the American's store without understanding what was happening.

Leo threw himself against the automatic doors. The edge of one of them scraped his shoulder through his T-shirt. He slumped into his father's arms, still screaming. When the fat man in the saggy pants continued toward the counter, Amador saw the storekeeper appear on the other side of the door. Amador held Leo's head to protect him. The storekeeper stood there for a few seconds. When the doors closed, he raised an arm in the direction of the cash register.

"All right, man, I'm coming!" he yelled to the fat guy, who was carrying a four-pack of beers in one hand and complaining. "Anyway, this guy's first. And it's after ten, so you can't buy alcohol."

The moisture from Leo's saliva reached Amador's chest. He remembered splashing water on his face and telling himself, *Your son's completely normal. Everything will work itself out.* A far-off echo began to reverberate in his head. *Alma's crazy, Alma's crazy.* It was the voices of a crowd of children. *Alma's crazy.* Amador and his friends had yelled it at the girl who was nothing more than a fist gripping a table leg. The voices began to grow louder inside Amador's head. *Alma's crazy!* He wanted to cover his ears. He didn't because it would have meant letting go of Leo, who was now trembling in his arms.

"Was it all a lie?" the boy babbled against his father's chest.

Amador squeezed his son while the overwhelming chorus of children continued in his head. Then a deeper voice, an adult's, stood out amid the screaming pack. *Alma's crazy!* It was his own voice, which continued to repeat the slogan with which he had made Alma cry so many times. *Alma's crazy!* the voice yelled again, so deep now that Amador felt it reverberate in his ears. Suddenly, all the children's voices began to distort. They grew slower and softer. And slower and softer still. Until they stopped. Until they stopped and left only the deep voice. Until Amador was forced to listen to his own voice.

Your son's crazy, he heard himself say.

Amador detached himself from Leo with an abrupt movement. He left him standing there beside Victoria, who was looking nowhere in particular, with his head down. He ran back to the car and closed the two doors that were still open. The intermittent warning sound stopped. He rested his backside against the trunk and let himself slide down until he was hidden.

Amador sat on the ground so that his son wouldn't see him cry.

Leo wanted to take a step forward and head toward the BMW, but his mother grabbed his shoulder to stop him.

"Give him a minute," she said. "Stop thinking only about yourself."

The man with the crutches observed the entire scene from inside his car. When he saw the boy and his parents get back in the BMW and leave the Open, he drove forward to move closer to the crutch that had slid along the ground. He picked it up.

He was glad now that he had stumbled as he had tried to get out of the car to stop the boy. He was also glad that he had been distracted with the call and hadn't seen him return to the store.

"This was absurd all along," he said.

Then he bent down and felt for his cell phone in the footwell.

21.

AARÓN

Sunday, June 11, 2000

As Aarón left University Hospital, his car's wheels screeched on the hot pavement. A man dressed in green ran after him, raising his arms in his direction before giving up. Aarón let out a cackle, exaggerating it and distorting it. He returned along the same highway, without paying attention to his speed. He checked the rearview mirror to make sure the police car he'd seen in the parking lot wasn't following him. Another cackle ended abruptly when he had a terrible thought.

No boy was born that day.

The hospital receptionist had said it. Aarón blinked hard and shook his head.

"It's not possible!" he yelled at the car.

Maybe the boy could've been born somewhere else, but he forced himself to reject the idea—it would be impossible to check all the hospitals.

He felt dizzy in his stomach and noticed his thoughts beginning to race. The daylight seemed to be growing more intense. He mentally went over the numbers written on the pages on his table, in the living room of his apartment. A stream of calculations passed through him from the inside out, like a jet of pressurized soda shooting from a boy's mouth. He smelled chamomile.

He remembered Sr. Palmer telling him his date of birth: March 10, 1947.

"It can't be!" he yelled again. "They all matched!"

But doubt awakened somewhere in his mind. Maybe not all of them.

He reached Arenas's main street and drove across it. He had to stop in front of the school when a shirtless man with a sunburned chest covered in white hair showed him a stop sign. Behind him, two men were putting up a traffic light beside the crosswalk. On the opposite side of the road, another traffic light, lying on the sidewalk, was waiting to be hoisted. He could almost hear a hum from the stream of images and numbers inside his head. He closed his eyes until someone honked a horn behind him.

He parked the car outside his apartment block and ran to the entrance. He pressed the button to call the elevator but, a second later, he set off up the stairs.

He left the door open, with the keys in the lock. He reached the table, spread the papers out on it, and began pointing at each of the circles he'd drawn for each robbery. He checked the birth dates and death dates of each person, which he had gradually been adding to the diagrams. His mind made the calculations automatically, without effort. He started with the first robbery and finished with the last.

"It can't be," he said again as he ran his finger over Sr. Palmer's name on the piece of paper headed *May 12, 2000*.

His knees gave way and he had to grab a chair to stop himself from falling. He rested his elbows on the table.

"You have to reach the end. Sometimes you think you're smarter than you are." Aarón said the words into the air, words of the only professor at the university who'd failed his work. "It's not possible."

He struck his forehead several times with his left fist. His hand began to tremble when he placed it on the piece of paper depicting the night when David was shot. May 12, 2000. He positioned the tip of a ballpoint pen on the circle where he'd written Sr. Palmer's surname. The newspaper had indicated that Sr. Palmer was fifty-three years old. And Aarón had taken it for granted that it had to match one of the ages that were always repeated: *53 years, 3 months, and 2 days.* Under the numerical rules of the stack of papers he had on the table, for Sr. Palmer to be that exact age on May twelfth, he must have been born . . . "On February tenth, 1947," he said. He read what he'd written, beginning to understand the mistake he'd made. "Because sometimes I think I'm smarter than I am." The pen fell onto the table when he covered his face with both hands.

It's no good giving the correct answer if you don't explain how you arrived at it, the professor had said to him, with his feet up on the desk in his office. Aarón had defended himself, saying there were things he felt he knew without needing to understand them. To which the professor had replied: *It seems to me that sometimes you think you're smarter than you are. And no man of science can allow himself that luxury. The risk you run is that you end up changing reality to fit your calculations, and not the other way around.*

He peered through his fingers to look at Sr. Palmer's name again and the date he had allocated to him so that everything would match up.

"Changing reality to fit my calculations . . . ," Aarón said, recalling the professor's words.

When he understood how serious his error could be, he savored the bitter taste of his own mistake.

He got up to go close his apartment door, like a scientist locking himself in his laboratory when on the verge of discovering something important. Back at the table, he picked up the pen and crossed out the incorrect birth date he had attributed to the American. Beside it, he wrote the real one, the one Sr. Palmer had told him in the store that afternoon: March 10, 1947.

One month later.

He scanned the circles representing the rest of the individuals present in the most recent robbery. He checked the details of the Cañizares boy, the son of the owner of the university bookstore. Aarón had visited her at the store to find out how the youngster was after the incident at the Open, and somehow, he had managed to ask her on what day her son was born. She had replied with the date that Aarón expected. He now underlined the information to confirm its accuracy. Moving the pen over the page, he also checked the gunman's date of birth. Héctor Mirabal had obtained it straight from the police file. Aarón underlined that, too. He moved on to the circle representing the man who'd called emergency services with his cell phone. Aarón had obtained his home telephone number. After a couple of conversations in which he made the most of his status as a friend of the victim, he built enough trust to be able to ask the man his date of birth. Another correct date. Aarón underlined the information again.

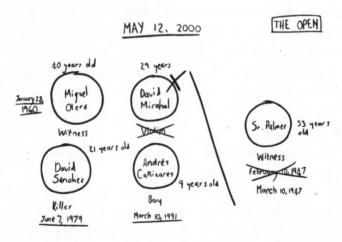

Those three ages, those three birth dates, were correctly noted.

Then Aarón focused on the only person who remained uncorroborated. A new fear crystalized somewhere in his chest when he rested the pen on David's name. Because he already knew what he was going to find.

Sr. Palmer's and David's details were the easiest to obtain. That was why Aarón had left them until last. And that was why, when he had reached them, overexcited after finding that the dates and numbers had matched across the preceding eighteen people, Aarón had let down his guard. He had assigned a birth date and age to Sr. Palmer, taking for granted that it would follow the pattern. In the case of David, who he well knew was born on February 3, 1971—the very same day as he was—he hadn't thought it necessary to specify his age in years, months, and days. Hence, beside his name, he had simply written *29 years*.

His stomach tightened again.

He looked at the notes for the people of that age in the previous robberies. *29 years, 4 months, and 9 days* was the age of one of the witnesses in 1909. The same age as the robber who shot Antonio Canal II in 1950. And exactly the same age as the young guy working at the gas station in 1971: *29 years, 4 months, and 9 days*.

Cold, thick sweat covered his hand when, for the first time, he calculated David's exact age on the day the bullet intended for Aarón hit him.

David was *29 years, 3 months, and 9 days* old that day.

One month younger than he should have been. One month younger than all the others.

One month.

Sr. Palmer and David's ages diverged from the pattern by one month.

"And what does this mean, now?" asked Aarón.

He got up and stood looking at the table. He felt the cold travel down his back. He assumed it was still day, because the sun had made his steering wheel searing hot only a few hours ago. He remembered the reddened chest of the man who'd stopped him on the street where the Open was. He touched the back of his neck and confirmed it was hot. An electric current that didn't hurt but depleted him was set off inside his brain.

He turned around.

He was startled when he began to understand.

No boys were born that day, not at that hospital.

He crossed the living room in the direction of the kitchen. He stepped on the trash can's pedal and rummaged through the cardboard boxes and food waste. One by one, he took out the pieces of the airline tickets to Cuba that he had torn up the previous day. He arranged them on the breakfast bar. He completed the impromptu puzzle almost without error, placing the pieces in position at first glance until the four tickets were whole again. His two, and David's two. His heart began to beat hard, anticipating what he was going to find.

He checked the flight's departure date: June 10.

"Yesterday," he said.

Sweat began to pearl on his forehead, as if from the electric heat that emanated from his head. He returned to the living-room table and picked up a blank sheet of paper. He wrote a new date on it in large characters.

He was depicting a new robbery.

He traced five circles and beside each of them wrote the ages that had always matched. Inside of the circle he'd positioned by the store counter, he wrote Sr. Palmer's name. And this time, he added the correct age: *53 years, 3 months, and 2 days*. Under the circle to which he assigned the age *29 years, 4 months, and 9 days*, he added the word *Victim*. When he went to write a name inside of the same circle, he thought his hand wasn't going to respond. Finally, it did.

And the name that Aarón wrote for the victim was *Aarón Salvador*. Himself.

At the top of the page he had written *June 12, 2000*.
"Tomorrow," he said out loud.

JUNE 12, 2000

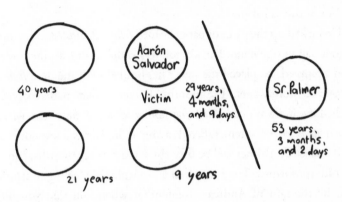

He slumped into the chair and held on to the table with the entire length of his arms. A new thought emerged in his head and escaped through his lips.

"That's why David isn't dead." He bit the inside of his lip. "David isn't dead."

Andrea had repeated it so many times since the day of the robbery. His mother had, too. It had been right in front of him all along.

"David isn't dead," he said for the third time. "He doesn't count, and I wasn't going to be here."

He looked at the piece of paper he'd just written his name on. Tomorrow he would be twenty-nine years, four months, and nine days old. On June 12, 2000. But he wasn't meant to be in Arenas that day. He couldn't have gone to the Open. Because he'd left the love of his life and decided to travel to Cuba with his best friend on the designated date. Nothing would have made him stay.

Nothing.

Nothing except a gunshot that left his friend prostrate in a bed. Nothing except his feeling of guilt and his discovery of something that would obsess him, like the robberies depicted on the pages he had in front of him. A grotesque laugh, filled with terror, escaped his mouth when he understood.

"All of this is for me."

He picked up the piece of paper headed *May 12, 2000* and crumpled it into a ball in one hand. David's robbery didn't count. In the position it had occupied, he placed the new one, headed with the date *June 12, 2000*. One month later. The month's difference that made everything match. Like it always had. *I'll bring your medication tomorrow. We have an agreement, right?* he remembered saying to Sr. Palmer a few hours ago.

"Because Sr. Palmer will be fifty-three years, three months, and two days old, tomorrow." He recognized an inexplicable feeling of triumph when he thought of Andrea. "Remember when you said you didn't believe in destiny? Well, all of this is a fucking ploy by the bastard. Because the real robbery at the Open's going to happen tomorrow. And this time I have to be there. The fourth out of five. Tomorrow it's my turn. It's tomorrow that the boy will be born."

The living room, and the entire apartment, began to spin around him. He felt the table move under his arms. Somehow, the wall to the left became the one to the right, and the chair rocked back and forth as if the floor had turned to waves of wood. He felt his stomach rise to his throat. He struggled to stand. He had to walk with his arm stretched out to touch the wall and keep his balance. He reached the bathroom just in time to vomit into the toilet. With each retch, he felt the blood pumping in his head and pulsing in the hemorrhage in his eye.

He emptied himself.

When he got to his feet, the room continued to undulate under him. He sat on the toilet and rested his head in his hands, pressing his eyelids with his palms until he saw two enormous white spots. He tasted bile at the back of his throat. He tried to clear it, to exhale, and what came from his mouth was a groan originating in his stomach, the sound of a man accepting the certainty of his own death.

"No."

Aarón dried his eyes. He was surprised by the gravity in his voice. The cold left his body, and the exhausting activity inside his head stopped. The moisture seemed to suddenly disappear from his hands. His heart rate stabilized at a normal speed—he felt it in his neck. He enjoyed the serenity for a moment. Then he got up.

He knew what he had to do.

He searched in the kitchen first. Then in the living room. He looked under the papers on the table. Lifted the cushions on the sofa. He didn't remember going to the bedroom since he'd arrived, but he searched there, as well. He returned to the bathroom and looked under the toilet bowl. He stood still. He turned his head and closed his eyes. Then he remembered.

He opened the front door and found what he was looking for. He grabbed the keys he had left in the lock when he closed the door. He slammed it shut again. He inserted the key and turned it to the left, four times. He took out the key and squeezed it with the rest of the bunch in his left hand. He walked to the large living-room window, pulled up the shutters. He narrowed his eyes, expecting sunlight, but was left openmouthed when he found himself looking at the orangey darkness of a night lit only by streetlamps and a first-quarter moon. He opened the window and could feel the warmth of the air. Someone had lit a barbecue. Without hesitating, as if everything was part of a daily routine, Aarón swung back the fist he held the keys in and then threw them with all his might.

"You're not going to get me!" he yelled. He heard the distant sound of the keys landing on the pavement. "Nothing's going to make me leave this place."

He emptied coins, his cell phone, and his pharmacist's ID badge from his pocket onto the bedside table. He slumped onto the bed without undressing. He wanted to sleep.

Only when the sun came up did he understand how absurd it had been to think he could fall asleep. He spent several hours lying in bed, watching the morning light climb the bedroom wall, before the telephone rang. It was the landline. He let it ring. There was a moment of silence. Then his cell phone began to vibrate on his bedside table. He reached for it and held it in front of his face to see who it was.

"Drea," he tried to say, but his throat didn't work as it should have and the word was just phlegm.

"Aarón?"

"Drea." The second time was better. "It's me. I'm at home."

"I just called you at home."

"I'm in bed," he said, and regretted it immediately. "Drea, you're not going to believe what I've discovered. I was right." He sat up on the edge of the bed. His own smell reminded him that he'd been wearing the same clothes for twenty-four hours. "But I got some of the calculations wrong."

"I don't want to know," she said. "I'm not interested, you hear me? I didn't even want to call you. It's about the pharmacy."

"The pharmacy?" He swallowed some kind of sour remnant in his mouth and screwed up his nose. "What is it?"

"They're going to fire you," she said. She paused, like she would have to see the reaction on his face had he been in front of her. "You haven't been in all month. All month! Your boss had to call me. You won't even pick up the phone."

"I won't pick up the phone?" He wanted to sound surprised, but he remembered the many missed calls he'd seen on his cell phone at some time and ignored. "Where are you? I can hear people."

"At the mall. Aarón, listen to me. You're going to get fired, do you hear me? How're you going to pay for your apartment? How're you going to pay, huh? Are you going to lose everything because of that heap of paper on your table?"

"You gave me a burst blood vessel," he said. He stroked it through his eyelid.

"A burst blood vessel?" Andrea's voice seemed to soften, but she didn't allow it. "You have no idea what state your boss is in. He's been running the pharmacy by himself for an entire month. He's put up with it for this long because of what happened to David, but now he's really pissed. You have no excuse. And to top it off, Sr. Palmer's wife showed up saying you hadn't taken her husband his medication or something. Your boss found out you've been getting free gas in exchange for delivering the American's medicine to his store."

"Why should he care?"

"Don't ask me. But he wasn't very happy about it. He wants you to show up at the pharmacy today. That's the first thing. But he also wants you to go to the Open to do something about your . . . your shady deal. Aarón, get up, right now, and get yourself to the pharmacy. He's giving you one last chance. You're going to lose your job."

"I can't go out today. It's today that the fourth robbery's going to happen, and—"

"This again?" she cut in.

"Drea, listen to me. You don't understand. I can't go out today. I'll go tomorrow. I'll start tomorrow. I promise."

"Aarón—"

"I can't go out today," he insisted. "I included David's robbery as part of the series, and it turns out I got it wrong."

"Stop! Please, stop." She sighed. Aarón imagined her with her cheeks puffed out, letting out air. "I'm going to hang up."

"It's the fourth robbery today. It's my turn."

"Aarón," she said. He thought he heard a slight sob. "If I have to go take the heat for you at the pharmacy, or fix this business with your shady deal with the American . . ."

"What shady deal!? Hang on a second. You? Why would you go?"

217

"Aarón, please, wake up, you're going to get fired!" she yelled. "If you don't go, I'll have to go for you. I'll make something up. I'll tell them you're still in a bad way, Aarón . . . I don't know. But I swear, if I—"

"Andrea." He walked around the room with his free hand resting on his waist. "Andrea, listen to me. Don't even think about going to the pharmacy, and especially not the Open. You can't. And you're not going to, do you hear?"

"So what should I do? Stand by and watch you lose everything? I am *so* mad at you, but I'm not going to let you destroy your life like this."

"All right." Aarón held his hand up as if showing someone he wasn't armed. "All right. I'll go. I'll go to the pharmacy, today, without fail. But promise me you won't go there. I'll take care of my boss and the American, but you must not go to the store or the pharmacy. Promise me you won't." He gripped the cell phone with both hands.

"Promise me you really will go. I can't even trust you anymore," she said.

"I will. I promise."

"You'd better. It's your job and your home. Not mine. You've already lost . . ." She broke off. Aarón knew what the unsaid words were.

"I'll go," he repeated, and Andrea couldn't have understood the sacrifice and declaration of love contained in his words, the consequences leaving the house that day could have for him. "The bastard has it all planned out," he murmured.

"What did you say?"

"That you can stop worrying. I'll be there. I'll go back to work today," he said, thinking of the keys he'd thrown out the window.

"By the way," she added, her voice vibrating with joy, "David's started showing signs of improvement. He hasn't opened his eyes yet, but the doctors are saying he's on his way back. He's going to get better. I hope you go see him."

"I will," he said. "It's what had to happen. He had to get better." He smiled at the confirmation that David's robbery had just been a trap. That it didn't need to have any victims.

"I'm going to call you tonight to make sure you went to the pharmacy and fixed the thing with the American."

"Talk to you tonight. And if not—"

Aarón had wanted to say goodbye somehow, but Andrea hung up on him. His words dissolved into the dry, sour saliva that a sleepless night produces. He took a deep breath, almost tasting the chamomile. He threw the cell phone on the bed. He dropped his shoulders and stood with his arms outstretched on either side of his body, his gaze absent.

"It can't be altered."

Even so, he refused to give up, so he started searching for a solution to the two problems he faced.

First, how to get out of the apartment.

And second, where to obtain a weapon to take to the American's store.

"So you think you're smart enough to make me go, you bastard?" he said. "We'll see who's smartest."

From his wardrobe he took the first T-shirt he found. He rubbed his armpits with the one he'd just taken off. He looked at the cell phone on his bed and considered calling his mother. She was the only person apart from Andrea who had another set of keys. He certainly couldn't ask Andrea to bring hers. How would he explain that he'd thrown his own through the window after locking himself in? Aarón looked around him and imagined what his mother would say if she saw the house in the state it was in. The news that he was on the verge of losing his job might even have reached her, so he abandoned the idea.

He pulled on the clean T-shirt and looked at the window right above his bed's headboard. He thought about it for a few seconds before climbing on the bed. At some point in the night, he'd opened the window, hoping for a little cool air that never found its way in. He leaned out. Right underneath him—at not such a great distance, in fact—was one of the landscaped areas that led to the communal pool. He crawled back over the bed and headed to the living-room table, which was up against the window through which he'd thrown his keys.

He couldn't stop himself from taking one last look at the pile of papers. He examined the sketch of what he had assumed would happen tonight at the Open. He saw his name and Sr. Palmer's. Under his circle, he reread the word *Victim*. He shuddered. He wondered who the witnesses would be. Under the last circle, he had written *Killer*. He picked up the pen.

"Not if I get you first and you become the victim," he said out loud.

He crossed out that circle. He also struck several lines through the word *Victim* under his own name. His eyes came to rest on some details he had highlighted days ago. A box, framed several times with the same pen until the paper was torn at the corners of the rectangle, contained two lines of words:

August 14, 2009

Victim: the boy

JUNE 12, 2000

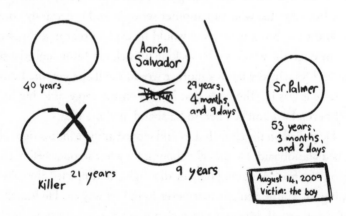

He smiled, aware of his miscalculation. Everything was going to happen one month later. Or wouldn't happen at all.

"Not if I manage to do away with the killer tonight and all this madness loses its meaning."

He threw the pen onto the table with a triumphant expression, and it slid across the surface until it hit the stone from the lake. The one he'd collected from the bottom to give to Andrea the night it all began. The one she'd returned to him ten years later, the day they broke up, a month ago now. Aarón felt his heart accelerate. A month without Andrea was much longer than he ever wanted to live without her. Now he saw it clearly. He wasn't missing anything. Because there was nothing without her. *You can give it back to me whenever you want*, Andrea had said before leaving the stone on the dashboard of his car. Aarón picked it up now and put it in his pocket. He could return it to her that night.

He positioned his hands on either side of the window frame. Down below, there was grass.

"You can do it," he persuaded himself.

He rested his left foot on the table and pushed himself up to step with his right foot onto the windowsill. Several papers fell to the floor. With both feet in the window, he turned around and looked back inside the apartment. He crouched so that he was able to grip the windowsill with his hands, then lowered himself out of the window until he was hanging.

Aarón closed his eyes, and let go.

He felt a slight pain in his ankle when he set off toward Héctor Mirabal's house.

22.

AARÓN

Monday, June 12, 2000

"Aarón."

A hand hit him in the face. Something dug into his back.

"Aarón, wake up."

Wetness descended his chin as fingers grabbed it and shook his head. The thing digging into his back began to really hurt. What was it? Then he remembered. It was the corner of the wall that framed Héctor Mirabal's front door.

"Héctor?"

Aarón said the name while he was still dreaming, uttering it from a shadow-filled place, a world of just two dimensions: the liquid on his chin and the stabbing pain in his spine. The word became a question of which Héctor could only have heard the last syllable.

"Héctor!" Aarón repeated, shouting this time.

He suddenly opened his eyes, fully awake in a second. The sharp brick on the corner where he'd sat to wait scraped his side. He wiped the saliva that had escaped from the side of his mouth with the back of his hand. He blinked until he was able to bring Héctor into focus.

Crouching in front of him, Héctor was holding his police officer's cap in his hand between his legs, his forearm resting on one of his knees in a pose that was as cop-like as it was friendly. Aarón could feel Héctor's other hand on his face. It was warm. Behind his silhouette, the sky was black—it was night again. Some high-pitched whining started up on the other side of the door.

"Man, are you all right?"

Aarón looked from side to side, found his bearings, and pushed himself forward to gather in his legs. He crossed them in front of himself before rubbing his face hard.

"What're you doing here?" asked Héctor.

"Did I fall asleep?"

"You tell me."

Héctor stood up with an agile movement and pulled Aarón up by the arm. Once he was on his feet, Aarón closed his eyes for a few seconds to ride out the sudden head rush. Inside the house, claws were scratching the door.

"I came looking for you this morning," Aarón started explaining. "I guessed . . . I guessed you were on duty, so I sat down to wait for you. I must've fallen asleep. No surprise—I didn't sleep at all last night."

Héctor stretched out his little finger and thumb on one hand, held it to his ear, and opened his eyes in a questioning expression.

"I left my phone at home. I had to leave"—he hesitated for a second—"suddenly."

"Because of my brother, right?" Pushing aside his nightstick, Héctor pulled a large bunch of keys out of his pocket.

"Because of David?" asked Aarón.

"Of course you don't know." He shook his head and looked down at the ground. "Seeing as you haven't called me for a week."

Héctor pushed his front door open. The dog's snout appeared first, and then the animal leapt euphorically between his owner's legs. Aarón didn't know how to respond until something clicked in his head.

"David!" He wanted to hide his excitement, but he sounded like a game-show contestant remembering the correct answer at the last second. "That's what you're talking about. Is it that? He's better, I know. Drea told me this morning. That's why"—the lies escaped from his mouth before he could contain them—"that's why I came. That's why I was waiting for you."

He indicated the place where he'd sat. An image of himself that morning appeared in front of him, ringing the doorbell until he thought it would catch fire, until he heard a window opening on the neighboring house and the dog losing his voice on the other side of the door. He remembered sitting down and hugging his knees, rocking. He remembered resting his head on the wall just for a second.

"That's why I'm here," he repeated, and he pushed the door, from inside the house now, to stop seeing the brick that had scraped his back.

Héctor had turned on a bunch of lights in record time while the dog danced back and forth in erratic movements with his ears bent forward. He also turned on a pedestal fan, one of its blades creaking as it began to turn. Héctor unbuttoned his uniform shirt with a single hand. He took it off and hung it on the back of a white armchair. Aarón could see drops of sweat among his chest hairs.

"Fuck me, this heat!" He waved his arms. "She told you? I thought Drea and you . . . you know. But you shouldn't have waited for me, buddy. Everyone there's looking forward to seeing you. They called me this morning. I was supposed to work until eleven tonight, but my head was all over the place. Man, I'd started thinking he'd never wake up. My boss just gave me permission to go home. He said it's no big deal leaving Carlos by himself for a couple of hours."

He finished undoing his laces and dropped both boots on the floor. The dog stuck his snout in one of them. Héctor smiled at unpredictable moments while he spoke. Barefoot now, he approached Aarón and grabbed him by the shoulders.

"And what about you, buddy? You had me worried. All this time without hearing from you. I called you a few times. Still a mess, huh? Don't hold it against her if my mother says something to you tonight." He struck Aarón's right shoulder as if they were chatting in the locker room after a game. "She finds it hard to understand why you haven't been to see him. But it's over. What matters is, my brother's all right. Fuck, what a fright, man. I still can't believe it. I don't think I've breathed easily since that guy called from the Open."

Héctor undid his belt and hung it on the chair, next to the cap. Aarón fixed his eyes on the belt. On the handgun. Héctor dropped his pants and jumped out of them.

"OK, let me get dressed and we can go," he said, smiling.

Héctor set off up the stairs, and Aarón remembered him chasing him and David up the staircase in the Mirabal family home when they were teenagers, to give them a beating for spying on him while he kissed Patricia, or Alicia, or both of them that one time, in the basement.

The dog shot off after him.

"I . . . I've got to go to the pharmacy first!" Aarón yelled a moment later up the staircase. "I have to take care of a few things with my boss!"

Aarón could hear Héctor moving around.

"Héctor? I said I have to go to the pharmacy to speak to my boss!" he repeated.

"All right, man," Héctor shouted back from upstairs.

Aarón was opening and closing his hands on either side of his body. If he was going to do it, he had to do it now. He dried his palms on his pants before approaching the white armchair. He jumped when he realized he was treading on Héctor's uniform pants. He smoothed his hair back and wiped the corners of his mouth with his fingers. Now.

It was a quick movement.

The metallic sound was drowned out by the fan's creaky blade.

"Crappy situation with the pharmacy, buddy," Héctor said as he came down the stairs. "You should've gotten sick leave for depression or something. But man, why've you been waiting for me, then?" he added as he pushed his head through the neck of his T-shirt.

With the T-shirt on his shoulders, he looked left and right.

Aarón wasn't by the white armchair.

Or at the door.

Because at that moment, Aarón was running toward the Open like a child running from his parents to get out of something scary. His ankle was pulsating, painfully, at each step. The first time he stopped to regain his breath, bent over and gripping his knees, he took the revolver out from under his T-shirt and held it in his left hand.

That's almost a kilo you're holding, Héctor had explained to Aarón the winter the Arenas Police Department accepted him, making his father proud. *It's a thirty-eight. They make us keep the first chamber empty so we have time to count to five before firing. This is Arenas, after all— nothing ever happens here. Hey, buddy, I'll call my brother and we can go shoot some cans, what do you say?* Aarón laughed into the asphyxiating heat of the night when he remembered what Héctor said to finally persuade him: *Come on, man, you're only fifteen once. Enjoy it. When're you going to get another chance to try it? When're you ever in your life going to need to fire a weapon?*

Breathing heavily in an empty alleyway, Aarón looked at the revolver.

He pointed it up to the sky and pulled the trigger. The cylinder advanced to the next chamber.

The echo made him cackle again.

The pavement turned yellow and violet as it reflected the light from the neon sign that said *OPEN* at the American's store. Aarón walked at a slow but determined pace, his arms barely swinging to each side of him. He smelled gasoline. A warm breeze washed over his skin.

At each step, he felt the cold metal on his belly.

A car honked behind him to make him get out of the way. It parked parallel to one of the gas pumps. Aarón heard the driver say they'd been lucky to make it, the tank was empty.

"Can I fill it?" his son asked.

"Sure, but be careful. If you get gas on those shorts your grandma just gave you . . ."

The boy got out of the car and pulled on the hose. Before he'd finished inserting the nozzle in the tank, four drops fell onto his shorts and four dark-brown circles appeared on the fabric on one of his legs.

"Here, why don't you go pay?" his father said.

Aarón stopped at the store's entrance. He stood there for a few seconds before making the final step. When he did, the doors opened in front of him with a plastic squeak. The cold air coming from inside made his stomach contract. The revolver's barrel dug into his thigh.

This can't be avoided, he thought.

As soon as he was inside, he surveyed the store. He recognized Sr. Palmer behind the counter with his back to him, his head surrounded by white hair. He was watching television, the volume up to full. He also recognized one of the Moreno brothers, who stood reading a car magazine in the newspaper section. Aarón identified him as Jesús Moreno, the youngest of the three, whose brothers had thrown him out of the swimming-pool business not long ago—the whole town knew about it. With two teenage children and in dire straits.

The hair on Aarón's arms stood on end. He rubbed them hard, as if he were cold. Still standing at the entrance, he saw a third person.

Now we're four.

It was a young man wearing a cap. The peak was over his eyes, and he was examining one of the shelves down the second aisle. Where the beers were. He was hitting his right leg with his hand, drumming out the beat of a song in his head. From the way he was pinching his bottom lip, he seemed to be in a state of complete concentration. The song must have reached its climax, because the young man played an imaginary drum kit on the cans and finished with a few plucks on his invisible guitar.

Aarón held his hand to his fly to feel the mound from the pistol. When the young man with the cap noticed the movement and looked at him, Aarón pretended to scratch his crotch. The eyes of the air guitarist were a brown so light they seemed amber. He picked up a can of Heineken and turned it around, checking something.

Aarón searched in the confectionery area, where sometimes he saw a crowd of kids after school. Now it was empty. He headed slowly toward the counter. On the way, he inspected the three aisles.

Where is he?

Sr. Palmer saw Aarón's reflection in the circular mirror that hung from the ceiling, the one that reflected the white rays from the fluorescent tubes that lit the establishment. He peeled his eyes from the screen, lowered the volume, and got up from his chair.

"Aarón!" he yelled. "I'd given up on you. Don't tell me they're going to fire you. Your boss was here an hour ago asking for explanations about the free gas. As if I'm his employee. *Asshole,*" he said in English. "I didn't pay any attention. I told him I'd talk to you, that it has nothing . . ."

Aarón turned around when he heard the automatic doors. The blond boy walked in with a couple of bills in his hand.

". . . to do with me, and that . . . ," Sr. Palmer continued to grumble somewhere.

The American's voice gradually melted into the air until it disappeared, like magic ink dissolving in water until it was transparent. The boy, rubbing one of the legs of his shorts, walked on with his head down.

And that's all five of us.

Aarón's eyes traveled from the boy to Jesús Moreno, who was now leafing through a magazine with a naked blonde on the cover. From him they jumped to the young guy in the cap, and Aarón saw that he was hiding a can of beer in each pocket of his pants. A prick in his neck preceded the next image. Sr. Palmer was moving his lips and waving a hand with his forefinger outstretched, but Aarón heard nothing, because the American's speech had become waves of deep, unintelligible sound. He was vocalizing more and more slowly, and seemed to take an eternity to utter a single word. Droplets of saliva were shooting out from his mouth.

Something brushed against Aarón's leg.

Touch became vision when the boy passed him, approached the counter, and held up the bills. His movements were slow and heavy, as if he were submerged in water.

Another prick in the neck. The Moreno brother's face appeared. He was still looking at the magazine. Aarón could almost imagine the handgun hidden in the black jacket of the man who could no longer afford to bring up his children or buy the porn magazine he was holding. While Aarón tried to find reasons Jesús Moreno would want to rob the store, one of the waves of distorted sound brought with it a strange noise.

A metallic click.

Another prick in the neck. The young guy in the cap was looking at Aarón with wide eyes. Suddenly, his hand went to his back pocket to—

"Palmer, grab the boy!" yelled Aarón. Time was moving at its normal speed again.

The cell phone the air guitarist had just taken from his back pocket dropped to the floor. The battery shot out and ended up under one of the refrigerators at the back of the store.

"Holy shit! What the fuck?" exclaimed the American in his native language. He was struggling to breathe and holding his chest.

"Grab the boy!" Aarón yelled again through one side of his mouth. Seeing the boy remain motionless, Aarón turned to him. "Get behind the counter. Go!" He pointed the gun in an attempt to indicate where he should go.

As the child went around the counter, a damp patch grew on the dark brown of his shorts. When he reached the other side, he hugged the American's legs and closed his eyes. Sr. Palmer was searching among his drawers for his capsules to stop the out-of-control machine his heart had become.

"You two!" roared Aarón. He aimed the gun at Jesús Moreno first and then at the beer thief. His hands were so moist he was afraid the weapon would slip through them and fall to the ground.

"Get on the floor! Both of you!"

Aarón smelled his own adrenaline. It was a bitter smell that stuck to his throat.

"I'm sorry, I'm sorry," said the youngster in the cap. He took the two cans out of his pockets and put them back on the shelf. "I'm sorry, it was just a couple, I was going to pay for the rest. I swear, I was going to pay for them. I have money. My band's doing well. We're . . . we're not Dover, but . . . but we put on our own concerts. If only we were Dover. I'd die a happy man if I wrote a song half as good as 'Serenade.' But I didn't want . . . I didn't want to bring up dying—I'm nervous. It's that gun, it's making me . . ."

He kept talking as he knelt. Then he lay facedown. When its peak touched the ground, the cap fell off his head. He held both hands behind his neck. With his forehead pressed against the floor, he continued to mutter something.

Aarón aimed the weapon at Jesús Moreno. The magazine had fallen from his hands. He was holding up his palms so Aarón could see them.

"Too close to the jacket," he said. "Arms up."

Jesús Moreno ignored him.

"I said arms up!"

His hands remained where they were.

"Up!"

"I can't," he said. It was little more than a whisper, because the voice was trapped behind a throat tight with fear. "I'm trying, but I can't."

Aarón gestured at the floor with the gun to instruct him to lie down.

"Like him," he said, turning his head toward the young man with the cap.

Jesús Moreno slumped down. His knees crunched when he hit the floor, like eggs cracking. With the help of his elbows, he slowly brought his whole body down. He placed his hands behind his neck and turned his face before resting his cheek on the cover girl's bare breast.

"Which one of you is it, then? Which one?"

Aarón was moving the gun from side to side. He was blinking at a frenetic rate to alleviate the irritation from the sweat over his eyes.

"Aarón, what're you doing?" The American's voice interrupted his thoughts. Sr. Palmer was holding the child's head in trembling hands. "If this is because of David—"

"Shut up!" Aarón ordered.

Sr. Palmer's shoulders flinched, and he squeezed his eyes shut.

"It's not for David anymore, it's for me." Tears mingled with sweat around his eyelids, and his burst blood vessel burned. "All of this, it was all for me."

The blond boy's father looked in the direction of the store. He was striding toward the entrance when he sensed something was not right. The first thing he saw through the glass was a man lying on the floor. Then two hands appeared, holding a gun. They were white, the fingertips almost purple. The father contained his initial instinct to go in and returned to his car in search of his cell phone.

Aarón explained to Sr. Palmer: "One of those two guys there, the ones on the floor, one of them was going to kill me tonight."

And what if it was the old man who was going to do it? a voice in his head said.

"You wouldn't hurt me, would you?"

"What the . . . ," Palmer began instinctively. "What're you saying? You're Ana Salvador's boy, come on."

"It's one of these two," said Aarón. He aimed the revolver at the floor again. "It's you, isn't it? Those yellow eyes have been making me nervous since I came in. Or you, Jesús. Why don't you do away with your brothers instead? They were the ones who played you. Come on, which one of you came here to rob the store? Which one?"

Aarón approached the young man with the cap and crouched down to frisk him. He was still babbling, and Aarón noticed he was trembling. After searching his clothes, he only found a wallet and a pine-tree-shaped air freshener in his back pocket. Aarón threw the little tree at a row of shelves.

"I knew it had to be you," he said to Jesús Moreno, before getting up and taking a couple of steps toward him. "Why're you wearing a jacket in this heat? I think you know how warm the evenings are in June around here, don't you? What're you hiding in that jacket, huh? What're you hiding in there?"

"Please," Jesús begged in a stifled whisper. "I've just come from an interview. My brothers and I—the business, they got rid of me a few months ago."

"We all know what happened. You know what we're like in this town. Sr. Palmer makes sure all the information keeps flowing."

Aarón crouched down next to him. He searched in all the jacket pockets. In the pants. The smell of shit caught him by surprise. It was as pungent as the samples that, when he was studying at the university, reached the laboratory after a two-week delay.

He shot up, revolted.

The racing thoughts started up in his head, and this time they were painful from the outset.

It's not them. These two are more frightened than you are.

Behind his eyes, all the way to the back of his neck, an electric charge made his shoulders contract. Aarón narrowed his eyes as if it would ease the pain.

Have you really not figured it out yet? his mind asked him.

He walked backward to separate himself from the two men on the floor. His hands were freezing. They were beginning to feel numb. He looked at Sr. Palmer, and the gun pointed at him.

It can't be him.

The old man lowered his head while he recalled Ana Salvador cleaning Aarón's lips, crouching with her skirt above her knees. He closed his eyes and thought of his wife. He pressed the child's head against his legs.

Aarón let out a cry of pain when the images were projected in his head so brightly it burned his eyes.

If it's not those two cowards or the American, it can only be . . .

"Tell the boy to come out," said Aarón.

Sr. Palmer shook his head. "No."

Aarón frowned, squinting in his characteristic way. Sr. Palmer identified the mannerism as one that had been his since he was a child. And it had remained identical into adulthood.

"Tell . . . the boy . . . to come out," Aarón repeated with difficulty.

"No, Aarón, put that gun down," the American said with as much conviction as he could muster, not realizing he had said it in English.

The pain in Aarón's head was increasing with each small effort. It hurt him just to listen to the words.

"I want that boy here in front of me!" he yelled. The blood pumped with such force in his temples and neck that he thought he was going to lose consciousness.

Sr. Palmer repeated that he wasn't going to let the boy out, but the youngster untangled himself from his legs. The American's fingers barely touched his golden hair when he tried to stop him. With his shorts soaked and his face moist, the boy came out from behind the counter.

He looked Aarón in the face and said, "What?"

The electric current continued to overload Aarón's brain. The dates again—*not if I get you first and you become the victim*—and the numbers—*it can only be him*—slammed against the inside of his head—*there's always a victim, there's always a killer*—with a force that turned the spasmodic pain—*they've never killed the boy*—into an unbearable, continuous buzz.

Until there was so much energy that the mechanism shut down. And the lights went out.

From the darkness, Andrea's voice reached him. *You didn't think the boy was going to kill you, did you?* it said.

And then Aarón understood.

Andrea, or her voice, was right. And that was why her voice no longer sounded like a thought, but was so clear that Aarón looked around him to make sure she wasn't there.

"Now do you realize?" she said. "It was easy. Don't you see it's your turn to be the victim, no matter how many times you crossed it out on the piece of paper at home? It's you. And I only see one gun here. Did you really think it could be the boy?"

The voice changed pitch with each word. It was Andrea's, but sometimes it sounded like David's. Sometimes it was Aarón's own. He closed his eyes.

"You could shoot right now in any direction and the bullet would ricochet and hit you between the eyes. That bastard destiny, remember? You said it yourself." The voice was Andrea's again.

Aarón shrieked to drown out the tangle of voices, but they still wormed their way through his agonizing screams.

"Time for you to decide," said the imaginary Andrea. "You can shoot one of these people, but it won't make any difference, because they're like David. They're just actors in your death scene. Do you remember how you explained it to me? You were right about everything! I don't like admitting it, but it's true. There you are, the five of you, each with your role to play. We don't need to ask them how old they are, do we?"

Aarón covered his ears and tore his scalp with his fingernails. He felt icy metal on his ear. It did nothing to silence the voices inside him.

"You can shoot these people for no reason or put yourself out of the picture, which is what has to happen. Who would've guessed, huh? Victim and killer are the same person in this fourth robbery."

Aarón bit his tongue.

"Victim and killer are the same person. A good one, don't you think, Aarón?"

And then Andrea, David, or he—or all of them at the same time—said the final words.

"Best of all, that person is you."

The blond boy's father began to wave his arms when the howl of the far-off siren grew louder. The blue lights of two police cars appeared in the distance.

Andrea, who was wearing a new T-shirt bought at the shopping mall and heading right then to the Open to ask the American if Aarón had shown up to solve the problem with his boss, looked up in the direction of the sirens. She saw a man waving his arms at the police cars and pointing at the store. She held her breath.

Andrea heard the gunshot before she exhaled.

Her legs began to work of their own accord. She ran toward the store. As she crossed the forecourt, a boy came out from inside. He hugged the man who had been waving his arms on the street.

"It's Aarón Salvador!" someone yelled from inside.

Andrea charged at the doors. A police officer tried to prevent her from going in, but when she recognized Aarón's sneaker at the end of a leg stretched out on the floor, nothing could have stopped her.

More than the pain, it was the cold and the darkness that surprised Aarón when the bullet passed through his head.

Then his senses faded one by one. His open eyes didn't see Andrea kneel next to him.

His wounded tongue could no longer taste her lips when Andrea pressed hers against his and blew to help him breathe.

Nor did his dead sense of touch enable him to feel Andrea placing her hands behind his head, covering the wound to keep his life from spilling through the hole, the gray substance wetting her fingers and T-shirt.

Without his hearing, Aarón couldn't listen to Andrea say, "Please don't die, I believe you."

It was when Andrea rested her forehead against Aarón's blood-soaked chest that the sweet smell of chamomile entered his body.

And Aarón knew that Andrea had arrived and was with him.

As always.

As always.

Unsure whether his hand was responding or not, he imagined himself putting it in his pocket. He took out the stone from the lake.

And although Aarón wanted to say one thing to Andrea—*Warn the boy. I miscalculated, it will happen a month later, on September 14*—his lips said something else.

"Come in the water," he said.

And water was the last thing Aarón thought of.

After that, there was nothing.

23.

ANDREA

Friday, August 14, 2009
Toulouse, France

The gunshot sound woke Andrea.

Slumped on the kitchen table, in the dark, she jerked her shoulders as she suddenly straightened. It took her a few seconds to come out of the nightmare. The nightmare that always ended with the image of her resting her head on Aarón's blood-soaked chest. The one that had been recurring for nine years, and more frequently in the last month.

With her eyes open but still unable to make out the shapes in the room, the sudden light that appeared on the table and the vibration that accompanied it startled her. In reality, it had been the movement of her cell phone, turning itself on, that had woken her.

Andrea rubbed her face hard, as if it would help her wake up. She snatched up the cell phone and held it against her face.

"What happened?" she said right away. She swallowed hard and held her breath.

At the other end of the line, the man sighed in his car.

"David, please." Andrea increased the urgency in her voice. "Tell me what happened."

"Nothing happened."

Outside the American's store, David placed the crutch he'd just gathered from the ground on the passenger seat.

"Nothing happened," he said again. "I told you. No-thing."

Andrea listened to David's words and closed her eyes. For a few seconds, the nightmare began to play in her mind again. *Don't die, I believe you.* She shook her head to try to stop it.

"The boy didn't show up?" she persisted.

"The boy came. But he went into the store and came out on his own two feet. No one shot him or kidnapped him. Nothing happened to him in the store. Well, the poor kid looked terrified, of course. With everything we made him believe, I'm not surprised the poor thing—"

"You let him go in?" Andrea contained her urge to scream at him. "You were supposed to be there to stop him from entering."

"Andrea." He paused to make sure she was listening. "Leave it. Stop, seriously. The kid went in the store five minutes ago on the date Aarón said. And nothing happened to him. How many times do I have to say it? Nothing. Aarón wasn't well. He was wrong about everything."

Andrea listened to David saying the words she had repeated so many times to herself. It made it sound more real. And she refused to accept it.

"I don't understand how you could've let him go in after everything I told you," she said, still clinging to the story.

She'd refused to believe the story herself when Aarón tried to explain it to her with that heap of papers. Andrea had seen them again the night Aarón died. Carlos, Héctor's partner, stationed at the entrance to the building cordoned off with police tape, gave in to Andrea's pleas and let her into Aarón's apartment. It went completely against official procedure, but Carlos was moved when he saw her squeezing her nose with two fingers as if it would help her stop crying. She was shaking as she made her way up to the second floor. Her pants were soaked in blood.

Her hands were still moist between the fingers with Aarón's saliva. A circle was darkening on the blue T-shirt she'd bought that morning. When she walked into the apartment, she saw the papers piled up all over the table. The photocopies of the newspapers. The squared paper torn from the spiral-bound notebook. The pile of stapled paper on the laptop keyboard. Filled with regret, she remembered how she had thrown them in his face. She stood looking at the papers without knowing what to do for the five minutes Carlos had given her. Then she heard the elevator bell and the sound of boots approaching along the corridor. At that moment, through the mess of paper and ink, she caught sight of a box framed several times with the same pen until the paper had torn at one of its corners. Inside the box, occupying two rows, were the words:

August 14, 2009

Victim: the boy

Andrea felt the sticky heat of a masculine hand on the left side of her chest. Carlos was gripping her firmly. Aarón's voice reverberated around her head, and she couldn't tear her eyes from the piece of paper. *And this time it's going to be the boy who gets killed.* Andrea reached out and grabbed the rectangle of ink, blowing all the air out through her mouth. Without even closing her eyes, she let herself lose consciousness.

"Hey." David's voice crackled in her cell phone. "Are you listening to me?"

"I didn't hear the last thing. The signal went," she lied. She remembered the pain in her eyelids and temples when she woke up in the ambulance that night.

"I was saying the boy ran away before going in the Open. You can guess how scared he was. He didn't give me time to yell to him. Thank God. Just imagine how ridiculous it would've looked. Then I started calling you. I don't know when he went back in. Suddenly I heard screaming, and when I looked the kid was coming out of the store. His parents were there waiting for him. His parents, Andrea. Do you realize what we've put him through?"

Andrea stood up in the darkness of the kitchen. She turned on the light, and her eyes hurt when her pupils contracted. Emilio would be upstairs. He probably hadn't even noticed that she had spent the evening shut away in the kitchen, looking from the clock to her cell phone and from her cell phone to the clock. Just as he hadn't noticed that she had barely slept next to him the last three nights.

"So what should we do now?" she asked David. She opened a drawer and took out a box of medication. The pharmacy packaging made her eyes well up. "You know the boy's name, don't you? Your brother helped you find it. You told me it was Leo something-or-other."

She swallowed two pills without water.

"Andrea." He raised his voice to sound authoritative. "Enough. Seriously, stop. Period. It's over. I'm not going to let you end up like Aarón. Do you hear me? This has gone far enough. I should've made you forget it when you came to my house. Nine years without seeing you, and you suddenly show up for this."

He was referring to the last Saturday in February, the day the new attraction was unveiled at Aquatopia. Just after Andrea spoke to Leo, and as she tried to escape Arenas for the second time, her foot had stepped on the brake to stop her. Then Andrea had driven, almost with her eyes closed, toward David's mother's house. Ruth had opened the door, looked at Andrea with her blue eyes, and hugged her as she cried for what was clearly not the first time that day. *I want to see David*, Andrea had said. Ruth led her through the house. Several times, she asked Andrea why she'd left Arenas in the way she did.

They reached David's bedroom. The room he'd grown up in and where he'd played cowboys with Aarón. And the one he'd returned to after waking from the coma, because he struggled to look after himself with the crutches and with almost half his body paralyzed. When David saw Andrea walk in, he couldn't say anything. He just held out his arms—one of them in reality remaining pressed against his torso—and lowered his face to let himself be hugged. Andrea hugged him. She touched his face. Kissed his forehead. She said sorry for disappearing. And started to tell him why she had returned to Arenas. She told him what Aarón had been doing during the last month of his life. About the obsession that drove him to shoot himself in the head at the Open.

"I told you. It was all nonsense," David continued on the telephone. "I bet you, if I start studying a bunch of random dates, I'll end up finding patterns. How could it have been true? Andrea, seriously, we've been over this. It was Aarón. He must've been racked with guilt, feeling responsible for what happened to me. A total mess—I don't even want to think about it." He paused. "He made up all those numbers to give meaning to my accident. To believe he could still save me."

"No," said Andrea. She walked around the kitchen table with her free hand on her forehead. "The thing is, I wasn't able to explain it to you very well. Because I didn't pay much attention when he told me. All I remembered was that the kid was born on the same day you were shot. May twelfth." She remembered the receptionist at the hospital refuting this detail. "God, I should've paid more attention." She thought she heard Aarón's clicking ankle. "He had a lot of papers. A lot. On his table in the living room. He'd calculated the exact dates. He said it all matched . . ." She thought of the hospital receptionist again and added, "I don't get it. Aarón mentioned exact intervals. He gave the months and days. He calculated the date when the kid was going be killed. It all started on the day you were shot."

"And the date he calculated was *today*. Today, Andrea. August fourteenth. You showed me the piece of paper."

During that conversation in David's bedroom, Andrea had taken the piece of paper she had kept from her final visit to Aarón's apartment out of her pocket. The one she snatched up as the policeman came to usher her out. She had unfolded it. It was moist and crumpled. *You kept this for nine years?* David had asked. And Andrea had nodded, pressing her lips together to stop herself from crying, stroking Aarón's handwriting with her thumb. *This is the date he wrote down. It's going to happen on August fourteenth. And we have to stop it. We owe it to Aarón,* she had said.

"The boy's just been into the Open, that's what I'm telling you," David's voice went on in the cell phone. "He's just been in and nothing happened. What more do you want? What more do you need to realize it was all made up?"

"You saw the boy," Andrea reminded him. David fell silent at the other end of the line. "You didn't believe any of what I told you at your house, but . . . but then you saw the boy. You saw him on the TV and called me. You saw the same thing in him that I saw. You saw Aarón in that kid, tell me you haven't forgotten that."

"Andrea," David sighed, "all I saw was a kid who reminded me of Aarón. So what? It wasn't even a physical resemblance. It was . . . *something.* I don't know what. And now we've seen it was nothing."

Two days after the event at Aquatopia, David had been watching a television on the ceiling of a rehabilitation room. Without sound, and while he stretched and tucked in his left leg with the help of a machine, he observed the cheerful faces of dozens of the town's children at the water park. That was when the boy appeared on the screen. David stopped the movement of his leg. The machine stopped making its noise. He looked at the television with his pulse racing. And then the boy frowned, squinting in a familiar way.

"No." Andrea raised her voice. "Don't say that. When you saw the boy, you started to believe it. Why else would you have called me? Why did you ask your brother to help you identify the kid? Huh, David? Tell me why you did all that if it was just . . . *something.*" She imitated the way he had said it. "Come on, tell me!" Andrea was yelling, without caring whether Emilio could hear her. "Tell me why you went to the Open tonight if you didn't believe anything that Aarón discovered!"

After yelling, Andrea separated the cell phone from her face. It was a few seconds before she held it to her ear again.

". . . thing you asked me to do," David was saying.

"What?"

"I said I would've done anything you asked me to do," he repeated. "That's why I called his house. You asked me to do it. It was what you wanted me to do, for fuck's sake. Did I feel something when I saw that boy on the TV? Sure, but it was because I saw it just after what you'd told me, after seeing how messed up you were." He stopped for a moment. "Suddenly everything was full of hidden messages and cursed numbers."

"Don't make fun of Aarón."

"Look, Andrea, I'm at the fucking Open. Sitting in a car, spying on a child. And do you know why? Do you know why I'm acting like an insane person? For you. So I can tell you from here, from the American's store, today, August fourteenth, that everything that Aarón discovered was bullshit."

"Don't say—"

"Andrea," David interrupted. He grabbed the steering wheel and rested on it to shuffle in his seat. "Nothing happened. He was wrong from the start! Did they kill me? As far as I'm aware, in the end I didn't die in my supposed . . . what did he call them?"

"Scenes," she said. "I remember that word. He talked about a scene that was repeated again and again."

"Well, they can't be repeated that much. Because it hasn't been repeated. I'm alive. The kid's alive."

"But Aarón isn't."

Andrea sank back down onto one of the kitchen chairs. She heard footsteps over her head. Then an idea emerged in her mind.

"Aarón isn't alive," she repeated, almost in a whisper. "Aarón died." She said the next word at speed, excited by her discovery. "Maybe—"

"No, Andrea, it's over," David cut in. "What happened with Aarón was his own doing. He committed suicide. He killed himself. It was like cheating. He manufactured the situation so that what he wanted to happen would happen. To make it real."

Andrea wanted to counter his argument. She wanted to say something. She didn't know what. The excitement of the discovery vanished and left a dark void in her chest. Perhaps it was time to let it be.

An orange beam appeared under the kitchen door. Emilio had turned on the light in the adjoining living room. Andrea thought of Emilio, the man who'd saved her and given her a new life.

"Maybe you're right," she said. "Maybe I should forget it."

The kitchen door opened. Emilio looked surprised to find Andrea on the telephone, but he quickly smiled and headed to the refrigerator. Andrea returned his smile. She nodded as if listening to David—who wasn't saying anything—and left the kitchen. She went to the far corner of the living room. She had an idea.

"Hey," she said in a low voice, "I'm going to ask you one last thing."

"Why're you talking like that?" asked David. "And what're you going to ask me? I'm not doing anything else related to this business. Nothing, is that clear?"

"It'll be the last thing, I promise." She fell silent, waiting for a concession from David that didn't come. "Could you get hold of a video of the interview with the boy at the Aqua? Send it to me here, to my house?"

"No way. I told you, I don't want to have anything to do with this anymore. I'm not going to do it."

"It'll be the last thing." Andrea's shoulders tightened and she pressed her face against the wall. "You know people at the local TV station. It'll be a piece of cake. I bet your brother can help. He can obtain anything with that badge of his."

"Andrea, I'm not doing it. I don't want to do it, and it won't do you any good, either. You need to stop this. You need to let it go."

"And I will, I promise," she said, without knowing whether she was lying. "I'm going on vacation with my husband next week"—Andrea looked at the closed kitchen door—"and I swear it'll be the beginning of a new life. But I want to see that boy. To be sure the resemblance is just a coincidence. See him one last time and say goodbye to Aarón forever. Please."

David was silent.

"Fuck's sake," he finally said. He had never been able to refuse Andrea anything. "All right. I'll try. I will *try*, but I'm not promising anything."

"Thanks, David, thank you."

The kitchen door opened. Emilio came out with a sandwich in his hand. To disguise the true nature of the telephone call, Andrea raised the volume of her voice and said, "Yeah, I'm going on vacation with Emilio." She approached him. "We've booked three weeks away. Twenty days doing nothing."

She put an arm over his shoulders. He invited her to take a bite of his sandwich, and Andrea bit into it. She stopped chewing when she heard David's question.

"Where're you going?"

The voice came out clear from the cell phone. Emilio heard it, too. Andrea wanted to hurry up and swallow, but her husband jumped in ahead of her. "To Cuba!" he yelled cheerfully. Emilio didn't understand why whoever was on the other end of the line clicked his tongue in a sound of disapproval.

Feigning a carefree expression, Andrea slapped her husband on the backside, inviting him to go upstairs.

"I'll be right there," she said.

When she heard his footsteps on the second floor, Andrea spoke again.

"David," she said.

"To Cuba?" he blurted. "Are you serious? You have three weeks off and you're going to Cuba, of all places? You need to put an end to this. Seriously. And I bet your husband doesn't know anything about it."

"I want to go on the trip that Aarón never managed to go on," explained Andrea. "It could be the perfect chance to get closure on all of this."

Andrea heard David take a deep breath and expel the air noisily. She also heard him starting his car's engine.

"All right, Andrea, it's your call," he said. "But take care of yourself. And don't let it be nine years before you come see me in Arenas next time."

"I won't," she said, "I promise. I want to go visit Aarón's mother. I haven't seen her since it happened."

"She's not well," David said in a low voice. He thought of the dark silhouette some people had seen appearing behind the curtains in the main bedroom of the house at the end of the dirt road. Looking in the rearview mirror, he went in reverse gear and left the Open's parking lot. Then he stopped the car, hesitated, and added, "But it's not your fault. None of it's your fault."

"I know, David," she said, "I know."

She remembered Aarón saying his best friend's name. The dark void returned to her chest. Throwing her head forward, she made her hair fall over her face. She hung up and put the cell phone in her pocket.

Then, as she did some nights before going to bed, she headed to the chest of drawers at the entrance. She opened the bottom drawer. And squeezed the stone from the lake in her right hand.

Monday, September 14, 2009

Andrea and Emilio returned from their vacation to Cuba a month after her last conversation with David. With her back against their front door, she felt the tickle of Emilio's fingers climbing from her hips to her breasts. She turned to escape his hands and pushed the door with her own. They went in laughing.

"I'm not going to unpack for a whole week," said Emilio.

Then he took off his shoes without using his hands, flinging them away like a teenager would. He threw the letters he had under one arm onto a table. Andrea smiled. She lifted her hair with both hands and shook her head to air the back of her neck, her elbows pointing outward. Emilio approached and stroked her armpits. Andrea jerked forward, tucking in her stomach. She laughed.

"Stop tickling me," she ordered.

"Like this?" he said. He pinched her belly with two fingers.

Andrea was still laughing. She grabbed his wrists and, straining, pulled his hands around her back. She held them to the curve at the beginning of her buttocks. He rested his chin on her shoulder and breathed through her hair.

"You still smell of suntan lotion," he whispered in her ear. "You're stunning with such dark skin and blonde hair. The change of color was a good idea."

Andrea closed her eyes and tried not to think of Aarón.

"I'd been wanting to go blonde again for a while," she said.

She wondered whether she would ever be able to use chamomile-scented shampoo again. She tried to distract her mind from the memory of Aarón with images of their trip to Cuba. And she held Emilio tight, like a shipwrecked woman clinging to a splintered mast. After a few seconds, Andrea opened her eyes. Her chin was resting on Emilio's shoulder, her lips kissing his neck.

That was when she saw the envelope.

The yellow envelope on top of the pile of letters Emilio had taken from the mailbox. Her name and address written in black marker. She instantly recognized David's handwriting. Andrea squeezed her husband harder.

"Hey, hey," he said. "You're going to strangle me to death."

Without taking her eyes from the envelope, Andrea separated herself from Emilio.

"We still have tonight," he joked. "I'm going to take a quick shower, then we can have lunch, and I think I'm going to take a nap." He kissed one of her cheeks. Then he returned to the front door, brought in the suitcase they'd left outside, and closed it. "Don't touch the suitcase. I'll unpack tomorrow."

Andrea nodded, maintaining a forced smile. She let it drop when Emilio set off up the stairs. When she heard him close the bathroom door, she went over to the envelope and picked it up. She reread her name and address. She turned it around and found *D.M.* as the sender. She remembered the newspapers using the same initials to report on David's condition after the robbery at the Open. She opened the top flap of the envelope, looked inside, and took a deep breath.

She headed into the living room and knelt in front of the television. She inserted her hand into the envelope and extracted the disc. A card stapled to the plastic sleeve read *Leo at the Aqua*. David had also written an address on it, as well as *Tel:*, but hadn't added the number. Perhaps he reconsidered at the last moment. Perhaps he didn't want Andrea contacting the boy.

"I wasn't intending to," she murmured.

Her hands broke out in thick sweat as she placed the disc in the DVD player. The menu listed just one file. Andrea threw her hair back, rubbed her eyes, and breathed deeply. Then she pressed the button on the remote control.

Her eyes welled up right away.

The boy was sideways to the camera. Seeing his face, Andrea held two fingers to her mouth. A woman's hand was gripping the boy's shoulder hard from one side.

The voice of a female reporter Andrea couldn't see asked, "Hello, young man, what's your name and how old are you?"

The boy was pensive for a moment. Andrea saw the way he looked at the person gripping his shoulder. Then he turned to the reporter, pressed his lips together, and replied, "My name's Leo. And I was born on June twelfth, 2000. You work it out."

Hearing that, Andrea stopped blinking.

The video continued to play on the screen, but she no longer saw it. The light simply reflected off her pupils without acquiring meaning. She felt her stomach tighten. She stopped breathing.

A cold sweat covered the back of her neck.

The boy had said June 12, 2000.

With her eyes wide open, Andrea relived the recurring nightmare that always ended with her resting her head on Aarón's moist chest.

"I'm a bit weird, that's the problem," said the boy on the television screen.

The video ended and the screen reverted to the menu.

Andrea pressed the button on the remote control again.

"Hello, young man, what's your name and how old are you?" the reporter repeated.

"My name's Leo. And I was born on June twelfth, 2000. You work it out."

June 12, 2000.

A gunshot reverberated in Andrea's head.

It was so loud, her body spasmed. It brought back memories of their last conversation at Aarón's apartment. It made her remember a key sentence.

One's born when the previous one dies.

Aarón's voice was so clear in her head that it frightened her.

"One second," said Andrea.

She shot to her feet.

"One second, one second, one second." Her mind raced. "That boy was born on June twelfth, not May twelfth. He was born the day you . . ." She held both hands to her chest. "You were the fourth. David didn't die. David didn't count. His scene didn't count. That's why . . ." When Andrea invoked her next thought, her words turned to a sob. "That's why he looks like you."

She covered her face with her hands to focus her senses and concentrate on trying to remember Aarón's words. He'd said the victims were always born on the day the previous victim was killed.

"But how did he know when the boy would be killed?" she murmured into the palms of her hands.

A new memory echoed in her mind. The boy's age matches in *years, months, and days*. That's what Aarón had said.

"But what's the age, what's the age . . ."

She strained her memory to remember the numbers Aarón had mentioned to her. *Nine years . . .*

"Nine years and what else? It's no good to me if I can't remember the rest," she complained.

She pressed her eyes shut, and her mind was illuminated with the light of another memory. Her heart began to pound.

"No," she said in a sigh. She took her hands away from her face. "You started counting on the wrong day."

Suddenly she understood. She didn't need to remember the exact age of the boy. She just needed to know the difference in time between David and Aarón being shot. Because it was from Aarón's death that she had to start counting.

"June twelfth," murmured Andrea. Her mind quickly did the calculation. "Exactly a month later. It'll happen a month later. That's why it didn't happen on August fourteenth. Because the boy's going to be killed . . ." Her heart slowed to a stop. Andrea raised her left arm, turning her wrist. She held her watch in front of her eyes and read the date on the face: *09/14/09*. The word escaped from her mouth as a groan. "Today."

From the bathroom, Emilio heard the door slam. With a towel wrapped around his waist, he went out into the hall.

"Andrea?" he said into the staircase. "Is everything all right?"

Then he heard the car start up. From the window of their bedroom he saw his wife leave, without understanding why.

Inside the car, Andrea dialed David's number. She steered with the palm of her other hand, which also held the disc with the video of Leo on it.

"David," she said when she heard him answer. "I got the package, the video." She paused before yelling. "It's him!"

"Andrea?"

"It's him. It's the boy. The one Aarón said. It was all true." She gabbled the words as she looked in the rearview mirror to merge onto the expressway. "It was all true! The only one he got wrong was you. He started counting from the day of your robbery. But you didn't die! And one's born when the previous one dies! How did we not realize? How did you not realize when you watched the video?"

"I didn't watch it," he explained. "*I* want to forget the whole thing."

"It's today!" yelled Andrea. Several cars honked their horns around her. "They're going to kill him today at the American's store. We have to stop it. I need you to go to that kid's house and tell him—"

"I'm going to hang up," said David. "I swear I don't want to do it, but I'm going to hang up if you don't stop talking about this."

Hearing him, Andrea stopped. After a silence, she yelled, "Don't you understand? It's today! It's going to happen today! At the Open!"

"Just stop," David replied. His tone was weary.

"I'm driving to Arenas. To the address you wrote on the card. But I won't get there before ten p.m. I need you to help me and go—"

David hung up. Andrea was left with her mouth half-open. She looked at the screen on her cell phone as if she would find an answer there. She dialed his number again. His telephone was off. The car behind her protested with a honk.

Then the cell phone started to vibrate.

It was Emilio. Andrea threw the phone onto the passenger seat.

"Yes, I'm going to Arenas!" she howled at the device. "And yes, I had to drive!"

Andrea stepped on the gas. She felt the hardness of the pedal under her foot. A shiver ran down her back. She peered under the steering wheel and found what she feared. She'd left the house with bare feet.

24.

LEO

Monday, September 14, 2009

Leo heard his father come out onto his bedroom balcony behind him, but he kept his eye pressed against the eyepiece. He'd just focused on Saturn for the first time. When Amador cleared his throat, Leo separated his face from the telescope. He didn't turn around or say anything. In the dark, under the automatic shutter from which Pi hadn't seen the sky light up in a shower of stars an eternity ago, Amador spoke to his son. "Do you know what day it is tomorrow?"

Leo straightened. He looked up to the night sky and searched for Saturn again. Viewed with the naked eye, it disappeared into the mass of stars on one of the last nights of summer in Arenas.

"September fifteenth," he finally said. "Tuesday."

"Don't play dumb, you know what I mean." Amador took a step forward without fully reaching his son. "Tomorrow—"

"School starts," said Leo, finishing his sentence for him. Then his shoulders slumped, and he blew air out through his nose. "I know."

Amador, to whom Leo stood out against the black of the night behind him, remembered his father also letting his shoulders drop and sighing through his nose on the day he told him he wanted to study mathematics and not law, a declaration of intent that he never fulfilled because those slumping shoulders and that snort had been enough to persuade him to do what he had to do. He took another step forward and positioned himself to the right of his son. He looked up at the sky in the same direction as Leo. He put an arm around him, resting it on his shoulder. He put his other hand in his pocket.

They stood in silence for a while, looking without seeing Saturn.

Two crickets started a conversation somewhere.

"Have you seen a shooting star today?"

"You know what, Dad?" said Leo. He remembered himself lying on his bedroom floor, last summer, trying to open the shutter a crack. "I don't think shooting stars really exist. I've never seen one."

The temperature of Amador's skin changed when he remembered the punishment. He peeled his eyes from the sky and bent his head to look at Leo. His son's eyes were still fixed on some distant place beyond the stars. A silvery light outlined his nose and one of his cheeks. Directly under his chin, on the floor, his toes were moving up and down.

"You haven't seen . . . I don't know . . . Saturn, either," Amador improvised, "and you know it exists."

Leo smiled.

"I *have* seen Saturn," he said, and lifted his chin slightly. "It's right there."

Amador saw his son's chest rise as he breathed deeply.

"Dad," he said, "the summer's over."

"Technically, there's still a week. And it'll still be hot until October."

"It's not the same."

Leo fell silent for a few seconds before going on. A third cricket, its chirp a higher pitch, joined the chorus.

"Next year I think I want to go to a camp," he said. "There're still a lot of things I haven't seen."

Amador's stomach seemed to rise. And then fall.

"Dad, this year I'm going to try to make friends."

Amador knelt down. He hugged his son like he hadn't done since the last incident at the American's store, since the time he had to untangle Leo from his arms and leave him alone with Victoria looking at the ground, because a mass of voices in his head were trying to make him think his son was crazy. Since he hid behind the car so that Leo wouldn't see him putting his head between his knees to stop himself from hearing those voices.

"Of course you will. Everything's going to be different this year," he whispered in his ear.

When he let go of him and looked at him straight on, his son's face glowed with the moon's bluish light, looked back at him expectantly.

"Can I stop going to see Dr. Huertas?" he asked.

"Not yet," Amador answered with a shake of his head. "He's back next week. We have to go to the practice and tell him what happened in August. He'll know what we have to do."

Leo lifted his bottom lip and nodded. Then he looked down at the floor. A warm current of air brought with it the smell of whatever Linda was preparing in the kitchen.

"I asked Linda to make your favorite dinner. You need to eat and get an early night. You have a big day tomorrow."

Leo nodded again without saying anything. Pi suddenly appeared and began purring, rubbing his head against one of his owner's legs. Amador stood.

"Let's go," he said.

Leo looked at the sky one last time before taking something round out of one of his pockets. He screwed it onto the eyepiece and moved the telescope into a horizontal position.

"Let's go," Leo repeated.

He thought about putting his arm around his father's waist, but stopped himself. He clenched his fists on either side of his body. He walked beside Amador, wishing the next day would never come.

They crossed the balcony, guided by the dim light from the waning moon. In Leo's bedroom, which was in darkness except for some luminous pools of silvery light, the stars on the ceiling glowed in the form of green dots, giving off the light stolen from the sun in the day and from the bulb on the wall during many nights of secret reading. Amador dipped his head to avoid the shutter. Leo went in right behind him and looked up at the ceiling. Amador copied him, and smiled when he remembered the day they'd stuck the stars up there and how Leo had gotten angry whenever he'd misplaced one.

"See, son? You said you've never seen a shooting star, but you've been sleeping with this above you for years."

Amador crouched and pointed at a sticker of a star with six points and a curved plastic tail as a trail. Leo located it without needing to follow Amador's finger.

"It's not the same. And anyway, this sky isn't complete."

That surprised Amador.

"We never finished it?" he asked. "But I promised you we'd buy whatever stars we needed so it was the same as in the book I gave you," he remembered out loud.

An echo of Leo's laughter, the laughter he'd let out when Amador lost his balance and almost fell off the ladder, reverberated in his head almost as loudly as the sound of the crickets that were still chirping outside.

"You also said that would be a black hole."

Leo indicated the empty corner of the ceiling where the stars had stopped. Amador recognized the last luminous dot, the one that finally cricked his back when he stuck it up there. He remembered Leo with an empty sticker sheet in his hands, running his fingernail along it several times, hoping to find some forgotten star. He also remembered the face he pulled then, how he'd looked at the celestial map in his book and then at that empty corner father and son were now looking at again.

Amador, squatting, took his son's outstretched hand.

"Would you like us to finish it today?"

Leo's face lit up in the middle of all that darkness. He smiled, without showing his teeth, just for a second.

"You said I had to eat and go to bed. Tomorrow—"

"Is the first day of school," said Amador, finishing his sentence. "I know. But I also told you that everything's going to be different this year. And you're going to start off with a complete sky above your bed." He spoke with the excitement of a boy about to get up to some mischief, like eating candy in a store without paying for it, behind his mother's back. "Let's tell Linda to put the chicken breasts on hold."

"Chicken breasts in breadcrumbs?" asked Leo, his smile now wide across his face.

"What do you think?"

Leo laughed properly for the first time in months. Amador leapt up and groped for the light switch on the other side of the room. They both squinted when the light came on and made the entire universe suddenly disappear. Leo found his sneakers under the bed just before his father pointed at the ceiling with his thumbs and asked, "I got them from the American's store, didn't I, Commander?"

Leo froze, his right foot just halfway into a sneaker. He looked at his father.

"Leo."

The seriousness in Amador's voice and the severity of the look he gave him made any explanation unnecessary. Leo finished putting on his shoes while trying to hide the trembling in his hands. He preferred not to say anything, in case the words got caught in his throat.

Amador turned off the light and they left the room.

Leo recognized the cold on his back.

"Why's Linda saying you told her to wait half an hour to serve dinner?" The sound of Victoria's heels and voice surprised them as they headed to the front door. "Don't tell me you've forgotten that your son starts school tomorrow."

Amador turned around. Victoria was speaking as she walked toward them from the entrance to the living room from the garden. The crushed ice in the glass she held jingled with every step. It reminded Amador, with total clarity, of the sound made by the ice cubes in the double whiskey his father had been drinking on the night he'd pointed out a certain Victoria Cuevas to him at a convention of weary old lawyers in Prague, when he'd said into Amador's ear that she was the type of woman who was of interest to him.

"We're heading to the Open for a second."

"Hmm. What's this, some new kind of shock therapy I haven't been told about?"

She finished the question just as she arrived in front of her husband and son. The sound of her heels stopped. But not the tinkle in her glass. She held out her free hand and pinched Leo's nose, then took a sip of her drink before continuing.

"Or are you running away in the middle of the night?" She looked back and forth from Amador to Leo until her eyes came to rest on the boy. "Are you going to snub your classmates like that? They must be *dying* to see you tomorrow."

The way she pronounced that word—*dying*—turned Amador's stomach. *Her name's Victoria Cuevas. She's a top lawyer*, Amador Cruz Sr. had said. *Trust me. You want that woman to be the mother of your children.*

"We're going to buy some stars for the ceiling."

Victoria let out one of her loud guffaws, throwing her head back in an exaggerated gesture.

"Come on, son, let's go," Amador said.

He opened the door and held an arm out in Leo's direction to indicate he should go ahead of him. Leo turned away from his mother and walked outside.

"OK. Do what you want. I'm going to start eating. Linda will take your uniform up to your room in a moment," she said, raising her voice. "She'll wake you in the morning for breakfast. I'll pick you up at the gate, opposite the Open. You know the spot, on the other side of the street. Same as always. Let's see when—"

"That's great," Amador cut in.

He didn't say anything else. He went out and closed the door behind him. It slammed harder than he intended.

Leo was waiting outside. His mother's words had made his stomach tighten. He pictured himself barefoot on the sidewalk, looking for the shade from the traffic light to ease the burning on the soles of his feet. They climbed into the Aston Martin. Amador turned the ignition.

Victoria listened to the car drive away. She headed to the sofa, shaking the contents of her glass. She sat down, crossed a leg over the other, and put her drink on the table. She began clicking her fingernails together. Hooking her forefinger under her thumb before releasing it. She remained there for several minutes. Staring at the wall. Swinging the foot that hung a short distance from the floor.

Then she heard a vehicle's engine. She screwed up her nose when she judged that Amador couldn't have had time to go to the store and back. The screech of the vehicle braking hard made her begin to worry. It was as if something was about to hit the house. Soon after, the doorbell started ringing incessantly.

When Victoria opened the door and discovered the barefoot woman, she knew immediately that something wasn't right.

Amador and Leo drove toward the Open with the windows down. Leo looked at his father. When Amador nodded, his son leaned half his body out through the passenger window and let the warm air hit his face. He closed his eyes and imagined himself lifting his arms to celebrate an imaginary victory, though his imagination wouldn't allow him to create anything he wanted to celebrate. His father thought he saw a contained impulse when Leo moved his hands slightly.

"You can put your arms up if you want," he told him.

Leo, cleaving through a deafening wind outside with his eyes closed, didn't hear him.

He came back inside the car as they approached the center of town, now lit by orange streetlamps with clouds of insects around them, like giant suns in an entomological solar system. When they'd negotiated a traffic circle and entered the Open's street, Leo's eyes fell on the other side of the road, where the school was. It seemed strange to him that the empty building he was now looking at could cause the sweat that dripped from the base of his back. He could almost feel the jolt of electric pain from Slash's stomping foot again.

Everything's going to be different this year, his father had just said. Leo shook his head the way someone would to shake off guilt. He managed to put the stream of images that seeing the school had triggered out of his mind. He promised himself that this year his solitary lunches in the cafeteria would end. As would the solitary waiting on the other side of the street. He would no longer lock himself in the restroom stall, his feet up on the toilet bowl so they wouldn't find him, looking at his watch to make sure he left ten minutes after the others. *Always the last one* was Mom's usual greeting.

"Everything's going to be different this year," he repeated, as if it were a motto.

"What's that?"

"Nothing, Dad."

The Open appeared on their right. With a sudden turn of the wheel, Amador, who had been distracted looking at his son, drove into the parking lot. He pulled up behind another car that was just then starting its engine.

"I don't think I'm in the way here. Anyway, you won't be long, will you?"

Leo turned his head to face his father. In the background, through the windshield, he might have seen a university student carrying a pile of books under his arm, going into the store to buy a few cans of Red Bull to see him through the night of study he had ahead of him.

"You're not coming with me?" Leo asked.

One of his hands began to tremble, and he trapped it under his leg.

"No, son, there's no need. Take this." He took a twenty-euro bill from his front pocket. "It'll be enough, won't it? And make sure that old man gives you the right change."

"The old guy's not there anymore. There's another man."

"Well, don't let him rip you off. Come on, go, it'll be quicker. Your mother said she was about to start eating, and—"

"I know it's not that," Leo said as he grabbed the bill. "What you want is for me to go in alone. You don't care about Mom."

He waited for his father to get angry. Instead, Amador's expression tightened first, then relaxed, as if someone had disarmed his defenses after uncovering his biggest secret.

"Son." He turned off the engine. "If you really want things to change, you have to start changing them yourself. This is something you have to do. You know there's no danger at the Open. We've been over this."

Leo put his other hand under his leg.

"Dad," he began. When he knew what was about to happen to his voice if he kept speaking, he fell silent.

"Go on, Leo."

Amador grabbed the steering wheel with both hands, as if the car were still in motion. He signaled the Open with his chin. The neon sign blinked over the automatic doors. They opened when a man went in, leaving a German shepherd puppy tied to one of the posts, the same posts where Leo's classmates left their bicycles.

A wave of terror rose from Leo's stomach to his throat when he thought about going back into that place alone.

"I don't want the stars anymore," he said, without a tremble in his voice. "Let's go home." He threw the bill onto his father's lap.

Amador's fingers stiffened around the wheel. "Don't make me . . . ," he murmured, more to the dashboard than to his son. He was afraid the fuse was close to igniting.

"I don't want them."

"Get in there, right now!" Amador yelled suddenly, unable to contain it. He was also unable to contain the blow he dealt the wheel with one of his hands. Two tiny drops of saliva hit the windshield.

Leo jumped in his seat and looked at his father with his shoulders hunched. Amador was looking back at him out of the corner of his eye, his body facing forward, his head barely turned. Leo didn't like the way his father was breathing. Slowly, he freed one of his hands and picked up the bill from his father's lap. He didn't care if Dad saw him shaking now. But he wasn't shaking. He grabbed the money without taking his eyes off his father's. Amador gestured at the entrance to the Open again. The steering wheel leather squeaked under his hands. "I'll wait for you here," he said.

Leo opened his door. He got out without another word. When he closed it and found himself alone, facing the Open again, he considered running. He halted the impulse by contracting his toes. He squeezed the moist bill in his fist.

And he began to walk.

Amador followed his son with his eyes. The image of Leo blurred. He dried his eyes with the back of his hand.

This is going to take time. Your son's not well. You know that, don't you? he thought.

Before he could stop himself, like he'd stopped so many things for so many years, Amador screamed something unintelligible into the empty car. It loosened up his contracted throat and enabled him to vent his despair in a single heaving sob.

Then he saw the doors open.

He also made out Leo letting past a man dressed in a leather jacket. With a sadness that he allowed himself to listen to for the first time in his life, he remembered the way Victoria had just mocked her own son at the door to their home.

Suddenly he heard the incessant honking of a car approaching at full speed down the Open's street. Amador dried his eyes and turned around to see what was making the racket.

His heart stopped when he recognized Victoria.

She was traveling in the passenger seat of a car he didn't know. Half her body was hanging out, like Leo's had been a few minutes ago. She was waving her arms. Amador made out the silhouette of another woman at the wheel. She was gesturing wildly with an arm outside the window, and screaming at the windshield. Victoria was screaming, too, her hair blown back by the force of the air. The car headlights changed intensity in electrical spasms.

Amador could not move.

Then he heard a skid beside him.

Victoria stumbled as she tried to get out of the stranger's car. She hit the ground face first.

Andrea bolted toward the store. Tears flew behind her. She felt the heat of the road surface on the soles of her feet, now black with tar and gasoline.

She ran with all her strength.

A flash turned the present Open into the Open of nine years earlier. Andrea ran toward Aarón. She imagined her own skin tinted with the blue reflection from the police lights. She remembered the sneaker at the end of a leg lying on the floor in the store. She felt the moisture from Aarón's chest on her forehead.

Andrea screamed to return to the present.

She considered going straight through the doors. Smashing them into a thousand pieces.

The opening system wouldn't respond in time at the speed she was going. She would have to cut herself to shreds before she could hold the boy in her arms.

Hold Aarón in her arms again.

That was when the first gunshot rang out. The first of three.

Andrea drew blood on her right foot when she stopped dead and skidded on the grit.

Victoria felt a pain in her stomach that was much more intense than the one sometimes caused by the feeling of being ashamed of her own son.

Amador's pupils dilated until the glow from the neon hurt his eyes. His body jerked three times, once for each shot, but he couldn't separate his hands from the steering wheel.

Andrea fell to her knees when she saw the man in the leather jacket run out toward a car waiting for him, with the engine running, by a gas pump. The dog at the door was barking and fighting against a leash that was too short. Inside the store, a thin man waved his arms and screamed for help.

Victoria managed to push herself up with both hands. She spat out dust from the ground. She walked toward the Open's doors and passed Andrea, whose face was buried in her hands, her elbows resting on her knees.

For several minutes, Amador's open eyes saw nothing.

He didn't see Victoria going into the store.

He didn't see Andrea pulling at her hair before falling to one side.

Amador saw nothing until the siren of an ambulance that appeared in front of him flicked a switch in his brain and brought him back to reality.

A reality in which he knew his son was no longer there.

He cried out.

The car door opened. Amador let himself practically fall out. His elbow hit the hot pavement. The pain made him cry out again.

Then he heard a deep, slow, distorted echo.

"Leo!"

Amador heard himself scream his son's name.

EPILOGUE

Monday, September 21, 2009

A week later, Victoria opened her son's bedroom door.

She waited on the threshold for a length of time she was unable to measure, too afraid to go in, before taking the first step. Something changed in the air as soon as she was inside, something electric that made her whole body prickle. She thought she heard a warm whisper just behind her ear. In reality, the silence was total. The school uniform was hanging from the wardrobe's doorknob. On the bed, the bedspread was still wrinkled, marking the place where Leo had sat for the last time. Victoria held her neck in both hands, resting her arms on her chest. She spent another indeterminate amount of time standing there with an absent gaze, as she had so often in the last seven days. Then she spotted something. She went out onto the balcony and took hold of the telescope. When she tried to fold it and couldn't figure out how to do it, she had to contain an urge to smash it against the floor. She left it in the same place, as if that were what she had wanted to do all along.

Back in the bedroom, she bent down to grab hold of the bedspread at one of its edges. For a moment she looked at the folds in the fabric. A volatile image of Leo, with his back against the wall, reading, began to form in front of her eyes, and she stopped it before . . . She pulled hard. The wrinkles in the material disappeared. The imaginary Leo vanished.

Victoria felt her eyelids burning. She slapped the bed a couple of times before sitting on it. With her back straight, she crossed her legs and rested her head on the thumb of her right hand. With her fingers, she pressed her lips against her teeth. Her throat hurt through the back of her neck. She felt the tears land on one of her calves before she knew she was crying again.

Something came away from the ceiling over the bed, landing near her. She picked it up and played with it in her fingers. A tiny circle of white plastic.

At some point, she heard the sound of knuckles on the door.

"Señora?"

"Don't come in."

Victoria's voice sounded firm. Her tears had dried now and had formed a layer of salty varnish on her face. When she went to the door, she saw Linda with her head bowed, not daring to look her in the face.

"I'm going, señora."

"You didn't need to tell me. Leave your keys in the kitchen and go."

Then the doorbell rang.

"Has someone come to pick you up?" asked Victoria.

Linda shook her head. She took a step back when she sensed the señora approaching her. Victoria slammed the bedroom door shut behind her.

"Leave it. Go out the back, through the garden."

"Señora, I'm so sorry—"

"It's too late."

And it was too late. Linda's secret—the second envelope, the one she took from the mailbox and handed to Leo behind his parents' backs—had burned for five nights on her pillow. Then it had begun to burn on the tip of her tongue. And in the end, she had to let it out to prevent it from turning her to ashes. She told Amador on the sixth night that Leo never saw. She explained to him that she'd found another letter for the boy, in the mailbox. That it had been on the morning when the cat jumped onto the breakfast table and marked the señora's rug. That she hid it and showed it to Leo downstairs, where the washing machine was. That it said practically the same thing as the first letter. That she wanted to protect Leo by letting him see it first. That she had tried to stop him from reading it, but that Leo had been too quick for her and opened it right there. That later she didn't know what he'd done with it. And that . . .

Amador hadn't let her finish. He just asked her what she would do if she stopped working for them, because she was going to stop working for them due to the *serious consequences of your carelessness*, which were the words Amador used. *Go back to my country and hug my little girls*, Linda had replied, thinking about the daughters who hadn't grown up, pinned to the wall above her bed. And when Victoria learned that this had been her response, that Linda had had the temerity to say she would go to hug her daughters, she had yelled at Amador to throw her out of the house right then. *She'll go tomorrow morning. We don't need another scene*, he had replied. And then Victoria had run to Leo's room to hug him, but her hand had frozen when she touched the door handle that she no longer knew how to turn.

"Go out through the garden," she repeated.

The doorbell rang again, a high-pitched note and two deeper ones.

Linda looked up at Victoria. When she tried to say something, the señora shook her head. The words disintegrated on her tongue before they existed. Linda would have liked to go into Leo's room to plump up his pillow.

She turned around and started heading downstairs toward the living room. Halfway down, she heard her name and stopped.

"Linda," said the voice that reached her from behind her back, "when you hug your daughters, think about why I can't hug my son." The voice paused. "If you'd told us about that letter—"

"That letter wouldn't have changed anything. You hadn't hugged your son for a long time," Linda found the courage to say, driven by a sudden heat. After regaining her composure, she continued down the carpeted stairs.

The doorbell rang a third time. Linda looked at the suitcase she'd left by the front door. She crossed the room in that direction. When the doorbell rang a fourth time, she felt it vibrate over her head. She remembered the señora's order. She picked up the suitcase and opened the door.

Outside a man and a woman were waiting, the man supporting himself on a pair of crutches. Linda left the house, and the suitcase bumped against one of the crutches. She apologized. Then she extended the handle, let out a mouthful of air, and walked away from the house that had never been her home. The suitcase wheels got caught every few paces on the gravel path.

"Hello?" Andrea said into the house. "Victoria? It's Andrea."

Victoria was standing with a lifeless hand on the door handle she'd forgotten how to turn again. She squeezed it hard before letting go as if it burned. She rested her head against the door and stroked it with both hands. She pressed an ear against the wood to listen for her son moving around inside the empty room.

"I've brought what you asked for," she heard the voice downstairs say.

Victoria started heading down the stairs. At first, she moved slowly, resting both feet on the same step before moving on. Then she regained her strength and walked to the entrance, making her heels click like a tribe that bangs its drums before mounting an attack.

Through the doorway, standing next to Andrea, she saw a man who could have been well built, resting on crutches. He had one eye open and the other almost closed. Victoria thought there was something disconcerting in his rictus and the outline of his lips. There was also a beautiful serenity in his incomplete gaze and a kindhearted quality to his half smile.

"Is it him?" she asked Andrea.

Andrea nodded. She expected Victoria to invite them in. She didn't. She just looked David up and down with a fixed expression.

He felt uncomfortable. He didn't know what to say.

"So you brought it?" Victoria asked.

Andrea hesitated. She closed the zipper on her purse. She thought about taking David by the arm and leaving this woman who was looking down on them to be consumed by her own pain.

"Is Amador there?" Andrea asked.

Victoria yelled Amador's name, forcing her exhausted throat.

He heard his wife's voice over the melody of "Seasons in the Sun," which was playing at full volume on the speakers in his study.

"He probably can't hear me," Victoria explained. "When he shuts himself in his study, it's as if the world doesn't exist. But don't worry. I'll watch it with him."

After saying that, Victoria held a hand out in front of Andrea and David's faces. Andrea pressed the purse against her stomach. She looked at David. He picked up on the doubt in his friend's eyes. But then he nodded and gestured at Victoria with his head.

Andrea understood. She opened the zipper on the purse. In the tense silence, it sounded like the gear assembly of some industrial machinery. She took out the disc. Stapled on its plastic sleeve was the card showing the words *Leo at the Aqua*. She looked at David again. He gave an expression of consent. Andrea placed the disc in Victoria's hand.

"It's what Aarón would've wanted," she said to her.

Victoria looked down. She was silent. Andrea noticed a slight tremble in her chin.

"Thank you," said Victoria.

Then she snatched back her arm.

And closed the door on them.

Outside, David pulled Andrea toward him. She rested her forehead on his shoulder.

"It's what Aarón would've wanted," David repeated.

Inside the Cruz house, Amador was going down the stairs after Victoria beckoned him. He found her in the living room, standing in front of the television. When he saw his son on the screen, he had to make an effort not to fall.

"I'm a bit weird, that's the problem," he was saying.

Victoria looked up at her husband. Then she walked toward the center of the room. She picked up the telephone and placed it on her shoulder. Amador could see her, blurred, through the glassy filter of contained tears.

"Please, who're you calling now?" he managed to ask. Inside his pocket, he squeezed the photograph of a San Francisco coffee shop.

"This wretched town's local TV station," Victoria replied. "I gave a lot of money to that fat girl so they wouldn't broadcast the footage of Leo. They'd better brace themselves."

Her fingernail, the one she'd been clicking against her thumbnail, cracked above the flesh.

ABOUT THE AUTHOR

Photo © 2019 Abel Trujillo

Paul Pen is a bestselling Spanish author whose four novels have been translated to many languages. *The Light of the Fireflies* was his first book to be translated to English, selling more than one hundred thousand copies worldwide. This book was followed by *Desert Flowers* and *Under the Water*, with which he reaffirmed his unmistakable brand of literary suspense and ability to create a deeply immersive reading experience for the mind, heart, and nerves. Now, his debut novel of almost ten years ago, *The Warning*, is being published in English for the first time, finally offering readers around the globe the chance to read a story already adapted to the big screen in 2018. Motion pictures of *The Light of the Fireflies* and *Desert Flowers* are also in development, the latter scripted by Pen himself. In his capacity as scriptwriter, Pen is working on a forthcoming Netflix series while he writes his next novel.

ABOUT THE TRANSLATOR

Photo © 2017 Colin Crewdson

Simon Bruni translates literary works from Spanish, a language he acquired through total immersion living in Alicante, Valencia, and Santander. He studied Spanish and linguistics at Queen Mary University of London and literary translation at the University of Exeter.

Simon's many published translations include novels, short stories, video games, and nonfiction publications, and he is the winner of three John Dryden awards: in 2017 and 2015 for Paul Pen's short stories "Cinnamon" and "The Porcelain Boy," and in 2011 for Francisco Pérez Gandul's novel *Cell 211*. His translation of Paul Pen's novel *The Light of the Fireflies* has sold over one hundred thousand copies worldwide.

For more information, please visit www.simonbruni.com.